Dinner At
The Beach House Hotel

Judith Keim

BOOKS BY JUDITH KEIM

THE HARTWELL WOMEN SERIES:
The Talking Tree – 1
Sweet Talk – 2
Straight Talk – 3
Baby Talk – 4
The Hartwell Women – Boxed Set

THE BEACH HOUSE HOTEL SERIES:
Breakfast at The Beach House Hotel – 1
Lunch at The Beach House Hotel – 2
Dinner at The Beach House Hotel – 3
Christmas at The Beach House Hotel – 4
Margaritas at The Beach House Hotel – 5
Dessert at The Beach House Hotel – 6
Coffee at The Beach House Hotel – 7 (2023)
High Tea at The Beach House Hotel – 8 (2024)

THE FAT FRIDAYS GROUP:
Fat Fridays – 1
Sassy Saturdays – 2
Secret Sundays – 3

THE SALTY KEY INN SERIES:
Finding Me – 1
Finding My Way – 2
Finding Love – 3
Finding Family – 4
The Salty Key Inn Series . Boxed Set

THE CHANDLER HILL INN SERIES:
Going Home – 1
Coming Home – 2
Home at Last – 3
The Chandler Hill Inn Series – Boxed Set

Holiday Hopes
The Winning Tickcts (2023)

For more information: **www.judithkeim.com**

PRAISE FOR JUDITH KEIM'S NOVELS

THE BEACH HOUSE HOTEL SERIES

"Love the characters in this series. This series was my first introduction to Judith Keim. She is now one of my favorites. Looking forward to reading more of her books."

BREAKFAST AT THE BEACH HOUSE HOTEL is an easy, delightful read that offers romance, family relationships, and strong women learning to be stronger. Real life situations filter through the pages. Enjoy!"

LUNCH AT THE BEACH HOUSE HOTEL – "This series is such a joy to read. You feel you are actually living with them. Can't wait to read the latest one."

DINNER AT THE BEACH HOUSE HOTEL – "A Terrific Read! As usual, Judith Keim did it again. Enjoyed immensely. Continue writing such pleasantly reading books for all of us readers."

CHRISTMAS AT THE BEACH HOUSE HOTEL – "Not Just Another Christmas Novel. This is book number four in the series and my introduction to Judith Keim's writing. I wasn't disappointed. The characters are dimensional and engaging. The plot is well crafted and advances at a pleasing pace. The Florida location is interesting and warming. It was a delight to read a romance novel with mature female protagonists. Ann and Rhoda have life experiences that enrich the story. It's a clever book about friends and extended family. Buy copies for your book group pals and enjoy this seasonal read."

MARGARITAS AT THE BEACH HOUSE HOTEL – "What a wonderful series. I absolutely loved this book and can't wait for the next book to come out. There was even suspense in it. Thanks Judith for the great stories."

"Overall, Margaritas at the Beach House Hotel is another wonderful addition to the series. Judith Keim takes the reader on a journey told through the voices of these amazing characters we have all come to love through the years! I truly cannot stress enough how good this book is, and I hope you enjoy it as much as I have!"

THE HARTWELL WOMEN SERIES:

"This was an EXCELLENT series. When I discovered Judith Keim, I read all of her books back to back. I thoroughly enjoyed the women Keim has written about. They are believable and you want to just jump into their lives and be their friends! I can't wait for any upcoming books!"

"I fell into Judith Keim's Hartwell Women series and have read & enjoyed all of her books in every series. Each centers around a strong & interesting woman character and their family interaction. Good reads that leave you wanting more."

THE FAT FRIDAYS GROUP :

"Excellent story line for each character, and an insightful representation of situations which deal with some of the contemporary issues women are faced with today."

"I love this author's books. Her characters and their lives are realistic. The power of women's friendships is a common and beautiful theme that is threaded throughout this story."

THE SALTY KEY INN SERIES

FINDING ME – "I thoroughly enjoyed the first book in this series and cannot wait for the others! The characters are endearing with the same struggles we all encounter. The setting makes me feel like I am a guest at The Salty Key

Inn...relaxed, happy & light-hearted! The men are yummy and the women strong. You can't get better than that! Happy Reading!"

FINDING MY WAY- "Loved the family dynamics as well as uncertain emotions of dating and falling in love. Appreciated the morals and strength of parenting throughout. Just couldn't put this book down."

FINDING LOVE – "I waited for this book because the first two was such good reads. This one didn't disappoint.... Judith Keim always puts substance into her books. This book was no different, I learned about PTSD, accepting oneself, there is always going to be problems but stick it out and make it work. Just the way life is. In some ways a lot like my life. Judith is right, it needs another book and I will definitely be reading it. Hope you choose to read this series, you will get so much out of it."

FINDING FAMILY – "Completing this series is like eating the last chip. Love Judith's writing, and her female characters are always smart, strong, vulnerable to life and love experiences."

"This was a refreshing book. Bringing the heart and soul of the family to us."

THE CHANDLER HILL INN SERIES

GOING HOME – "I absolutely could not put this book down. Started at night and read late into the middle of the night. As a child of the '60s, the Vietnam war was front and center so this resonated with me. All the characters in the book were so well developed that the reader felt like they were friends of the family."

"I was completely immersed in this book, with the beautiful descriptive writing, and the authors' way of bringing her characters to life. I felt like I was right inside her story."

COMING HOME – "Coming Home is a winner. The characters are well-developed, nuanced and likable. Enjoyed the vineyard setting, learning about wine growing and seeing the challenges Cami faces in running and growing a business. I look forward to the next book in this series!"

"Coming Home was such a wonderful story. The author has a gift for getting the reader right to the heart of things."

HOME AT LAST – "In this wonderful conclusion, to a heartfelt and emotional trilogy set in Oregon's stunning wine country, Judith Keim has tied up the Chandler Hill series with the perfect bow."

"Overall, this is truly a wonderful addition to the Chandler Hill Inn series. Judith Keim definitely knows how to perfectly weave together a beautiful and heartfelt story."

"The storyline has some beautiful scenes along with family drama. Judith Keim has created characters with interactions that are believable and some of the subjects the story deals with are poignant."

SEASHELL COTTAGE BOOKS

A CHRISTMAS STAR – *"Love, laughter, sadness, great food, and hope for the future, all in one book. It doesn't get any better than this stunning read."*

"A Christmas Star is a heartwarming Christmas story featuring endearing characters. So many Christmas books are set in snowbound places...it was a nice change to read a Christmas story that takes place on a warm sandy beach!" Susan Peterson

CHANGE OF HEART – *"CHANGE OF HEART is the summer read we've all been waiting for. Judith Keim is a master at creating fascinating characters that are simply irresistible. Her stories leave you with a big smile on your face and a heart bursting with love."*
Kellie Coates Gilbert, author of the popular Sun Valley Series

A SUMMER OF SURPRISES – *"The story is filled with a roller coaster of emotions and self-discovery. Finding love again and rebuilding family relationships."*

"Ms. Keim uses this book as an amazing platform to show that with hard emotional work, belief in yourself and love, the scars of abuse can be conquered. It in no way preaches, it's a lovely story with a happy ending."

"The character development was excellent. I felt I knew these people my whole life. The story development was very well thought out I was drawn [in] from the beginning."

THE DESERT SAGE INN SERIES:

THE DESERT FLOWERS – ROSE – "The Desert Flowers - Rose, is the first book in the new series by Judith Keim. I always look forward to new books by Judith Keim, and this one is definitely a wonderful way to begin The Desert Sage Inn Series!"

"In this first of a series, we see each woman come into her own and view new beginnings even as they must take this tearful journey as they slowly lose a dear friend. This is a very well written book with well-developed and likable main characters. It was interesting and enlightening as the first portion of this saga unfolded. I very much enjoyed this book and I do recommend it"

"Judith Keim is one of those authors that you can always depend on to give you a great story with fantastic characters. I'm excited to know that she is writing a new series and after reading book 1 in the series, I can't wait to read the rest of the books."!

THE DESERT FLOWERS – LILY – "The second book in the Desert Flowers series is just as wonderful as the first. Judith Keim is a brilliant storyteller. Her characters are truly lovely and people that you want to be friends with as soon as you start reading. Judith Keim is not afraid to weave real life conflict and loss into her stories. I loved reading Lily's story and can't wait for Willow's!

"The Desert Flowers-Lily is the second book in The Desert Sage Inn Series by author Judith Keim. When I read the first book in the series, The Desert Flowers-Rose, I knew this series would exceed all of my expectations and then some. Judith Keim is an amazing author, and this series is a testament to her writing skills and her ability to completely draw a reader into the world of her characters."

THE DESERT FLOWERS – WILLOW – "*The feelings of love, joy, happiness, friendship, family and the pain of loss are deeply felt by Willow Sanchez and her two cohorts Rose and Lily. The Desert Flowers met because of their deep feelings for Alec Thurston, a man who touched their lives in different ways.*

Once again, Judith Keim has written the story of a strong, competent, confident and independent woman. Willow, like Rose and Lily can handle tough situations. All the characters are written so that the reader gets to know them but not all the characters will give the reader warm and fuzzy feelings.

The story is well written and from the start you will be pulled in. There is enough backstory that a reader can start here but I assure you, you'll want to learn more. There is an ocean of emotions that will make you smile, cringe, tear up or outright cry. I loved this book as I loved books one and two. I am thrilled that the Desert Flowers story will continue. I highly recommend this book to anyone who enjoys books with strong women."

Dinner At
The Beach House Hotel

The Beach House Hotel Series
Book 3

Judith Keim

Wild Quail Publishing

Dinner At The Beach House Hotel is a work of fiction. Names, characters, places, public or private institutions, corporations, towns, and incidents are the product of the author's imagination or are used fictitiously. Any resemblance to actual events, locales, or persons, living or dead, is coincidental.

No part of *Dinner At The Beach House Hotel* may be reproduced or transmitted in any form or by any electronic or mechanical means, including information storage and retrieval systems, without permission in writing from the author, except by a reviewer who may quote brief passages in a review. This book may not be resold or uploaded for distribution to others. For permissions contact the author directly via electronic mail:

wildquail.pub@gmail.com

www.judithkeim.com

Wild Quail Publishing
PO Box 171332
Boise, ID 83717-1332

ISBN# 978-0-9968637-8-0

Dedication

This book is dedicated in loving memory of Barbara Bova, without whose friendship, support, and encouragement, The Beach House Hotel series and my continuing pursuit of writing might not have happened. I'm so grateful to her!

CHAPTER ONE

Rhonda DelMonte Grayson and I stood at the top of the front steps of The Beach House Hotel, the seaside mansion in Sabal, Florida we'd turned into an upscale, boutique hotel. As the limo rolled through the gates of the property, I crossed my fingers behind my back.

With Rhonda due to give birth in the next two months, I needed all the help I could get while Rhonda and her husband Will welcomed their child into their family and the world. Bernhard Bruner was our last hope of finding a suitable general manager for the hotel out of the group of candidates we'd screened.

"I hope we like him," said Rhonda. "The last two applicants we talked to were doozies. I'm tellin' ya, Annie, I'm not going to take any bullshit from a guy thinkin' he can boss us around."

I smiled, used to the way Rhonda thought and spoke. My proper grandmother would shudder in her blue-blooded grave, but Rhonda wasn't even aware of the language that hid a big, loving heart.

The limo continued toward us.

"I hope *he* likes *us!*" I said, giving my crossed fingers a squeeze.

Below a lock of bleached blond hair that fell on her forehead, Rhonda's dark eyes sparkled. She elbowed me. "Here goes."

Before the limo even pulled to a stop, Rhonda and I eagerly

made our way down the steps to greet Mr. Bruner. An older man in his fifties, he'd come highly recommended to us as the perfect choice to oversee a property like ours. But would he be willing to work with us?

We'd interviewed several other men who weren't exactly thrilled with the idea of having to work under the guidance of two women. But The Beach House Hotel was our baby, and we weren't about to simply hand it over to someone else—no matter how much we wanted and needed some time to ourselves.

Paul, our driver, stopped the limo, got out, and hurried around behind the car to open the passenger door.

A shiny black shoe appeared, followed by creased gray slacks. Dressed in a navy blazer, starched white shirt, and conservative tie, the man who stood so straight before us had a sharp, blue-eyed gaze. Beneath his nose, a trimmed mustache brushed the top of his lips. His stern appearance reminded me of my old, middle-school principal.

As we exchanged greetings, a black and tan dachshund jumped out of the car and sat at her master's feet, looking up at me with what I thought of as something of a smile. Charmed, I stooped to pat her head.

"And who is this?"

"Trudy," Bernhard said. "She goes everywhere with me."

Rhonda and I exchanged glances.

"Uh, we weren't told about her," said Rhonda.

Bernhard picked the dog up. She gave him a lick on the cheek and turned bright dark eyes to us, wagging her tail furiously.

"If it's a problem for me to have her here, we can end this visit right now." Bernhard's words weren't unkind, but there was no question as to his intentions.

I reached over to give Trudy another pat on the head and

grinned when she licked my hand. I loved dogs, but Robert, my ex, had been allergic to them. And any kind of pet had been out of the question in my grandmother's formal home, where I lived after my parents were killed in an automobile accident.

Rhonda glanced at me and shrugged. "It's okay with me, Bernie."

Bernhard stiffened. "My name is Bernhard."

I placed a hand on his arm. "Among ourselves, our staff is quite informal. Rhonda likes to give people nicknames. It's a sign she likes you."

I held my breath as I waited for him to say something. If he and Rhonda couldn't get along, it would never work.

"All right. A few of my friends call me Bernie, but, in business, I like to use my full name." He set the dog down and stood staring at the façade of the hotel.

The two-story, pink-stucco building with its red-tile roof spread before us. I recalled the first time I'd seen it and how impressed I was with its design and features. By anyone's definition, the seaside estate was gorgeous.

"Can we give you a quick tour of the property?" I asked. "Normally we'd usher you in through the front door to give you an idea about the arrival that guests enjoy. But with the dog, and your long day of travel, you might want to stretch your legs and start the tour outside."

"Good idea," Bernie said. "I want to see everything."

Rhonda and I pointed out the putting green in the front circle of the hotel and led him over to what was once a large multi-car garage. Now, its second floor held an apartment for Manny and Consuela, the two people who'd been with us since before we opened our hotel, and an apartment for Troy, who was managing our day spa. On the ground floor, we'd set up a small laundry for towels and special linens, leaving some garage space still to park the hotel's limo and the occasional

VIP's car. The day spa was attached to the building near the laundry. Behind it, there was a tennis court, a shuffleboard court, and horseshoe pits.

I watched Bernie's face for a sign of approval as he took in everything, but he gave nothing away. "Let's have a refreshing drink by the water," I said, "after which we can take you through the public areas and show you a number of rooms before we sit down and discuss the job."

Bernie nodded agreeably.

While Rhonda went inside to talk to Consuela, I walked Bernie around the side of the hotel, past the herb garden the chef had recently established, and out onto the beachfront. Beneath a palm tree, a ground-level, wooden deck held a few tables and chairs. Guests frequently had lunch there, or, in the evening, enjoyed a cocktail while watching for the elusive green flash of a Gulf Coast setting sun.

I was amused to see Trudy run off for a sniff here and there before dutifully returning to Bernie's side.

The late January day was cool for Florida, but Bernie seemed to enjoy the shade as he sat waiting for Rhonda to reappear.

"You're certainly welcome to take off your coat and loosen your tie," I said.

He shook his head. "No, that wouldn't do." He gave my sandals a disapproving look.

"We like our guests to relax and enjoy themselves. While a dress code for dinner is suggested, we all like a bit of informality during the day," I quickly explained.

He nodded, but didn't comment, making me wonder if the man ever relaxed.

Rhonda walked toward us, followed by Consuela carrying a tray of drinks and snacks.

Bernie stood as they approached.

"Bernie, I'd like you to meet Consuela," Rhonda said. "She and her husband Manny have been with me since my ex and I bought The Beach House before Ann and I converted it to a hotel. Consuela is a whiz in the kitchen, and her husband is well...my Manny around the house." Rhonda let out a raucous laugh.

Bernie's mustache twitched and a glint of humor lit his eyes.

At the sight, I filled with relief. Rhonda was Rhonda, and though it had taken me a while to get used to her ways, I loved her and her carefree manner.

Bernie sat down and watched as Consuela placed the drinks before us and set a plate of cookies and a bowl of nuts on the table. "Thank you, Consuela," he said, smiling at her.

She left us, and Rhonda described how the kitchen staff had grown after hiring Jean-Luc Rodin as chef to prepare evening and some luncheon meals, along with his sous-chef, Carl Lamond.

"It continues to be a growing operation," I said. "The locals like to come to the hotel to dine and hold special events, and we've encouraged them to do so."

"Yes, I've read all about dinner at The Beach House Hotel. You've got a fine operation," Bernie said. He slipped a cookie crumb to Trudy, who wagged her tail in appreciation.

"C'mon, let's show you around the place. I think you're gonna like it," said Rhonda, rising to her feet.

I smiled. Rhonda was as proud of the hotel as I was.

Inside, we explained how we'd configured rooms downstairs for the small, discreet, private meetings our VIP guests demanded. Bernie nodded with approval at the small dining room where senators and other government officials sometimes met and where guests could entertain and dine alone.

As we continued our tour, Bernie asked discerning questions about the property, guest services we offered, staffing issues, and other aspects of the hotel operation. I knew then he was truly interested.

By the time we'd shown him the entire hotel, including the Presidential Suite, the Bridal Suite, and a few typical guest rooms, Bernie seemed as excited as a reserved man like him could show.

"Well, whaddya think?" said Rhonda as we led Bernie to our office.

"You've got a very impressive operation here. I'm sure I can be of help to you."

The three of us sat at the small conference table in the office. After going over his résumé, probing his past experiences, and discussing his management approaches, Rhonda and I shared hidden smiles.

I checked my watch. "I realize you have another appointment. Thank you so much for coming here, Bernie." I rose and shook his hand. "It's been a very productive meeting. We'll get back to you as soon as we can. As we have told you and others, as part of the compensation package, any general manager we hire will be given the use of the small house on the property for his residence."

"That's very nice." He shook hands with Rhonda and smiled at both of us. "Thank you for your time. I'm sincerely interested in this position and would love to have the opportunity to work with you."

We accompanied Bernie and Trudy to the front entrance of the hotel, where we made arrangements for the limo to drive him downtown.

Standing on the steps of the hotel, watching his departure, I turned to Rhonda. "Well?"

Rhonda shrugged. "He's a little uptight, but I think we can

get Bernie to loosen up. He's the best of the lot, Annie. His references are excellent, and his résumé is outta sight. Let's take a chance on him."

"Okay. Him and Trudy," I said, smiling. With Rhonda's baby due and our busy season upon us, we needed help. I just hoped by bringing Bernhard Bruner into the mix, we weren't about to make a horrible mistake. We'd made a few along the way.

CHAPTER TWO

E arly one morning a few days later, I was outside talking to Bernie when Tim McFarland, our front desk manager, hurried across the lawn to me. "Ann, you've got an emergency call on the hotel line. From Liz. And she's crying."

My heart fell to my feet. My daughter Liz, at college in Boston, was usually calm and easy going.

"Excuse me, but I've got to take this," I said to Bernie. Before he could answer, I was hurrying toward the front entrance of the hotel.

I raced inside, through the lobby, past the kitchen, and into my office. My heart pounded as I picked up the phone. "Liz?"

"Mom?" I heard the quiver in her voice before she burst into tears. "Something horrible has happened. There's been a terrible accident. Dad and Kandie ... Dad ... they're both dead!"

The room began to slowly rotate around me. Gripping the edge of my desk, I lowered myself into my desk chair. "Oh my God! Oh, Liz. I'm sorry. So sorry." Tears sprang to my eyes. My ex had ditched me for Kandie— Kandie with a K as the voluptuous receptionist in our office had always called herself. As hurt and angry as I'd been when it happened, I would never wish something like this on either one of them.

"What happened? When did it happen?" I asked, feeling sick as I tried to get my mind around the shocking news.

"Last night. I got a call from Dad's lawyer, Jack Henderson, a few minutes ago. He told me Dad and Kandie went to the club for dinner, and on the way home, Dad lost control of the car on the icy back roads he liked to take. They hit a tree at a pretty good speed."

"Oh no! That's awful, simply awful," I said, imagining the gory details. In the past, I'd been forced to ride with Robert when he'd driven faster than I liked. There was no stopping him.

"And, Mom?" Liz's sobs became louder. "Mr. Henderson reminded me I now have custody of little Robbie. What am I going to do with a two-year-old?"

"You have custody of him? What about Kandie's family?"

"Both of her parents are dead, and neither Dad nor Kandie wanted anyone else to take him. I didn't mention it to you earlier because both Dad and I thought it would never come to anything. But I signed an agreement to take care of Robbie if anything happened to them. Dad told me both he and Kandie wanted this, as I'm Robbie's half-sister."

"Where is Robbie now?"

Liz sniffled. "With the babysitter at her house. As soon as I'm dressed, I'll get him and go over to Dad's house."

"I see..." I tried to imagine this scenario. Liz had told me all about how undisciplined Robbie was. I couldn't imagine her trying to take care of him and going to school.

"Oh my God! Mom, do you think he knew he was going to die? He had me sign the papers right before Christmas not that long ago." She began to sob even more hysterically.

"Liz, listen to me, honey. Your father, no doubt, was simply trying to put things in order. With the business in trouble, he probably wanted to tie up loose ends."

"Mom, I don't know what I'm going to do. Angie and Reggie are back at school, but I haven't called them yet. I need you. Please, you've got to come to Boston and help me."

Still fighting the sickening news, my stomach whirled. "I'll be there as soon as I can. In the meantime, you'd better go and get Robbie and take him to your father's house. A little boy is going to be very confused and unhappy with his parents gone. You need to be there for him."

"Okay. Let me know when you're going to arrive, and Robbie and I'll meet you." She hung up, leaving a buzzing phone in my hand.

Stunned, I hung up and sat in a stupor, trying to fathom all that had happened. My hands crept to the pendant I always wore—the pendant Vaughn Sanders had given me before we were officially engaged.

I lifted the phone and punched in his number, hoping I could catch him between takes for his role on the soap opera, *The Sins of the Children*.

The phone rang and rang. I left a message for him to call me and began checking flight schedules to Boston.

Rhonda burst into the office. "Annie? Is everything okay? Tim told me there's some kinda emergency."

Tears filled my eyes and spilled over. I didn't love Robert anymore, but my heart ached over his early death and his leaving a young, motherless child alone ... well ... there was Liz. I myself had been left an orphan at six and knew the emptiness Robbie would always feel.

"What is it, hon?" Rhonda said, patting me on the back.

"Robert and Kandie were killed in an auto accident last night. They slid off an icy road and crashed into a tree."

Rhonda plunked down into a chair, facing me. "Oh my God! That's terrible. I know I've called him a lot of names in the past but this ..." She shook her head. "He was a rotten bastard to you, but he didn't deserve something like this. And what about their little boy? Poor kid."

"That's the other thing. Apparently, Robert had Liz agree to be Robbie's guardian if anything happened to him and Kandie. Both of Kandie's parents are deceased and she had no siblings. So Liz signed those papers before Christmas when she was staying with them."

"Oh, Annie, what a mess. Poor Liz. I'm so, so sorry. How's she gonna take care of him and finish school?"

"That's what I have to help her figure out. She was just getting back into her schoolwork. Now I don't know what will happen. I'm flying up to Boston as soon as I can."

Rhonda rose and gave me a hug. "You go. Don't worry about the hotel. I'll help Bernie get settled in the house and his office. It's more important for you to be with Liz at this time."

I tried Vaughn again without success. I hung up and hurried home to pack warm clothes for the trip north.

I'd just slammed my suitcase shut when Vaughn called. Hearing his calm, steady, "*Hello,*" I burst into tears.

"What's wrong, Ann?" His obvious concern caused more tears to flood my face. I steadied myself. "It's Robert and Kandie. They were killed in an auto accident due to icy roads. Liz is now guardian of Robbie, and I need to fly to Boston to help her settle things."

"My God! What a horrible thing! I'm really sorry to hear this. Is there anything you want me to do? Do you want me to fly to Boston to be with you?" Vaughn's voice was full of compassion.

"Yes ... no ... oh, I don't know. Until I get things sorted out, be there for me like you always are. I have no idea how long I'll be there, but I'll let you know. I can't believe something like this has happened." A sob caught in my throat.

"How's Liz taking it?" he asked.

"She's very shaken by the whole thing and overwhelmed by the idea of suddenly being responsible for a toddler. Before Christmas, Robert had her sign papers agreeing to that. Both Robert and Kandie wanted her to have him if anything happened to them." I paused. "Liz wondered if Robert had any premonitions of something like this happening. I told her I didn't think so, but I wonder too."

"It's hard to know for sure, Ann, but I personally doubt it. I think it's an unexpected tragedy, a part of life," Vaughn said, reassuring me. "And I'm truly sorry that it happened."

"Thanks. I needed to hear that. I love you, Vaughn," I said. "I'll be in touch. I've got to go now or I'll miss my plane."

"Let me know if I can help. Love you too," Vaughn said.

How lucky I am to have him in my life, I thought and picked up my suitcase.

CHAPTER THREE

Boston's cold and rainy wind gusts jabbed at me as I stood shivering on a sidewalk outside Logan Airport. I hugged my winter coat closer as I waited for Liz to pick me up. Patches of snow and ice were still evident on the sides of the roads within the airport. I was so thankful I'd taken the chance over two years ago to leave Boston and move to Florida and The Beach House Hotel.

I braced myself for greeting Liz. She was hurting so much. At the thought of her taking on the care of Robbie, mixed feelings whirled inside me. I knew it wasn't Robbie's fault that his presence had caused me such pain, but I associated him with his obnoxious, young mother and the cruelties of my ex. Robert had used Robbie's birth to brag to me about finding a new, younger woman to produce the boy he'd always wanted.

My teeth were chattering by the time Liz drove up in a van. Seeing me, she swerved over to the curb, got out of the car, and rushed into my arms, sobbing. I patted her back and stared into the face of the little boy looking at me through the backseat car window. Raindrops streamed down the outside of the window making it seem as if they were his tears.

My heart went out to him. *Poor little guy*, I thought, giving Liz a last squeeze before urging her toward the van. Drivers stuck in traffic behind her beeped their horns impatiently.

Inside the car, I turned to Robbie, who was staring at me curiously. "Hi, Robbie, I'm ..." I stopped, not sure how to call myself.

"I've been calling you Grammy," said Liz, giving me an

apologetic look. "Wasn't sure what else to do."

I blinked in surprise, uncertain I was ready for such a title. True, my fortieth birthday had come and gone, but I didn't think of myself as old enough to be a grandmother. I'd been a very young mother.

Liz chuckled. "It suits you fine, Mom."

I brushed away my concern. After all, Rhonda was about to become both a mother and a grandmother in a matter of weeks. Turning back to Robbie, I smiled and said, "I'm Grammy."

His serious expression softened. "Gammy."

I smiled at him. Even with Robert's features stamped on his face—a permanent reminder of all that had happened between us—Robbie was adorable.

"Mom? I'm so glad you're here. I need you to help me with everything. There's so much to do. I've set up a meeting with Dad's lawyer for tomorrow morning. After I drop Robbie off to day care, we'll go into Boston."

"Where are we going now?" We were heading west into the suburbs.

"To Dad and Kandie's house. They'd just moved into a rental. Dad's business is all but gone. The staff was down to a secretary and himself." Liz blinked back tears. "It's all a mess."

I reached over and patted her shoulder. "We'll get it all straightened out."

We pulled up to a small, colonial-style home in a nice neighborhood. I couldn't help comparing it to the large home Robert and I had shared for so many years—the home he'd cheated me out of. Sadness filled me at all he'd lost because he'd been too egotistical to listen to the advice of others.

"Here we are," Liz said, turning to Robbie with a smile. She got out of the car and lifted him out of the car seat.

"Mommy?" Robbie said.

Liz shook her head. "No, sweetie. Mommy isn't here. It's you and me and Gammy."

My heart broke at the sight of tears rolling down his cheeks. I held out my arms to him. He shook his head and buried his face against Liz's shoulder.

"He'll get used to you, Mom," said Liz.

"I know. I'll give him time."

Liz led me inside the house, and I took a look around. Kandie had refused any of the family furniture she'd been offered, opting instead to buy all new things. The modern furniture, jammed into a space much too small for it, didn't suit the colonial style of the interior.

"Come into the kitchen," said Liz. "Robbie's play area is there." She took off Robbie's coat and hat, and I followed her. Dirty dishes were piled up everywhere. Used pots were sitting on the stove.

"Oh my! What happened?"

"I just haven't had time to clean up." Liz set Robbie down in a corner of the kitchen where a few toys were scattered. Straightening, she shook her head. "Kandie didn't like housekeeping. I swear she didn't do a thing to keep things nice. All she did was sit and watch television."

"Why don't I clean up the kitchen? It'll give me a chance to keep an eye on Robbie and get to know him a little."

"Thanks, I'll change the beds upstairs." She paused. "Guess I'll sleep in Dad and Kandie's room and give you mine. As soon as I get things straightened upstairs, I'll put Robbie down for a nap and then we can talk."

"Fine," I said, appreciating Liz's sensitivity about the bedrooms.

After I stacked dishes in the dishwasher, I scrubbed countertops and then attacked the stove. It, like the rest of the kitchen, had been sorely neglected. I remembered how fussy

Robert had been about having everything tidy in our house and wondered how he could have lived like this.

As I worked, I kept an eye on Robbie. He seemed quite content to sit and play with his blocks and a musical toy. There was something endearing about seeing him like that. I set aside my work and sat down beside him on the rug.

"Hi, there!"

Robbie studied me. "Gammy?"

"Yes, that's me. And you are Robbie. Can you say your name?"

"Wobbie. Obo Wob."

Liz walked in at that moment. I gazed up at her. "What's he saying?

She smiled. "Dad and I sometimes called him Robo-Rob—wind him up and let him go. It used to drive Kandie crazy." Tears leaked from her eyes. "I can't believe all this, Mom." She glanced at Robbie. "What am I going to do?"

I stood. "Let's talk after Robo-Rob goes down for a nap."

Liz picked up Robbie. "Okay, up you go."

As she left the room, Robbie stared over her shoulder at me. I gave him a little wave. Then I searched for a paper and pen. Liz and I had a lot to talk about.

That night, after Robbie had gone to bed, Liz brought out a red, expandable-wallet, file holder.

"We have to go through this," she said sadly. "When I signed the documents, Dad told me about this file. Inside are legal documents and other papers we should know about."

She handed me the huge file holder. "First, I'm going to pour us another glass of wine. We're going to need it."

I sat on the couch in the living room and waited for Liz to return.

She handed me a glass of the red wine we'd sipped at dinner and took a seat beside me. She gazed at me and let out a long sigh. "This is so weird."

"I would never have expected anything like this," I said, still shocked by all that had happened.

Liz opened the file and pulled out copies of both Robert's and Kandie's wills and some other papers. "See? Here is the agreement about my becoming Robbie's guardian. I see that Jack Henderson is executor of the will."

I studied the agreement. It seemed very clear.

"Mom? Dad told me if he could have chosen the perfect person to raise Robbie, it would be you. He said that if I had difficulty with him, I should come to you. Wasn't that sweet of him?"

I got up and left the room without answering her. In the small powder room off the front hall, I grabbed a tissue and let my tears flow. The man Robert had become in the last couple of years was someone I didn't even like. He'd made me seem so unlovable when he left me for Kandie, and then he'd railed at me in anger when I succeeded in business and he didn't. To think he'd trust his precious son to me in any way touched my heart.

Liz knocked on the door. "Mom? Are you all right?"

"I'll be right out. I just needed a few minutes to myself."

I emerged and Liz hugged me. "I don't think Dad ever really loved Kandie. Not after their crazy affair was over. I wish he'd never left you."

I lifted a hand in protest. "Let's not go there. As difficult as the divorce was to go through, I'm happier now than I've ever been. Vaughn and Rhonda and the hotel are my life now. And you, of course."

"And Robbie?" she asked.

I hesitated, and then said, "And Robbie. I'll do whatever I

can to help you and him, Liz."

"Good, because it's almost spring break, and I want to take Robbie down to Florida and leave him with you until I finish the semester. Then I'll have just one more year of school to complete for a degree. Maybe I'll do what Angie is doing and enroll in some online courses."

"Liz ..."

"Don't say a word. Just think about it. In the meantime, I've got to look into getting out of the lease on this house."

"No, Liz. If Jack Henderson is executor of the will, he will take care of it and everything else. But I think it's a good idea for us to know the state of things, so we can be sure Jack is doing his job and doesn't miss anything. What about bills? Did your father have a file for those?"

Liz led me into a small den. A laptop computer was set up on a desk. Beside the desk was a metal file cabinet. The only other thing in the room was a comfortable leather chair I recognized from the company office we'd shared.

"You start there in the file cabinet," said Liz. "I'll continue going through other stuff."

Looking through the metal cabinet, I found files for various household expenses—electricity, water, and the like. It felt strange going through papers that once might have related to me but now related to Robert's life with Kandie.

Liz brought me a file for a credit card. "Wow! Dad owes a lot of money on this."

"What about your father's life insurance? Is there anything in the files about that?"

Liz nodded. "He had a large policy, but I don't think he'd been paying the premiums. He mentioned something about that."

Silent, I shook my head. What had happened to Robert's common sense? Had things been so bad he couldn't even take care of fixed expenses? I looked around at the furniture. It was expensive. Maybe Jack could get enough money from selling it to take care of some of the debt.

Jack Henderson was the lawyer who'd handled the divorce for Robert. After all the tricks he'd tried to pull on me, I detested the man. Nevertheless, I sat quietly beside Liz in his office as we awaited his arrival.

Jack entered the room and smiled at me. "Ann, nice to see you again, although I wish the circumstances were different."

I didn't respond, merely nodded.

"And, Elizabeth," Jack continued. "I'm so sorry about your father and stepmother. Let's see what we can do to make things easier for all concerned." He turned back to me. "We'll put the past behind us and cooperate."

"Of course," I said politely. But I'd keep an eye on him.

By the time we left his office, we had agreed on most things. As Liz had asked, I would help care for Robbie while she finished school. And his living in Florida with me would be no problem. Liz would also take over Kandie's car, so she would be able to transport Robbie. Jack would deal with the lease on the house and contact the credit card company. As executor, he would handle settling the estate, which we all agreed was in a sad state. He would go ahead and sell what furniture and other possessions he could to help pay off debt.

Outside Jack's office, Liz turned to me. "I'm so glad you're here, Mom. Like Mr. Henderson says, you really are a good businesswoman."

"Be careful around people like him," I said. "He's a chameleon. I don't know why your father entrusted everything to him. But we'll keep an eye on him to make sure everything is taken care of."

Even as I reassured Liz, I hid my worries. With all the work at the hotel and now helping with Robbie, I was going to be more than busy—all at a time when Rhonda would be out of the office for a while.

We were heading back home when Rhonda called. "Annie? I've been trying to reach you. Is everything okay?"

"Liz and I are working out a few things. We just met with Jack Henderson, Robert's lawyer."

"Jack Henderson? Isn't he the asshole who tried to screw ya out of money?" Rhonda said. "How can you trust him?"

"I have to. He's the one handling Robert's estate, what little there is of it."

"Oh my God, Annie! Whaddya mean?"

"He left a lot of debt behind. And the life insurance policy he had has lapsed because of lack of payment. Apparently, he hadn't been paying on that for a long time. God knows why."

"And his little boy? And Liz? How are they doing?"

I waited until Liz had walked ahead to get into the car before answering Rhonda. "Robbie is going to be living with me for a while. Liz wants to finish school, and you know how important that is to me. I never got my degree, and I want her to get hers."

"Oh, Annie. How are you gonna manage him and the hotel with me bein' out for a while with the baby? Though Bernie is about to start the job, he needs to understand we still run the hotel."

"That, my dear friend, is something we're all going to have to work on. Right now, Gammy has to fill in for Liz and his parents."

"Gammy? Oh, that's adorable, Annie," gushed Rhonda.

Adorable? More like exhausting, I thought. Now that he was getting used to me, Robbie was beginning to act like any other two-year-old.

CHAPTER FOUR

Over the next few days, I took over the care of Robbie. As he became more comfortable with me, he turned into a whiny, difficult child who'd apparently never been disciplined. The words "no-no" had little effect.

While I babysat him, Liz went to a couple of her classes, so she could take important tests before spring break. In going through things in the house, she'd discovered Kandie's only things of value were the items of jewelry Robert had bought her. Liz wanted none of it.

As Jack had asked, I called an estate sales expert to come in and look at the furniture. The woman in charge agreed to handle the estate sale through her monthly auction. I called Jack to let him know that all of that could be done after we left for Florida and then gave him the woman's contact information.

Liz went to the DMV to transfer ownership of Kandie's van to herself. She hoped to sell it later for something smaller and more suitable to Florida. We sorted through personal, family papers and photographs and loaded the ones Liz wanted to keep into boxes.

I talked to Rhonda every day. Though she didn't come right out and say it, she needed me back there to handle Bernie. After she reported that Bernie and Jean-Luc had had a screaming match, I knew I couldn't wait any longer to go back home.

Liz and I packed up some of Robbie's special toys, clothes, and blankets and prepared to leave for Florida.

On the plane, Robbie sat between Liz and me. We'd arranged an afternoon flight to try to coincide with his naptime, but he was too excited by all that was going on around him to settle down. Finally, after going through a bout of crying that irritated everyone around us, he fell asleep.

"He can be so awful," murmured Liz.

"Remember all he's going through," I said. "He's spoiled for sure, but it's going to take him a while to get used to new rules and all the many changes taking place in his life. In the meantime, he's going to need a lot of love, even when you don't feel like giving it to him."

She gave me a quizzical look. "Was I ever this bad?"

I chuckled. "No, but you'd been taught 'no' meant 'NO'."

"Yeah," said Liz. "Kandie let him get away with murder. I don't think she really cared about him. She didn't give him much attention at all."

My heart clenched. Being a parent was the hardest job around, but all children needed to know they are loved. Though his tantrums were hard to take, I made a silent vow to help Robbie.

In the baggage claim area of the airport, Rhonda called to us, waved, and moved awkwardly toward us in an orange caftan. In just a matter of days, her baby bump had grown bigger and lower, and I realized her baby might not wait too much longer to see the world.

"Annie! I'm so glad you're here. There's lots going on at the hotel." She gave me one of her bosomy hugs and turned to Liz, who was holding Robbie.

"And who do we have here?" Rhonda tweaked Robbie's cheek, and he surprised us all with a wide smile. Her expression grew somber. She gave Liz the best hug she could under the circumstances. "I'm really sorry about what happened to your dad and Kandie. How are you holding up, honey?"

Tears moistened Liz's eyes. "Okay, I guess. Mom's been great. I'm flying back to Boston the day after tomorrow to finish school before the break."

We gathered our bags, picked up the stroller for Robbie, and headed outside. The warm air wrapped around me like a heartfelt welcome; I sighed with pleasure.

As we walked to her car, Rhonda pulled me aside. "I talked to Consuela about finding someone to help with Robbie. One of her neighbors is willing to be a part-time nanny."

"Great. Robbie's a handful. But Liz will have to approve of her, and we both need to spend a lot of time with him until he gets used to everything. Poor little guy is confused."

We caught up to Liz and went to find Rhonda's car.

As I sat in the backseat of Rhonda's convertible with Robbie, I felt the wind finger my hair. I turned to him and couldn't help smiling at the look of enjoyment on his face. His hair was being tossed about in the wind. We'd taken off his jacket so he could enjoy the warmth of the sun. Impulsively, I smiled at him and gave his hand a squeeze. He responded with a little giggle that touched me.

On the way to my house, we passed The Beach House Hotel. I craned my neck. It still felt strange not to pull into the hotel complex to the little house I owned there. Now, I rented the house to the hotel as living quarters for Bernie.

Rhonda drove into my neighborhood and then into the front circle of the house I shared with Vaughn. The imposing white stucco house with a tiled roof was one I'd always admired. It still surprised me sometimes that it was now where I lived and, more than that, it was the house Vaughn had bought so we could spend more time together away from the constant demands of the hotel.

We got out of the car, and I paused a moment to study the house. With five bedrooms and four and a half baths, it was elegant but not ostentatious. It extended across the lawn like a graceful bird whose wings were spread in flight. The large kitchen and huge lanai were the two features of the house I liked best. Vaughn, typical guy, loved the three-car garage and the pool and spa.

I unlocked the massive, wooden front door, and we stepped inside. Light-colored tile on the entrance floor led to the living room beyond, whose décor was brightened by a large Oriental rug in shades of light blue, cream, and gold. A large, white, U-shaped couch sat on the rug, waiting for the rest of the living room furniture we'd ordered to arrive.

Sliding glass doors filled most of the far wall of the living room and led to a screened lanai with a salt-water pool and spa. I suddenly realized how much work we would need to do to make the house toddler-proof. I quickly decided one of the first things I'd do would be to get either water wings or a small life jacket and then arrange for Robbie to get swimming lessons.

When Liz set Robbie down, he took off running.

"Hey, wait, Robbie!" Liz cried, but, laughing gleefully, he continued to run toward the kitchen.

She caught his arm, and he began to scream at the top of his lungs, "No! No!"

Rhonda and I looked at each other and shook our heads.

"She's got her hands full," I said, unable to hide the worry in my voice.

"It brings back so many memories," said Rhonda. "I guess I'd better get used to it."

"Who knew Liz would end up being a mother at her age?" I said.

"Or Angela?" said Rhonda. She elbowed me playfully. "So now we're both grandmothers. Not just me, huh?"

I laughed. I couldn't think of myself that way. Not yet. But the reality of what I was facing was unmistakable when Robbie ran toward me calling, "Gammy! Up!"

So conflicted I wanted to cry, I swung him up in my arms. Vaughn had bought this house just for us. And now the 'just for us' would include a little boy for the foreseeable future. At least until Liz was through this school year.

While Liz fed Robbie his lunch, I went into my office to make a few phone calls. I'd go into the hotel tomorrow. Today, I had to take care of things at home. We needed to have a safety fence put up around the pool. After making those arrangements, I called Troy Taylor, the young man who was in charge of the hotel's spa. He was an excellent swimmer who sometimes taught private swimming lessons. Even though it was our busy season at the hotel, I hoped he'd be able to help me out.

I quickly explained the circumstances to him and told him of my urgency. He responded with a promise to come by between spa appointments to get acquainted with Robbie.

"It'll be sometime this afternoon for sure," he said.

As I hung up, I was grateful for his enthusiasm, but I thought it might have something to do with Liz. He and Liz had had a thing going on between them at Christmastime.

"Robbie's down for a nap. Who was that on the phone?" Liz asked, coming into the room.

"Troy has agreed to give Robbie swim lessons. He'll stop by this afternoon."

Liz sank down into the chair in my office and gave me a glum look. "What am I going to do, Mom? How can I date?

How can I have a real life when I have to take care of my little brother?" Tears rolled down her cheeks. "It isn't fair that I have to give up my life for him. I didn't know what I was doing when I signed that agreement."

My heart went out to her. She was so full of life, so eager to make something of herself. Now, she was beginning to realize, some of her dreams were in jeopardy. I couldn't let her life be totally ruined by the dilemma she faced. I rose and went over to Liz to give her a hug.

"I'm sorry all of this has happened," I said. "We'll have to make the best of it. Robbie needs us. Things will get easier as we all adjust to a new routine. We need to make sure you have enough help so you can continue your schooling. Rhonda has found a woman to act as a day-time nanny for you."

"I love Robbie. I really do," said Liz, sniffling. "I just didn't want kids so soon; you know?"

I thought back to my own history. I'd been forced to leave college when I'd discovered I was pregnant with Liz. I'd married Robert and turned over my dreams for a business to him. He'd taken all the credit for the business I'd formed on paper. I let it happen, thinking we'd work together and be married for the rest of our lives. What a mistake that had been! I didn't want anything like that to happen to Liz. She was a young woman with a bright future—a hard worker who deserved a chance to fly.

"We'll help you," I said quietly. "But you're going to have to be a big part of it. You're legally bound to him as well as by blood. We can turn this into something wonderful for him."

Liz nodded, but the sadness on her face spoke of many things.

I called Vaughn and caught him at a good time. After

spilling my concerns over all that had happened so far, I told him what I wanted to do to the house. He quickly agreed to my plans to make it toddler-proof.

"Go ahead and do what you need to, Ann. The house is yours as much as mine. None of us wanted this to happen, and we're going to have to deal with it the best we can."

My heart squeezed with love for this kind, sweet man. "I love you more than I can tell you."

"When I get home, we can do a whole lot of...talking."

I laughed at the suggestive tone of his voice. I loved the way we flirted with each other.

We talked about his schedule, and I hung up with a promise from him to come to Florida as soon as he could.

Troy appeared as I was completing a list of furniture and other items we needed to convert a guest room into a little boy's room. Liz had left the house to buy groceries, diapers, and other supplies for Robbie.

"Hi, Ann," said Troy. "I'm here to check out the pool and to meet Robbie."

"Thanks for coming right away. I'm nervous about Robbie falling into the pool or off the dock and not being able to swim."

"Don't worry," said Troy. "I can teach him the skills and techniques to save himself. I'm certified to teach infants and toddlers how to survive in water."

"Wonderful." It was exactly what I needed to hear. All of us would try to keep an eye on him, but Robbie was an active little boy who didn't yet listen to warnings.

Troy shuffled his feet. "Uh...is Liz around?"

"She's gone to the grocery store, but should be back any minute." I checked my watch. "And Robbie is due to get up soon. Do you have time to wait?"

"I have no more appointments this afternoon. Mark is

holding down the fort, and Tammi is booked doing nails."

"Sounds good." We'd brought in Mark Spenser to assist Troy. Tammi had been doing nails for our customers from the very beginning.

I heard the sound of the garage door opening. "Here's Liz now."

"I'll help carry in groceries," Troy said.

He followed me into the kitchen.

Liz came through the kitchen door with a bag of groceries. At the sight of Troy, she dropped the bag on the floor and, sobbing, hurried into his arms.

I turned and left the room, giving them the privacy they needed.

As I entered the north wing of the house to check on Robbie, I thought of all the difficulties that lay ahead. It would take time to sort things out.

I tiptoed to the door of Robbie's room and peeked inside. He was sprawled across the double bed clutching the long-eared, stuffed rabbit he loved. His cheeks were flushed with sleep, giving him the appearance of a rosy-cheeked cherub.

He sensed my presence and opened his eyes. His brow furrowed at the sight of me. I waited for the crying to begin and was surprised by the curve of his lips. "Gammy?"

I sat on the bed beside him and brushed his hair away from his face. "I'm here, Robbie. I'm here."

CHAPTER FIVE

I watched as Troy and Liz worked together in the swimming pool to get Robbie accustomed to the water. He kicked freely and squealed joyfully when water splashed onto his face. When Liz let go of one of his hands, his head went under the water. She pulled him up into her arms and soothed his tears.

"Good boy, Robbie. You're doing well."

"Here, let me," said Troy. He took Robbie from her. "As soon as he'll let me work with him on some of the techniques, I will. In the meantime, we'll just play."

Observing the three of them together, I liked what I saw. Robbie was a brave little boy who loved attention. Liz and Troy worked well together, easy in each other's company, attentive to Robbie.

I called to her, "Liz, I'm leaving now. Paul is going to meet me at the store in the hotel van. He'll help me pick up the furniture you and I ordered for Robbie's room, along with a number of things to go with it. Troy, your father is bringing a safety fence to install around the pool. Is everybody going to be all right while I'm gone?"

Liz waved. "See you later."

Robbie was too busy playing in the water to notice.

Later, after Troy had helped put together the crib, I asked him to stay for dinner.

"Sorry. I have a date." He gave an apologetic look to Liz. "I didn't think you'd be in town."

"I didn't think I would be either." I knew her well enough

to know Liz was struggling to hide her disappointment.

"Izzie, me up," said Robbie. He held his arms up to her.

Sighing, Liz did as he asked and faced Troy. "Thanks for the help with the swim lessons."

"Yeah, well, see you around," Troy said.

Watching him go, Liz's eyes filled. "Guess this is going to be the story of my life," she said sadly.

I swung an arm across her shoulder. "Aw, honey. Give it time. Your situation is a surprise for everyone."

After an early dinner, Liz, Robbie, and I headed to the mall. Robbie needed a hat, sunglasses, and another bathing suit. In fact, Robbie needed a lot of even the basic things. As I'd tucked a few of Robbie's items into his new bureau drawers, I realized once more how Robert's financial situation had changed. The child didn't have adequate clothing. I'd do what I could to help, but it seemed so unfair for Robert to have placed Liz in such an uncertain, financial predicament. But like we'd all learned, life wasn't fair.

As I pushed Robbie in his stroller through the mall, I filled with pride at the smiles directed his way. With Robert's blue eyes and Kandie's dark hair, he was a handsome little boy.

His gaze flitted from one colorful object to another in various storefront windows.

"He loves this," I commented to Liz.

"Yeah, I don't think he got out very much. Just to day care and back," Liz said. "Kandie said it was too much of a hassle to take him anywhere."

No wonder he's enthralled with everything, I thought.

Liz's brow was creased with worry when she turned to me. "Mom? I don't want everyone to think Robbie is my baby." She glanced around. "I didn't even have a steady boyfriend when he was born."

"When you explain it, your friends will understand. Other

people don't matter."

Liz frowned. "And who is going to want to date me? I'm a mother to a kid that isn't really mine."

I placed a hand on her shoulder. "We'll all feel better about everything as we get used to it. Robbie is a darling little boy."

No sooner had those words come out of my mouth than Robbie shrieked and fought to get out of his stroller.

"Hey, what's going on?" I asked, trying to settle him in the stroller.

He pointed to a large Panda bear sitting in the window of a shoe store. "Mine!"

"No, Robbie, it's just a display. Let's go. We're going to get you some new jammies."

"Nooo!" screamed Robbie, fighting me. "Nooo!"

Liz took hold of the stroller's handle and quickly moved away, forcing Robbie to stay in his seat.

I followed her and Robbie's screams. Catching up to them, I said, "So that's what usually goes on?"

"Let's hurry up, get our things, and get out of here. Everyone's looking at us."

The clerk who waited on us was apparently used to screaming kids. I was not. No matter how much I tried to soothe him, Robbie continued fighting the stroller straps and screaming. I realized then that all the changes in his life had finally caught up to him. Liz wheeled him away while I finished up with the sales clerk. When the bill was rung up, I gasped at the total. And this, I suspected, was only the beginning of many more expenses.

On the way home, Robbie fell asleep in his car seat. In the quiet that followed, Liz turned to me. "Thanks for everything, Mom. If there's anything left of the estate, I'll pay you back."

"Okay. We'll see." I doubted there would be enough to pay for even the clothes Robert's son needed.

At the sound of someone in the kitchen, I sat up with a start. Then I heard Robbie's cry and it all came back—the accident, Liz, and Robbie. Leaning back against my pillow, I realized how much my life had changed...again. I closed my eyes. While my personal life might change drastically, my professional life had to remain steady, especially with Rhonda's new baby on the way. I got out of bed and hurried into the shower to get ready for the day.

When I entered the kitchen, Robbie was sitting in his new highchair, pounding on the plastic tray with a metal spoon. Her hair tousled, Liz was sitting at the kitchen table, holding her head in her hands.

"Where do you keep the little coffee containers for your coffee machine? I'm desperate for a good strong cup of coffee."

At the sight of my usually peppy daughter drooping like a wilted hibiscus blossom, my heart went out to her. I quickly found the little cups, put one into the machine, and pressed the button.

A few moments later, I handed her a cup of coffee. "Consuela is bringing Elena Ramos, a friend of hers, here for you to interview for a part-time nanny. Elena's sister Rita is going to be Rhonda's nanny. I understand these young women are very nice and are also accustomed to handling kids. Let me know what you think. I'll have a chance to talk to her later in the day if you like her."

"If she can walk and talk, I'll like her," teased Liz. "Seriously, though, Robbie has to like her too or it won't work."

"Good luck with her. Now, I've got to run. You can always reach me at the hotel." I gave her a quick kiss on the cheek and then went over to Robbie. "See you later, little guy."

"Gammy," he said, giving me a serious look.

My heart melted. I gave him a kiss and waved goodbye.

"Talk to you later," said Liz.

As I walked into the lobby of the hotel and toward my office, it felt like coming home. A sense of satisfaction wrapped around me as I took in the attractive décor of the living room and heard the buzz of conversation from the dining room.

As I stood there, a little black and tan dog rushed toward me, wagging her tail. "Hi, Trudy!" I bent to pat her and was rewarded with a quick kiss that made me laugh.

"Ahhh, Ann. She likes you. Always a good sign," said a deep voice, and Bernhard strode toward me. "Welcome back."

I stood and smiled at him. "How are things here?"

"Improving," he said.

I blinked in surprise, uncertain as to how to take that. I hadn't thought things were bad.

"How's the house? And are you settled in your new office?" A storeroom along the first-floor hallway had been converted to an attractive office for him.

"I'm still waiting for my printer. The first one we bought was defective. But my computer is up and running. And the house is nice. Very nice. I understand you used to live there."

"Yes. I recently moved to a different location. But I've always loved that house."

He smiled. "Trudy and I will be happy there."

I studied him a moment. He was wearing gray slacks and a long-sleeved white shirt. I couldn't help wondering what was behind his reserved appearance. He was a good-looking man in a somewhat severe way. His dark hair, gray at the temples, was brushed back from his strong features. His body was straight and tall and well-padded. I found it interesting that he poured so much affection onto his small, lively dachshund. I would have pictured him with a solid, unruffled, great dane.

"I'll see you later at the staff meeting," I said and moved away. I was anxious to speak privately to Rhonda.

When I stepped into the kitchen, Consuela greeted me with a hug. "Annie, I'm so sorry about all that happened. How is Liz? And the little boy?"

"I think we're all in a state of shock. Liz can't believe she's gone from being a free, easy-going student to the mother of a toddler. There's still a lot to work out. She'll be returning to Boston tomorrow to go back to school."

"I think she'll like Elena."

"I hope so. I'm going to be more than busy with the hotel while Rhonda's out with the baby."

Consuela waggled a finger at me. "I don't think we're going to have to wait too long for that baby. It's coming soon. I just know it."

I laughed. "I think you're right. I noticed it the other day."

After I grabbed a cup of coffee, I made my way into the office I shared with Rhonda. She wasn't there, so I turned on my computer to check figures. Glancing at the rooms income, I smiled with satisfaction. When I caught sight of the sales figures from the dining area, I frowned. Something was wrong. I got up and returned to the kitchen. "Consuela, when is Jean-Luc coming in?"

She gave me a worried look. "I don't know."

"What's going on?"

She glanced around warily and then whispered, "It's the new manager. He and Jean-Luc don't like each other."

Rhonda entered the kitchen. "Annie! I'm so glad to see ya! We missed you!" She gave me an awkward hug while protecting her belly. "We've got lots to talk about."

Consuela handed Rhonda a cup of coffee. "You might need this."

"Aw, thanks, honey. I guess I do. It was hard to get up this morning."

I followed Rhonda into the office, and after taking a seat at my desk, I turned to her. "What is going on between Jean-Luc and Bernie?"

Rhonda lowered herself into her chair and set down her coffee cup. Leaning forward, she shook her head. "They hate each other, plain and simple. I don't know what we're going to do about it, Annie. We need them both."

"Why are the figures in the dining room so low?"

"Jean-Luc refused to cook for us one night. I was afraid to tell you because you have so much other stuff going on. But we're going to have to get it settled."

"Okay, then. Let's get Bernie in here." I buzzed the intercom and was pleased when he picked up immediately.

"Hi, Bernie. Can you come to our office? Rhonda and I need to talk to you."

"Of course," he answered crisply and hung up.

In moments, he and Trudy appeared at the door to our office.

"Come on in," I said, indicating a chair at the small round conference table in our office.

I joined him and Rhonda at the table.

After laying the financial printout on the table so he could see, I said, "I understand we have a problem in the kitchen. As you can see, the numbers are way down."

He nodded. "But the savings on food items is way up. There's been a lot of waste in the kitchen. We can't have that, can we?" He gave me a look that challenged me to speak.

I gulped and drew a breath. "The chef is in charge of

ordering what he needs for the kitchen. Is that why Jean-Luc refused to cook one night?"

Bernie shifted uneasily in his chair. "Perhaps."

"The hotel's reputation is based on its good food as much as anything else. We can't do anything to stop that," said Rhonda.

"I thought you wanted me to run this hotel," said Bernie, drawing himself up. "That's what I intend to do."

"Our staff is like family to us," I said. "We respect one another and our choices unless it becomes a problem. We've been able to make arrangements with a local food bank to supply them with excess staples and the like, which gives us a tax credit."

"And the excess prepared food?" Bernie said.

"The staff is welcome to have it for lunch or to take it home," said Rhonda. "I like the idea that they can enjoy it and tell others about it."

"So be it," said Bernie. "But let's be clear. Am I or am I not to run this hotel? In the interview, you indicated you wanted me to step in right away to help you."

I took a moment to form the right words. "Yes, you were hired to help us run the hotel. I want you to think of it as yours, though in fact, it's ours. Rhonda's, mine, and yours, along with every other staff member. That's how we are able to succeed at The Beach House Hotel. Everyone working here feels a part of it."

Bernie rose. "I'm going to have to rethink things," he said stiffly. "Thank you, ladies."

Rhonda and I glanced at each other and watched silently as he left the office. Trudy followed behind him, bobbing along on her short, crooked legs, acting as offended as he.

"Annie, we can't have him just walk away from us!" Rhonda puffed.

I held up a hand. "Give him time to think it through. He's used to running large hotels like a dictator. We're very different."

When Jean-Luc arrived, I went to see him.

He smiled as I approached. "Hi, Annie. How are things in Boston? I was sorry to hear about the family's loss."

"There's still a lot to be done. Liz has brought her little brother to Florida. I'm going to have my hands full with him and the hotel." I cleared my throat. "Can we talk?"

He made a face. "If it's about Bernhard, I have nothing to say."

"Please, Jean-Luc, we need your help."

I waved him toward the office, and he reluctantly followed me.

As we'd done with Bernie, Rhonda and I indicated a seat at the table for Jean-Luc.

He took it, and we sat down with him.

"I understand you refused to cook one evening," I began.

Jean-Luc pounded the table with a fist. "No one, especially Bernhard, is going to tell me what I order for my meals."

"Exactly," I said, bringing a look of surprise to Jean-Luc's face.

He relaxed his hand. "You agree?"

"Of course," I said. "The kitchen is your domain."

"*Mais oui,*" he said, smiling.

"But Jean-Luc," I added. "Part of his job is to oversee expenses, so if he needs to know something about kitchen costs, we want you to cooperate. Okay?"

His lips curled with obvious distaste.

Rhonda reached over and patted his hand. "Look, Jean-Luc, if you can learn to get along with me in the kitchen, you can get along with everybody. Right?"

Jean-Luc's lips twitched with amusement. He glanced at

Rhonda. *"C'est vrai."*

I laughed when Rhonda looked as if she didn't know whether to be pleased or not.

CHAPTER SIX

That afternoon, I dashed home to check on things there. Liz had called me earlier, giving me a glowing report on Elena. As I walked into the kitchen, a short, attractive young woman greeted me with a smile that lit her face. Wearing a pair of black slacks and a crisp white blouse, she gave the impression of being very professional.

"I'm Ann Rutherford. You must be Elena," I said, taking in the confident way she held herself.

She smiled and extended her hand. "Pleased to meet you. Liz has gone out to pick up a few things, and Robbie is down for a nap."

"How are things going?" I asked.

"Good. Robbie isn't quite used to me yet, but I like him, and he seems to like me." She grinned. "Of course, at his age, he doesn't like the word '*no*,' but we'll work that out."

"I like what I hear about you. I know that anyone Consuela recommends will be good. She's a stickler for perfection."

Elena laughed, "Oh, yes. Everyone knows that."

"So tell me, what are your qualifications?"

"I'm the oldest of eight children. That's where I got my start. I've also taken a number of courses for becoming a trained nanny, starting with the basics like CPR and first aid, and, at the local community college, some education courses in childhood development. I've had various jobs in South Florida. Most recently, I was hired by a family in Miami, but I missed my own family and decided to come back here."

"Very good. Why don't we sit to discuss specifics?" I

indicated a seat at the kitchen table and lowered myself into a chair opposite her. "Liz mentioned you're available full-time during the week and will do weekend hours as required. Is that right?"

She nodded. "I'm available as live-in or not. Some of my customers preferred to have me stay during the work week and then work day shifts or only hours as needed over the weekend to give them more privacy."

I immediately thought of Vaughn. "Yes, I can understand that."

After discussing rates and specific job requirements, I rose, satisfied with our decision. "I'll draw up a contract for you to sign and have it ready for you tomorrow morning when you come in at seven. Is that all right?"

Elena stood. "That will be fine." She extended her hand. "Thank you very much, Ms. Rutherford."

Feeling ancient, I shook her hand. "Please call me Ann."

Her brown eyes sparkled with pleasure. "I'm glad I met you. Consuela talks about you and Rhonda all the time. She loves her new apartment at the hotel."

"We love Consuela. Manny too. They deserve whatever we can give them."

Elena was about to leave when Liz walked into the kitchen, carrying a couple of large bags.

"Mom! Isn't Elena great? I'm so happy she'll help us out."

She and Elena exchanged smiles.

"Me too. What did you get?" I asked, studying the over-sized plastic bags holding a number of odd-shaped things.

"Elena has a list of toys and books for kids Robbie's age. She wants to keep him busy in an educational way."

"Right," said Elena. "He seems to be a very bright boy."

I smiled at the look of pride that crossed Liz's face. She might not know it, but she was going to be a good guardian for her brother.

Liz and Elena began going through the items in the bag. I left them and hurried back to the hotel. We had several new arrivals scheduled, and I wanted to greet as many of them as possible.

By the time I returned home, Liz was giving Robbie his nighttime bath. From the shallow water in the tub, Robbie looked up and pointed. "Gammy." He held up a plastic truck. "Fuck."

Liz and I looked at each other and laughed.

"I'm hoping he gets the 'TR' sound down soon," Liz said, still grinning. She helped him out of the tub and began to dry him off. "I really like Elena. She'll move into the guest room next to Robbie's tomorrow morning. Is that all right?"

"Sure," I said, realizing the house Vaughn and I had thought might be too big for us had suddenly become drastically smaller. I was relieved the master bedroom area had its own wing.

That night, when I talked to Vaughn, I explained the latest plans, half expecting him to balk at the way things were turning out. But, true to his nature, he listened and merely said, "It'll seem easier when things get more settled. Funny how things turn out, huh?"

"When are you going to be able to come home?" I asked, missing him so much I ached.

"That's why I called." I could hear the smile in his voice as he continued. "I'll be home tomorrow night."

"Hurry," I said. "I can't wait to see you!"

He chuckled happily. "Good. I'd better go now. Love you."

"Love you, too," I answered, knowing those words were inadequate for the way I felt about him.

###

Promptly at seven, Elena appeared at the door, carrying a small, black suitcase.

"Good morning," I said cheerfully. "Robbie is just waking up."

Elena smiled. "Great. I'll go right to his room."

Curious to see how she was with Robbie, I followed her to his room.

Elena cracked open his door, peeked inside and said, "Boo!"

Through the crack, I saw Robbie stare at the door and then, smiling, he shrieked, "Boo!"

Elena opened the door and stepped inside. She began talking softly to him, reminding him of who she was, telling him about all the things they were going to do. All this was done as she lifted him out of the crib and quickly and smoothly changed his diaper.

I stepped out from the shadows in the hallway. "Hi, Robbie!"

He frowned from me to Elena and then pointed to me. "Gammy."

The smile that crossed his face charmed me. He seemed so alive, so interested in everything going on around him.

Elena stepped away so I could pick him up. I hugged him to me and carried him to the kitchen. After I got him settled in his highchair, I left him with Elena to go check on Liz. She was flying to Boston to return to school for the last couple of days before break and to follow through on funeral arrangements that she and Jack had made.

I tapped on her bedroom door.

"Come in," she called.

She was dressed and packing her suitcase when I entered

her room. She looked at me and sighed. "I got a text message from thc funcral home. They're all set for the burial tomorrow." Her eyes filled. "We're doing exactly what Dad asked. No service, just a private burial in the Rutherford plot. But it seems so sad to me."

"Do you want me to be there, Liz?" It was something I didn't want to do, but for Liz, I would.

She shook her head. "No, I think it would be a little weird, don't you?"

"Possibly, but it might make it easier on you."

"Thanks, anyway," said Liz. "Angie is having me to dinner tonight; she said she'd go to the funeral with me."

"That's nice." Though Rhonda's daughter Angela was expecting a baby sometime soon, she'd managed to stay in school, trying to get as much of her coursework out of the way before her baby came.

"Yeah, she's such a good friend," Liz continued. "I love her."

"Me too," I said, sitting down on the bed. "Is everything else under control?"

Liz nodded. "Thanks. I'll put the boxes of paperwork we packed up into Kandie's van and store them here when I drive back down. Then, I'll see about selling the car." She gazed at me with a sadness that dimmed the usual brightness of her blue eyes. "Dad was always so proud of all the things he owned. Now, it doesn't mean much, does it?"

I shook my head and wrapped my arms around her. "It's one of life's greatest lessons. Things are just things."

Liz began to cry softly.

"Oh, honey. I'm so sorry."

I rubbed her back, thinking back to the times she'd been hurting in the past. Comforting her like this was all I could do. Life would take care of the rest.

CHAPTER SEVEN

My heart beat rapidly as I waited for Vaughn to make his appearance in the baggage claim area of the Southwest Florida International Airport. Anticipation swept through me. I'd never tire of my excitement at seeing him again.

I noticed a commotion at the far end of the room, and then he appeared, a tall man in a crowd of people surrounding him, some asking for his autograph. With long strides, he walked toward me, his eyes focused on my face. As I returned his smile, I tried to ignore curious glances cast my way.

Vaughn pulled me into his embrace, and the world around us disappeared as I inhaled his particular scent and felt his strong arms around me. My man had come home to me.

"Let's grab my suitcase and get out of here," he said. "I can't wait to get home to relax."

"Home is a little different from when you last saw it," I gently warned him.

He gazed down at me with the dark eyes every female devotée of *The Sins of the Children* knew very well. "How are you doing with all the changes?" he asked as we walked through the baggage claim area. "And Liz? Is she holding up?"

"It's been a tough time, but Liz is handling it as well as can be expected. It's been difficult for her to lose her father this way. And she's not all that happy about suddenly having the care of Robbie. Who can blame her? Overnight, she's gone from happy college student to a young mother."

Vaughn gave me a thoughtful look. "It can't be easy for her."

"I've hired a nanny to help her and us out, but I'd forgotten what a two-year-old is like. Robbie's bright, but temperamental. I understand. The poor little guy has had to handle the loss of his parents and moving in with me—all in a short period of time. Liz and I both like his new pediatrician. She's tuned into his hurt and will help us deal with it if it becomes an issue."

Vaughn's suitcase came toward us on the baggage conveyer belt. Vaughn grabbed it and my hand, and we hurried out of the terminal.

As I drove down the highway to Sabal, Vaughn asked, "How's the new car?"

"Great! It's nice not to have to worry about my old car breaking down." I'd traded my worn-out Honda in for one of their new SUVs. Liz had wanted me to buy something fancy, but I was more like my staid, proper grandmother than even I'd suspected.

"And the hotel?" Vaughn asked.

"Okay, I guess. Wait until you meet our new general manager. I'm anxious to know what you think of him and his little dog."

Vaughn grinned. "You told me about the dog. My aunt had a dachshund when I was growing up. She and all of us loved him like crazy. Fritzie was his name."

"Trudy may be small, but she has Bernie well-trained to meet her every wish."

Vaughn chuckled. "You said he was a bit uptight. Is he fitting in with the rest of the crew?"

I shrugged. "Yes and no. He's stiff, but that's his nature. Rhonda's convinced we can loosen him up a little, but I'm not sure. It's a bit of a worry for me."

Vaughn reached over and gently squeezed the back of my neck. "I'm here to take away a few of your worries."

I laughed at the leering expression he gave me. Vaughn knew when he and I were making love, nothing else mattered.

We entered the house to find Elena in the pool with Robbie and Troy. When she saw us, Elena hurried out of the pool and wrapped a towel around herself.

"Hi, Ann! I hope you don't mind, but I'm learning how to teach Robbie to survive in the water."

"Of course not. I'm glad you'll be able to help him between swimming lessons." I took Vaughn's elbow. "Elena Ramos, this is my fiancé, Vaughn Sanders."

She smiled at him and held out her hand. "Pleased to meet you, Mr. Sanders. My mother loves your show."

Vaughn smiled. "Thanks. Please call me Vaughn. Guess we're going to be more like family while Robbie is here."

"Yes, but I'll stay out of your way as much as possible to give you and Ann your privacy."

I turned to Troy. "How's Robbie doing?"

"He's coming along," said Troy, ruffling Robbie's wet, dark hair. "He loves the water, but he doesn't like to get his face wet. I'm working on that."

"Gammy!" Robbie cried, pointing at me.

"Gammy? What is that going to make me?" said Vaughn, laughing.

"I'm sure he'll come up with something. Hard to believe we're grandparents already, huh?"

Vaughn nodded. "Though I suspect Ty and June won't wait too long after they're married. But nothing should stop us from being ourselves. Right?"

I chuckled softly at the sexy look he gave me and took his hand.

"Let me show you some of the changes in the house. You

already saw the highchair and other toddler items in the kitchen. The pool fence is easily removed for parties, but will remain up most of the time because of Robbie. We had a locksmith come in and install locks high enough on most of the doors to keep them out of Robbie's reach. We just have to remember to keep certain doors locked at all times."

As we walked through the living room, I said, "We've put safety covers on electrical outlets, and we've installed special openers on many of the cupboards in the kitchen, so he can't get in. I've already informed the hotel housekeepers that, when they come to clean the house, they'll have to be extra careful not to leave any dangerous cleaning supplies around."

"Wow!" Vaughn said. "I'd forgotten what it's like to have a toddler around. Especially these days, when there are so many rules and guidelines."

"I know." I'd raised Liz on a much more easygoing regimen, and she'd done just fine.

I led Vaughn into the guest wing of the house and showed him Robbie's room.

He studied the crib and the racing car theme Liz and I had put together and smiled. "Nice."

"Elena will use the guest room next door for the nights she'll be staying here, which will mostly be during the week. Liz is still in her room, and the other guest room will be for anyone else who comes here." I tightened my fingers on his hand. "Is it okay with you? I know the situation isn't what either of us envisioned when you bought this place for us."

He slung an arm around my shoulder. "What can we do? We have to help Liz. And as long as we keep our wing of the house to ourselves, I can live with it."

I released a little puff of relief.

Vaughn drew me to him and, gazing down at me, wiggled his eyebrows. "You going to help me unpack?"

"Later, big boy," I said playfully, knowing that wasn't what he was asking. "How about some lunch?"

He patted his stomach. "Sounds good. God knows you can't get decent food on an airplane anymore."

When we went back to the kitchen, Robbie was sitting in his highchair, eating pieces of cheese and small bites of apple.

"He's almost ready for his nap," Elena explained. "After I put him down, I'll be in my room."

I started to protest and stopped. I wanted her help with Robbie, but I wanted some alone time with Vaughn too.

I made Vaughn's favorite sandwich—ham and Swiss cheese on rye—and we took our sandwiches and iced tea out to the glass-topped table on the lanai.

Vaughn sat and leaned back in his chair. Lifting his face to the sun, he sighed with pleasure. "Sure feels good. New York is in the low thirties today."

"It a good time to be here," I said. "The hotel is full of people grateful to be able to sit in the sun like this."

After lunch, Vaughn said, "Why don't we eat dinner at the hotel? I'm hungry for some of Jean-Luc's food."

I smiled. "Whatever you want."

"And later," he said, eyes twinkling with mirth, "we can have our 'dessert.'"

I laughed at the game he was playing. "You got it."

As Vaughn headed into our bedroom to take a nap, I hurried back to the hotel.

When I walked through the front entrance, Bernie greeted me with a worried frown. "We have a problem."

My heart sank to my toes. "What's the matter?" Things had been going well when I'd left the hotel to pick up Vaughn.

"It's the PMS here at the hotel," he said grimly.

'Whaaat?" *Would he dare to be that much of a sexist?*

Bernie rolled his eyes at me. "The Property Management

System. The computers."

Chagrinned, my mind quickly switched gears. "What happened?"

"The whole system crashed. We have to get somebody in right away to fix it. The reservations system, the front office, guest folios, everything I need, they're all down."

At the idea of losing reservations and making guests unhappy, my stomach churned. I raced into my office. When we'd first set up the system, we'd used the Geek Guys in town. We needed them now. I punched in their number and tapped my toe, waiting for them to pick up. A message came on. I told them about our emergency and asked them to call back right away.

Bernie knocked at the door. "Any news?"

I shook my head and took a moment to stroke Trudy's smooth head. "I had to leave a message. Where's Rhonda? She might know of other people we can call."

Bernie frowned. "She said she was going to do some last-minute shopping for the baby."

I ignored the sign of disapproval on his face. We were women running this hotel, and that meant we had more than one role. Being a wife and mother was important to Rhonda. I understood that.

In a panic, I called Troy at the spa. He picked up right away.

"Hi, Ann. What's going on with the computers?" he asked.

"The system is down. We need to have someone help us get it back up. The Geek Guys didn't answer their phone. Do you have a friend who might be available to help us immediately?"

"As a matter of fact, I do. A buddy of mine is trying to set up his own computer service and repair business. He knows a lot more about that stuff than most. He's teaching a couple of courses at the nearby tech college. Want me to see if he's free?"

"That would be wonderful. In the past, the Geek Guys shop

hasn't always been quick to respond."

I hung up from Troy and turned to Bernie. "Troy has a friend who may help us."

"Good." Bernie let out a 'tsk' of frustration. "I was on a call with the office of Senator Byers when the system went down. I need to call him back."

At the mention of that name, a shiver crossed my shoulders. "Oh no! Not him! He's such a slime."

Bernie stared at me with surprise.

"After some awful publicity about Vaughn and me in my pool, he tried to get me to come to his room. It was so degrading, disrespectful ... humiliating."

"Ahhh, I see." Bernie's lips thinned with disgust. "We can't have that here."

"No," I responded, pleased by his attitude.

The phone rang. I snatched up the call.

"Okay," Troy said, "he's free and is on his way here. Chad Bowen is his name. He'll come right to the front desk. Good luck! I'm having to juggle things here a bit."

"Thanks," I said and hung up.

Trudy placed her little paws on my legs. At the pleading look in her brown eyes, I picked her up, careful to support her back. "Okay, little lady. Want to say hello?"

She responded with a kiss on the tip of my nose. Smiling, I gave her a little hug and set her down.

The look of adoration on Bernie's face as he picked up Trudy was touching. As I had before, I wondered about the stern-looking man who all but melted at the feet of this little dog. Impulsively, I said, "Bernie, why don't you come for cocktails and a simple dinner at my house tonight?" I quickly added, "And bring Trudy."

He smiled and bobbed his head. "Sounds great. What time?"

Vaughn, I was pretty sure, wouldn't mind this change of plans. I thought quickly. "Jean-Luc and Sabine can handle dinner, and Tim is scheduled on the front desk. Why don't we say seven o'clock? It won't be a late night." I wasn't about to give up playtime with Vaughn.

Bernie beamed at me. "Sounds good."

He left the office with Trudy, and I realized he was a lonely man.

I called Vaughn and told him what I had in mind. "I'll bring home some steaks if you're willing to grill them."

"Sounds good," said Vaughn. "I'm anxious to meet this new guy of yours."

"Whoa!" I said, laughing. "Bernie isn't my guy. You are!"

"Got that damn right," said Vaughn, keeping the game going.

"See you later," I said and hung up the phone just as Bernie led a young man into my office.

"Ann, this is Chad Bowen," said Bernie. "He's going to get to work on PMS now."

I stood and shook his hand, unable to stop from staring at him. Chad was tall and muscular. And with his strawberry-blond hair and bright blue eyes, he looked like a male model for a tourism ad for the state of Florida. *Not your typical desk jockey*, I thought.

"I'll take a look at the system and see what I can do," Chad said agreeably. "How long has it been since it has been checked?"

Heat flushed my cheeks. "Six months. I know I should have had it checked sooner, but we were busy preparing for a big wedding, and then the holidays came..." my voice drifted off at the looks of dismay on Bernie's and Chad's faces.

"Well, let's see what's happening," Chad said diplomatically. "For a hotel operation like this, I would suggest quarterly inspections and monthly tests in addition to the daily evaluations and backups that should be done during the night audit."

"Thanks," I said and sank down into my chair as Bernie and Chad left. Though he sometimes made me feel inadequate, I realized how much Rhonda and I needed to have Bernie around. Our personal lives were changing so rapidly it was affecting our everyday involvement in the business. Nevertheless, I needed to stay on top of things. The hotel was my baby in a way that none of the others was.

I looked over the financial report I'd printed off that morning. We'd had a good month. But the high season—January, February, and March—had to be good for us in order to carry the costs for the entire year. And in the hotel business, warm weather up north, cold weather in Florida, and numerous other factors could mean the difference between doing well and falling on our faces.

Rhonda came bustling into the office. "Annie, you won't believe all the things I bought for the baby. It was so much fun! I'm getting really excited now!"

"But what about the baby shower Dorothy wanted to give for you?" Dorothy Stern, our part-time office assistant, was thrilled with the prospect of having Rhonda's and Angela's babies around.

Rhonda waved away my concern. "I talked to Dorothy this morning, and we agreed that she would request each guest to bring gifts for the women's shelter I support. They need everything from diapers to toddler clothes. That way, we can celebrate my baby, but in a way to give to others. I'm thrilled with the idea."

"That's perfect." Rhonda had won $187 million dollars in the Florida lottery and certainly didn't need others to buy things for her. "I know people close to you want to be able to do something special for you."

"I feel so blessed to have so much that I want to share it. You know? Course, most of it is in trusts and all, but still..."

Rhonda's story was one I loved to hear. She was one of the lucky winners who'd had excellent legal and financial advice from the beginning. And though she technically had a lot of money, it was tied up in ways that prevented her from spending it in crazy ways. Still, she was one of the most generous people I knew.

"So what's this I hear about our computers?" she said, easing her pregnant bulk into her desk chair.

"The system must have gone down right after you left the hotel." I told her the PMS story and we shared a hearty laugh.

"I'm tellin' ya, Annie, every time I think we're learning all about the hotel business, something new comes up. Do you think we'll ever really know everything about it?"

I chuckled. "Not a chance. But we have to do the best we can. And now we have Bernie to help us."

"Yeah, he's a bit of a prick, but we need him because, Annie, I don't think this baby is going to wait too much longer to come into this world. I hope not, anyway. It's getting really uncomfortable to lug this kid around." She patted her baby bump affectionately.

We were discussing Chad and his qualifications when a knock sounded at the door and Chad came in.

"I've got things up and running, but you're going to need to install some upgrades, and I need to do some security checks. Maybe we can set up a time to do that late at night sometime this week."

I turned to Rhonda. "As you must have guessed, this is Chad Bowen."

She smiled. "I'm glad to meet you. Are you by chance Sadie Bowen's son?"

He grinned, "Guilty as charged."

Rhonda laughed. "She's in a theater group I used to belong to." She turned to me. "I sometimes worked on the sets for the annual musical show. Sadie is quite the talented singer."

"Yeah, too bad I didn't get those genes," Chad said, smiling.

"Would you consider becoming our IT guy on a part-time basis?" I asked him. "You were so quick to respond, I'm impressed. And now you're willing to work at night."

"Great idea," said Rhonda. "Will you do that for us, Chad?"

"Thanks. I'd like to. I'll draw up a proposal and then you can decide if you like my terms," Chad said, impressing me even more.

After he left the office, Rhonda turned to me. "I've always heard he's a good kid. And Sadie's had a hard time of it. I hope we can hire him. It would be good to add him to the family."

I smiled. It seemed our family was growing in all kinds of ways.

CHAPTER EIGHT

After greeting Jean-Luc and Sabine and making sure they were set for the dinner rush, I grabbed some steaks from the kitchen and hurried home to get ready for my evening with Vaughn and Bernie.

As I walked into the kitchen, the sight of Vaughn puttering around filled me with joy. He turned and smiled at me, and I rushed into his open arms.

"So, so glad you're home," I said, taking a moment to enjoy his presence, the feel of his arms around me. My life with the hotel was extremely busy, but mornings and nights without Vaughn were achingly lonely.

We broke apart, and I patted Vaughn's cheek. "I'm looking forward to the evening. Bernie seemed so pleased to be invited. And he's bringing his dog."

"That's a bit unusual, isn't it?" said Vaughn.

"Trudy isn't just any dog," I said, rising to her defense. "She's a real sweetheart—lively, affectionate, and full of personality. I'm falling in love with her."

He frowned. "Uh oh. Does that mean we're getting a dog?"

I laughed. "No, but if we were to ever get one, I'd want a dog like Trudy. Just wait until you see her."

I left him in the kitchen and went to check on Robbie. He was in the pool with Elena. My spirits lifted at the sound of his giggles as he played with her in the shallow end. She looked up at me and smiled. "Robbie loves the water. And he's getting better about getting his head and face wet."

"Good," I said. I stared at our wooden dock leading into the small inlet that served the eight houses in our neighborhood. A sailboat tied to the dock bobbed up and down in the water like a toy boat in a tub. The thought of Robbie or any other little one left unattended brought a chill racing across my shoulders.

I turned to Elena. "Tomorrow we'll have to take Robbie to get fitted for a life jacket. I don't ever want Robbie by the inlet or the dock without it."

"Okay. No problem," said Elena.

Feeling better about his safety, I went into my bedroom to change. As I removed my linen dress, I reveled in the peace and quiet of the room. The walls—painted a soft, warm, gray—met a darker-gray carpet that felt soft on my feet. The pale-gold duvet on the bed complemented the gold, tweed fabric of the overstuffed chairs that sat in front of a large window. The east-facing window overlooked a small, private lanai off the bedroom. On the opposite side of the room, sliding glass doors led to the family lanai and the pool overlooking the water of the inlet.

When I'd first seen the room, I was enthralled with the idea of having the sun available to it from morning until night. The window treatments guaranteed that it wouldn't cast too much heat into the space.

"Hey, princess," Vaughn called into the room. "Better hurry up. Our guests are arriving."

I quickly hung up my dress and grabbed a cotton sundress from the closet. Vaughn liked me in blue, and the blue of this simple dress matched the color of my eyes. I pulled a brush through my straight, dark hair and studied myself in the mirror over my bureau. I was a grandmother through unusual circumstances. Did being "Gammy" make me seem any older? I thought of the welcome home I had in mind for Vaughn and smiled. At least for tonight, it wouldn't.

I hurried into the living room. Bernie stood. Trudy barked and ran over to me, wagging her tail. I bent down and stroked her head, earning more wiggles from her. When I straightened, Bernie smiled his approval.

"Welcome," I said to him, and held out my hand.

He shook it solemnly. "It's good to be here. Thank you."

Vaughn stood by with a look of amusement as he studied the dog who looked up at him with a doggie grin. He turned to Bernie. "Can I get you that scotch now?"

"Yes, indeed. That would be nice."

Vaughn turned to me. "Glass of pinot grigio?"

"Perfect. Why don't we go out onto the porch? Perhaps tonight we'll be able to see the green flash."

"Green flash? What is that?' Bernie asked, following me onto the screened-in porch that overlooked the water, giving us a nice view of sunsets.

As I did with most new visitors to the Gulf coast, I explained, "If the atmosphere is just right, you can sometimes see a bright green flash at the moment the sun dips beneath the horizon. I've never seen it, but I never get tired of looking for it."

"Ahhh, sounds like a plan," Bernie said, smiling as he accepted his drink from Vaughn.

He sat in one of the comfortable, cushioned chairs. After being firmly told to stay down, Trudy sat dutifully at his feet.

Vaughn handed me my glass of wine, set the tray down on a nearby table and lifted his glass. "Here's to friendships!"

Bernie and I raised our drinks. After we each had taken a sip, Vaughn settled on the loveseat next to me.

"So, Bernie, tell me a little bit about yourself. I understand you've come to The Beach House Hotel from New York City.

The Brightly Hotel is a big, beautiful, busy property. I know it well. This is quite a change for you."

He looked at me and smiled. "A change I was more than ready for."

I'd heard all about the large, upscale hotel he managed, where people came and went in a hurry, about how he'd wanted to live life a little more slowly, and how ready he was to explore the resort end of the business by coming to a small property in the continental US.

Vaughn studied him. "Surely there's more to the story than that."

I could feel my eyes widen at the directness of Vaughn's questioning. Following procedures for conducting job interviews didn't allow Rhonda and me to ask too many personal questions. Rhonda and I knew Bernie was single. And from his glowing references, we learned that he was well-respected in the industry and that, away from the hotel, he was a bit of a loner, which we attributed to his formal manner.

The silence that followed Vaughn's question continued for a few awkward moments. Then, Bernie cleared his throat. "The woman I planned to marry was murdered a little over a year ago. It was a senseless death, a case of her being in the wrong place at the wrong time. She was riding the subway home, and a fight broke out between gang members. She became trapped between the groups, and during the battle, a stray bullet killed her as she was trying to get away." Bitterness crept into his voice. "I grew to hate everything about the city. I couldn't wait to get out of there."

Shock roiled through me. "Oh, Bernie, I'm so sorry. I had no idea."

He picked up Trudy and held her in his lap. "She's the only thing I have left of Louisa." His eyes shimmered with emotion.

Trudy gave him a kiss.

Watching them, I felt the sting of tears. I would never have imagined such a story behind our very stiff, very formal manager—a man, I now knew, who had a hurting heart.

Bernie patted Trudy and set her back down on the floor. "You see why I have her with me always."

I smiled. He was a true romantic.

"I'm sorry to hear about your girlfriend," Vaughn said. "Violence like that is the downside of living in a large city. I work in New York, but this has become home for me." He put an arm around me. "Here, with Ann."

Our conversation ended when Elena brought Robbie into the living room. "I thought you might like to say good night to Robbie," she said brightly. "I'm reading a few books to him before he goes to sleep, but he wanted to see you."

Dressed in the new pajamas Liz and I had bought him, he looked so much like Robert for a moment that I caught my breath.

Vaughn seemed to feel the tension in my body and held out his arms. "Come here, buddy."

Robbie hesitated, but then allowed Elena to bring him closer to us.

Vaughn ruffled his hair. "Have fun reading books. See you in the morning."

Robbie studied him and moved in front of me. "Gammy."

I lifted him into my lap and hugged him. He leaned against me a moment and then wiggled to get down.

"Sweet dreams, Robo Rob," I said.

His face lit up at the mention of his nickname. "Izzie?"

"Liz will be back soon. I promise."

Elena took Robbie's hand and he left the room, glancing back at me several times.

"Cute little boy," said Bernie. "So sorry about his parents."

"Thanks, it's been an awful surprise to everyone." I forced

a smile. "It's another reason Rhonda and I are glad to have you on board at the hotel."

"Ahhh, yes. I understand."

Vaughn rose. "I'm going to start the grill now if that's all right with everyone. Want to come with me, Bernie? We'll get another drink before grilling up some steaks."

"Sure."

Bernie and Vaughn left the room and I sat a moment, still shocked by Bernie's sad story. In his mid-50s, he obviously was still suffering from his loss. I wondered what other stories he had of his past.

I rose and decided to check on Robbie and Elena.

When I cracked open the door to his room. I saw Robbie sitting in Elena's lap, listening intently as she talked about the pictures in the book. Pleased by the way she was handling him, I silently closed the door and went into the kitchen.

I was putting together a green salad when Elena walked in. "Robbie's down for the night." She smiled. "I think he was exhausted from all the swimming we did."

"Thank you. You're so good with him," I said with real gratitude.

"He had a few tantrums today, but once he understands you mean what you say, he settles down." She chuckled. "One of my brothers was the very same way."

"Vaughn is cooking some steaks. Would you like to eat with us?"

She shook her head. "No thanks. If I'm through with Robbie for the day, I'd like to go and meet my friends for a while."

"Certainly," I said. "That was our agreement. You're free to come and go after Robbie has been taken care of."

She smiled. "Thanks. I'll see you later. I've got the key you gave me. I'll be quiet coming in."

She left as Bernie and Vaughn were bringing in the steaks. They were chatting comfortably with each other, and I thought, as I had so many times, that Vaughn was a real nice guy.

By the end of a very congenial meal, I thought the new, relaxed Bernie was a nice, all-around guy too.

Sated from our lovemaking, I cuddled up against Vaughn's strong body. It felt so good to have him in our bed, next to me. He cupped my cheek with his large, broad hand. "You are no ordinary Gammy,"

I smiled. "Good."

"How long do you think this arrangement with Robbie is going to stay this way? Liz will go back to school and be home in June and then what?"

I shook my head. "I wish I knew."

"Does this interfere with our plans to get married?"

Frowning, I pulled away from him and stared into his troubled eyes. "It shouldn't, should it?"

"We'd talked about a summer wedding. Should we wait until September when Liz is either back at school or on her own?"

My mind spun. "Maybe you're right. It's going to be a small, family wedding so I suppose it can be easily changed." Even as I said the words old resentments against Robert burned inside me briefly before I chided myself for being childish. Robert couldn't help dying and leaving Liz—and me—with our lives in an uproar.

"Let's not decide that now," Vaughn said.

At the sound of someone in the house, I sat up.

"It's just Elena," Vaughn reminded me.

I sank back against the pillows, more conflicted than ever

about the way things were turning out.

The next morning, I entered the hotel curious to see what kind of reaction I'd get from Bernie. Last night we'd been open and friendly in a new way.

As I stood at the front desk talking to our night clerk, I heard the clatter of nails against the tile floor and turned as Trudy rushed toward me.

Smiling, I knelt on the floor, and Trudy wiggled her way into my arms. "Hi, girl. Where's Daddy?"

"Good morning, Ann."

I looked up to find Bernie frowning at me. "We need to talk."

Concerned, I rose to my feet. "Sure, want me to come to your office?"

"Yes, please." Back straight and stiff, he led me into his office. Following behind him, I wondered where the pleasant, congenial man of last night had gone.

Inside his office, he indicated a chair for me before taking a seat behind his desk.

"What's going on?" I asked.

"I posted a schedule for the housekeepers. This morning, I discovered Ana had changed it all around. Either I'm in charge or she is. Which is it?"

My heart thudded at the anger in his voice. "Did she say why she'd done it?"

He shook his head. "Apparently it's spring break for the local schools and some of the women have family commitments. Their first commitment should be the hotel."

I drew a deep breath and hoped he'd understand what I was about to say. "We're lucky to have the housekeepers we do. They're good at their jobs. But they're also mothers and wives. And if they're willing to switch things around to cover their duties here at the hotel, I'm okay with it."

"But we need to know who's here and who we can expect," he protested.

"Surely you had department heads at the New York hotel. We'll make Ana head of Housekeeping and tell her she must report to you, instead of having you discover the changes to the schedule on your own. It's a growing operation and we're all trying to adjust to your new ways," I said, hoping to appease him.

"Okay, then, we're going to add more structure to the group, tiny as it is. Agreed?"

"Agreed," I said, wondering if Rhonda and I had made a mistake by bringing someone else in. Then I thought of Rhonda and her baby and all the changing demands of our families and realized I could never run the hotel without him.

Before I went to my office, I spoke to Ana. "It's important for you to inform Bernhard of any changes to the schedule."

"You know what it's like for us. A child gets sick, and if we can't find somebody to watch them, then we have to find someone to take our shift. Things were a lot simpler before Bernhard came."

"That may be," I said, "but he's going to help us make our operation a little more professional. You know how much we've grown. Now we have to be able to provide the necessary protocol, paperwork, and figures behind it."

She sighed. "Okay."

I left her standing at one of the maids' closets and went into the kitchen to grab a cup of coffee.

"*Buenos dias*," said Consuela. "You heard about Ana and Bernhard?"

I nodded. Nothing escaped Consuela's notice. "It's all settled. Are the cinnamon rolls ready?"

She grinned. "For you, *si*. A little hot for others."

I laughed and accepted a single sweet roll still warm from the oven. They were a weakness of mine.

Carrying the plate with the sweet roll, a napkin, and a cup of coffee, I carefully made my way into the office.

"Hi, Annie!" said Rhonda. "Look here! It's a house I think Angela and Reggie may like. What do ya think?"

I could feel my eyes widen. "Are you going to buy them a house?"

"No way. Reggie asked me to look for him." Her eyes moistened. "Annie, he's gonna do it. He's definitely going into business with Will. His parents are furious about it, but what's new? They're always mad about something."

I set down my coffee and the plate so I could give her a hug as easily as I could around the bulk of her pregnancy. "When did you find out?"

"Last night, Will made an official job offer, and Reggie accepted it. They've been talking about it for some time. Will figured he'd better know for sure before he thought of hiring somebody else. Nice, huh?" Rhonda's dark eyes sparkled. "I can't believe all my good luck. Now if only this baby will come. I keep telling him to hurry up."

"Him?" Though Rhonda and Will had chosen not to find out the sex of the baby, Rhonda was convinced her baby was a boy.

I looked at the photograph of the house Rhonda had pulled up on her computer. It was a nice but modest home in what was described as a family neighborhood with a community pool.

"Whaddya' think?" said Rhonda. "Nice, huh?"

"Very nice for a first home," I said. Gazing at her, I asked the question I couldn't hold back. "With all your money you could buy them a bigger house..." I let my words die out.

She smiled. "Will and I talked about it, and he pointed out that if Reggie didn't have to work for something like that, he might be one of those people who think they deserve it." Rhonda beamed at me. "Will's so smart."

I returned her smile. In Rhonda's eyes, Will was the best, the brightest, the most wonderful man of all. I could almost agree with her. Aside from the fact he was my financial manager, I loved him like a brother.

"How did your dinner with Bernie go last night?" Rhonda asked.

I took a sip of my hot coffee and sat down. "It was very interesting." I told her about Bernie's past.

"What an awful thing to have happened," gasped Rhonda. "Poor guy! Such a tragedy! We don't want him to be all alone. We'll have to introduce him to someone."

I waggled a finger in warning. "Now, Rhonda, we are not, repeat not, going to play matchmaker. That would bring us nothing but trouble."

"But, Annie, it's so sad for him to be lonely," pleaded Rhonda.

This time, I glared at her. "No. We've got our hands full introducing him to the staff. They're chafing at his insistence on being in charge of everything."

"You mean about the struggle between him and Ana? Consuela told me all about it."

I sighed. Nothing was sacred among our staff. "Bernie and I talked about setting up departments and running it like a big hotel. Even though we're small, it might be best to handle it that way. We're continuing to grow, and it's a lot different from when we started all this."

"Okay, I say we do it. We can't lose Bernie." Rhonda's expression grew even more serious. "When I talked to Angela last night, she told me she was gonna be with Liz all day today—for the private burial."

I sank down into my chair. "I can't thank Angela enough. I offered to go, but Liz didn't want me there. And, I admit, it would've been a little awkward."

"I think so too. I'm glad Angela and Liz are together. They're best friends after all. And where would we be if they hadn't been college roommates their freshman year?" Rhonda grinned at me. "So much has happened to us in such a short time, it sometimes seems unreal. Huh?"

I couldn't help smiling. Breakfast at The Beach House Hotel had turned into lunch and dinner at the hotel, with famous people coming and going along with others who'd discovered our gem of a small hotel. It made me feel as if all the worry and hard work that had brought us to this point was worth it.

CHAPTER NINE

R honda waved me out of the office. "Go! Don't keep Vaughn waiting. I'll cover for you."

I gave her a grateful wave and left the hotel. It was important to me to give Vaughn as much of my time as I could. We'd discussed it before he bought the house we were living in.

I drove past my small house on the hotel property, which was now serving as Bernie's home, and thought how much that house meant to me. I never wanted to sell it. It stood as a symbol of my determination to make a successful, new life following my divorce from Robert.

All was quiet when I walked into the house I now shared with Vaughn. I looked out at the pool. It was empty. Beyond the screened-in porch, I saw Vaughn washing down the small day sailer, a perfect sailboat for playing around on the inlet waters.

Before going down to join Vaughn, I decided to check on Robbie. I walked into his wing of the house and heard crying. Hurrying my step, I went to his room. Elena was sitting in a rocking chair with him, singing softly as he wept in her arms. She looked up at me with tears in her eyes.

"Someone is missing his Mommy and Daddy. When is Liz coming home?"

My heart squeezed in sympathy. "She should be here in a few days for spring break. She had a couple of course exams to take and her father's funeral to attend."

"Gammy?"

I knelt beside the chair and put my arms around him. "I'm here, Robbie."

He scrambled to get into my arms.

I sat on the floor and pulled him into my embrace. Rocking his sweaty little body, I thought of the twists of fate. And then I remembered what Robert had told Liz about my being the perfect choice to care for Robbie and vowed to keep him close. If someone had asked me to imagine such a thing two years ago, I would've laughed in her face.

"Were you able to get a life jacket for Robbie?" I asked Elena.

"Yes. Vaughn helped me pick it out."

I set Robbie on his feet. "Okay, Robo Rob I'm going to show you a sailboat." I turned to Elena. "Let's get the life jacket on him, and then I'll take him out to the dock."

While Elena fussed with putting on Robbie's life jacket, I quickly changed into jeans and a shirt.

Emerging from my bedroom, I almost ran into Robbie, who was standing before me—two arms and two legs sticking out of the yellow flotation device strapped around him. I laughed. "You really look like a Robo Rob now."

A small smile crossed his face.

I took hold of his hand. "Let's go."

Beyond the pool deck and lanai, the green lawn sloped down to the water. Robbie held my hand as Elena and I walked side by side.

Robbie suddenly jerked his hand out of mine and started running. With the bulk of the life jacket around him, his steps were awkward, but he was finally able to get some speed.

"Here we come," I called to Vaughn to give him a heads-up.

He caught sight of Robbie and went to meet him. Robbie stumbled into his arms. Vaughn lifted him up in the air and swung him around, bringing peals of laughter out of Robbie.

At the sight of them, my heart filled with love for them both. *Vaughn must have been such a great young father*, I thought, feeling a stab of disappointment that he and I would never have a child together. With my hysterectomy, that was impossible.

Vaughn set Robbie down and opened his arms to me. Keeping an eye on Robbie, I gave him a quick hug and then made sure Elena had a grip on Robbie's hand.

"How about a little sail?" Vaughn said to me. "There's a nice little breeze."

"Sounds like fun. Should we see if Robbie wants to go?"

"Sure." He went over to Robbie. "Want to go in the boat?"

Robbie pointed to the boat. "Boat."

"Okay," said Vaughn. "Let's go."

Vaughn led us onto the dock and over to the boat. "Better get in first, Ann. I'll hand Robbie to you. Make sure he sits down on the floor of the cockpit between the seats. It'll be more stable that way."

Vaughn held my hand as I hopped into the boat. As soon as I was steady, Vaughn lifted Robbie and handed him to me.

"Okay, sit here by me," I said to Robbie, and waited for Vaughn to come aboard.

After untying the boat, Vaughn settled inside, and quickly raised the mainsail. The breeze caught it, and the sail billowed out, allowing the boat to move gently forward.

As we moved away, Robbie and I waved to Elena, who sat on the dock watching us.

"This is a good way to start kids in boats. Nothing too strong, just enough wind to keep us moving," said Vaughn, sheeting in the mainsail a bit.

I looked down at the wonder on Robbie's face and chuckled. "I think someone might become a sailor."

"Good," said Vaughn. "It's another reason for him to keep

up with his swimming lessons. Both Nell and Ty are comfortable on the water because they took swimming lessons, and I got them started on sailing when they were about Robbie's age."

"Have you heard from your kids lately?" I asked, trailing my hand in the water outside the boat.

"Ty and June want us to come to San Francisco to see their new house. I told them we probably couldn't make it for a while. Nell is busy in DC and is still dating Clint. Guess it's pretty serious." He shook his head. "I have a feeling the family is going to get even bigger sometime soon."

"It would be wonderful if they could come here," I said. "I have yet to meet Ty and June, and you know I already love Nell." I'd heard and read awful stories about being a stepmother and hoped I'd never have to face some of the horrors others had.

Vaughn stroked the side of my face. "Get that worried look off your face. Ty will love you. If he doesn't, I'll talk some sense into him."

Robbie tried to stand up.

I restrained him. "No, sweetie. Better sit down."

"Noooo!" he screamed and began kicking at me.

"Hold on, son," said Vaughn. "We'll come about. Ann, duck your head."

The motion of the boat quieted Robbie. He looked up at Vaughn and smiled.

Vaughn laughed. "Okay, here we go."

The boat picked up speed and we headed back to the dock.

I lifted my face to the sky and watched white, puffy clouds play peek-a-boo with the sun, sending patterns of light and shadows on the water, telling a story like an old, silent movie.

"Ann, I wish I had a camera to capture you right now," said Vaughn. "You're beautiful."

"Gammy booful," echoed Robbie.

I smiled at Vaughn and ruffled Robbie's hair. It was these two who made me feel that way.

That night as Vaughn and I lay in bed, I brought up the subject that had been bothering me all day.

"Do you think it's going to be too confusing to Robbie to have him living here with us when Liz is his real guardian?"

Vaughn gave me a thoughtful look. "The most important thing for him right now is to have stability, which Liz isn't able to provide. We've all agreed it's important for her to complete her schooling. How can she take care of him and go to classes? And where is she going to live? Robert left her without any ability to take care of him financially. So, for the next couple of months, he'll be with us. After that, who knows?"

"I know, but you've gone to all the trouble of buying this house so you and I would have more time for each other. Now, things have changed. And with my work at the hotel increasing because of Rhonda's baby, I'm afraid I'm letting you down."

"Aw, my sweet Ann. Just knowing you're here for me is so important. These few years have been so hard for me. Even with all the so-called glamor of a show biz life, it can be very lonely."

"Rhonda thinks we should help Bernie find someone else."

Vaughn laughed. "I think I'd let that sleeping dog lie."

I grinned. "Me, too, but you know how Rhonda is."

"All too well," Vaughn said, chuckling.

I awoke to silence. When I rolled over, Vaughn's side of the bed was empty. I got up, threw a light robe over my nakedness and tiptoed into the kitchen to get a cup of coffee. At the sound of soft voices, I paused.

"Here it comes, Robbie. Better eat up your cereal, my man."

I smiled at the sound of Vaughn's voice and walked into the kitchen. Vaughn was now making the sound of what I suspected was an airplane as the spoon in his hand "flew" to Robbie's mouth.

From the seat in front of Robbie's highchair, Vaughn looked up at me and gave me a sheepish grin. "I was up early, and when I heard Robbie waking up, I thought I'd let Elena sleep in. It's been a long time since I played games like this. Ty used to love it."

I went to him and threw my arms around him. Nuzzling his neck, I said, "I love you, Vaughn. I really do."

Robbie stared at me with Robert's face and I stepped back. "Hi, Robo Rob."

He pounded the plastic tray of his highchair. "Gammy."

Vaughn went back to feeding Robbie, and I grabbed a cup of coffee. "I'm going to take a shower."

He wiggled his eyebrows at me.

"No hanky-panky." I pointed to Robbie.

A toddler in the house was making a big difference in our normal routines.

CHAPTER TEN

Later, in my home office, I was doing an analysis of the cost of wedding parties when my cell phone rang. Liz.

I quickly picked it up. "How did it go?"

She was quiet a moment before she answered. "Sad. It was so sad. Dad wanted a private burial and he got it. Thank God, Ange was with me. And she's promised to ride down to Florida with me in the van. Reggie will fly down later after he takes his last exam."

"I'm so sorry. I know how difficult this has been for you."

"Thanks. How's Robbie?" asked Liz. "I've been talking to Elena. It sounds like she and Robbie have been doing a lot of cool things together."

"He's doing well. She's very good with him," I said. "I'm glad we found her to help us."

"I should be home soon," Liz said. "I can't wait to get out of here."

"Drive carefully. Vaughn and I will both be glad to see you. We're here to help in any way we can, Liz."

"Yeah, I know. I've got to go. See you soon."

As we disconnected the call, my heart ached for Liz. The future she'd finally decided on was uncertain at best.

Three days later, Liz called from the highway outside Ft. Myers to say she and Angela would be home soon. They wanted to meet Rhonda and me at my house.

Rhonda and I left the hotel and drove to my neighborhood.

When I pulled up in front of my house, Elena was tossing a ball to Robbie on the front lawn. Vaughn's car was gone, as he'd left earlier to do some errands.

"Come on inside," I said to Rhonda. "We can wait for the girls there."

In the kitchen, I fixed a couple glasses of iced tea and sat down opposite Rhonda at the kitchen table, enjoying this rare moment alone with her.

"Did Reggie like the house you suggested? I asked.

Rhonda beamed at me. "He asked me to put a deposit on the house to hold it until Angela gets a chance to see it. I'm going to take her there this afternoon. It's the nicest house I've found in their price range. I'm thrilled they'll be living close by."

"I'm glad Reggie didn't suggest that either Will or you should help them. After meeting his parents, I admit I'm a little surprised he didn't."

"Yeah, me too. Katherine and Arthur Smythe are the kinds of people who'd think a starter home like this one was beneath them. My Angela has been very good for Reggie."

"I think so too." Reggie had been a bit of a jerk when Angela had brought him home to meet all of us. But he'd turned into a real nice guy. Best of all, he and Angela really loved one another.

"What about Liz?" Rhonda asked. "I thought she and Troy were dating. What will happen now?"

I shook my head. "I'm not sure. He's been dating other girls."

The sound of a car's horn beeping brought us to our feet.

"They're here!" cried Rhonda, hurrying out the kitchen door to the driveway.

I stayed right behind her, as excited to see them as Rhonda. As Liz pulled into the driveway, my heart filled with joy.

Beside me, Rhonda did a little dance. If she weren't so pregnant, I thought she might have jumped up and down.

Laughing, Angela got out of the car and was immediately swept up in Rhonda's embrace.

"Hi, baby girl!" said Rhonda. "I'm so happy to have you home."

Liz stepped out of the car and into my arms. "Whew! I thought we'd never get here. Florida is one long state."

I hugged her close to me. "I'm relieved you made it. I couldn't stop thinking of you making the trip under such pressure to get here."

Tears swam in Liz's eyes. "Everything in Boston is gone. Everything, but this van. I can't wait to get rid of it. I don't want any reminders of her."

I gave her a wry look. "You've got one big reminder. Here he comes now."

"Izzie! Izzie! I here," Robbie cried, running toward her.

Tears overflowed and rolled down Liz's cheeks. She swung him up in her arms. "Hi, Robo Rob!"

Elena approached quietly and stood beside me as we watched Robbie and Liz exchange hugs. "So sweet," she murmured.

But I knew the future wouldn't be all sweet. I turned my attention to Angela. She and I had formed a strong bond over the past few months.

We embraced and then I stood back, beaming at her. "It's good to see you, Angela. You look terrific."

"Thanks. I don't think it's going to be long before my baby is here." She rubbed a hand over her baby bump and glanced at Rhonda. "And Mom looks like she's ready now."

I smiled at Rhonda and froze. Her face suddenly contorted with pain. I rushed over to her and took hold of her hand. "Oh my word! Are you all right?"

Rhonda caught her breath and then let out a long groan. Liquid splashed at her feet. "Annie, help me!" she cried. "The baby's coming."

My mouth grew dry as I took in her pain and the fact that her water had broken. "Can you walk? We need to get you to the hospital."

She squeezed my fingers so hard, I yelped.

"Call 911 and get me inside," Rhonda cried between pants. "I've been having pains off and on all day, but I thought they were only the Braxton-Hicks kind. The baby isn't due for a couple of weeks."

Angela took hold of one of Rhonda's arms and I held the other as Liz dialed 911.

Wide-eyed, Elena picked up Robbie and took him inside, away from the action.

"Annie, grab some towels and a blanket and let me lie down on the kitchen floor. I don't want to ruin any of your rugs and I'm never going to make it to one of the bedrooms."

"But ... but ..."

"Annie, do it!" roared Rhonda, reminding me of our early days together when Rhonda drove me crazy with her bossiness.

Liz took Rhonda's arm while I hurried ahead to grab a blanket, towels, and a sheet.

I could hear a siren in the distance and realized the sound was coming closer. As I gathered things together, I prayed the EMTs would arrive on time to deliver the baby and that everything would be all right.

When I entered the kitchen, Rhonda was clasping the edge of the counter and groaning.

"Until the EMTs get here, try not to push," I said, spreading the blanket on the floor and layering towels on top of it.

"Don't push? Do you have any frickin' idea how to tell my

body that?" snapped Rhonda, before crying out with pain.

Liz, Angela, and I slowly eased Rhonda down on her back onto the towels on the floor. I lifted her dress and helped her remove her panties.

She groaned and bent her knees.

I saw the top of a head showing between her legs. "Oh my God, Rhonda! The baby's here." I turned to Liz. "Quick! Hand me a clean towel!"

"The EMTs are outside," cried Angela. She hurried out of the kitchen.

Seconds later, Angela reappeared with the medical people just as the baby emerged from Rhonda, landing on the towel I held in my arms. The baby let out lusty cries.

The EMTs quickly took over for me.

One EMT smiled and took hold of Rhonda's hand. "Ah, you're one of these mothers who like to surprise us, huh? Good job! We usually get here in time."

"Yeah? Well, I'm as surprised as you," she said.

Tears streamed down my cheeks as I squeezed Rhonda's other hand. "Oh, Rhonda, it's such a miracle," I managed to get out. "And she's beautiful. Absolutely beautiful."

Rhonda's eyes widened. "*She*? You said *she*? Where's my little boy?"

One of the EMTs handed Rhonda the baby. Rhonda held her close and traced a finger down her cheeks. Then she inspected the baby's hands and her feet. "Oh, Annie. She's beautiful, just like you said." Tears slid down her cheeks. "Wait until Will sees her. He's going to go crazy over her. She's the spitting image of him."

Angela knelt beside her mother and they embraced. "Mom, I'm so happy for you and Will. I called him. He's on his way."

I stood up and hugged Liz. "Such an exciting moment."

I noticed the paleness of her face, and smiling, hugged her

to me, so glad she was mine. And someday, I hoped, she'd know the joy of giving birth.

The EMTs swaddled the baby, helped Rhonda onto a gurney, and wheeled her out to the ambulance. I followed with the girls.

Will pulled up in his car, and, leaving the engine still running, got out and ran over to Rhonda. We watched as they embraced and inspected the baby together, crying and laughing at the same time.

The EMTs slid the gurney inside the ambulance and Will, his shoulders still shaking, watched as they drove away.

I went over to him. "Do you want me to take you to the hospital?"

He shook his head. "I'll do it." He turned around. "Angela? Come here, sweetheart. Let's go see your sister together."

Will drew Angela into an embrace, and I sighed with satisfaction. Angela had been unsure of Will at first. Now, it seemed they were close after all they'd been through together.

Liz and I were heading inside when Vaughn pulled up in his sporty convertible. "Whew! Good to see you. I was worried when I saw the ambulance leave the neighborhood." He got out of the car and put an arm around me.

"We're fine," I said, still bubbling with excitement. "And so are Rhonda and her new baby."

A frown knitted his brow. "What do you mean?"

I grinned. "Rhonda had her baby in our kitchen."

"It was really awesome," said Liz. "It all happened so fast."

"You're kidding me! Was it a boy like Rhonda thought?" Vaughn asked.

"No, but she's one of the most beautiful little newborns I've ever seen. And what a loud cry! She's Rhonda's baby all right."

Vaughn chuckled. "I'm glad everything's all right." He turned to Liz and threw an arm around her shoulder. "We're glad to have you home for spring break. How was the trip?"

Liz shrugged. "Tiresome, long, and sad. I'm happy to be here. For the next ten days of my break, I'll need some time to recover."

Vaughn and I exchanged glances. Later, when Liz was more rested, we'd have to talk about Robbie.

"Well, let's get you relaxed, shall we?" I said, leading her inside.

Vaughn went with me to the hotel to check on the status of things. Cody Craig of the rock group Chameleon was due to arrive with his French wife and young child. They were using the Presidential Suite, and I wanted to make sure they were nicely settled in. When I'd talked to Bernie earlier, things were a bit chaotic.

We arrived at the hotel as the last rays of sun left the sky. The outdoor mini-lights strung in the hibiscus bushes in front of the hotel and in the potted plants beside the double front doors glittered like lingering fireflies. I was pleased by it.

When Vaughn and I walked through the front entrance, Tim looked up at us from behind the front desk. "You here to see what all the fuss is about?"

"Fuss? What are you talking about?" I asked, immediately wary.

"It's Cody Craig's wife. She wants Jean-Luc to prepare a special meal for them in the Presidential Suite. Bernie tried to explain that it would be impossible, but she's not happy about it. She's making a lot of demands on all of us."

I pressed my lips together. We depended on well-known guests for their business and for getting better known as a hotel, but oftentimes it meant putting up with their egotistical nonsense. I turned to Vaughn. "Why don't you go ahead and have a drink in the lobby bar. I'll join you as soon as I can."

"Meet you there."

I went into the back of the house to the kitchen. Jean-Luc was slapping things around, muttering to himself in French. I knew enough of the language to realize how upset he was. When he saw me, he slammed a fist on the counter.

"Annie, I'm not here to wait on only one person. I serve everyone, *non?*"

"Yesss ..."

"That woman is going to drive me crazy. She wants this and she wants that. I have to take care of our other guests."

"You're absolutely right. Why don't you give me a chance to talk to Cody Craig and his wife and see if I can make them understand?"

Jean-Luc bobbed his head. "That would be good. I'm not a short-order cook."

I checked on the dining room. It was packed. Sabine was acting as hostess and overseeing the waitstaff. While I was standing there, Bernie rushed up to me.

"Glad you're here. One of our guests from New York is not feeling well. I've called the doctor that the hotel recommends, and he's agreed to see her, but only if I can drive her to his office."

"Okay, you take her. I'll try to get Cody Craig's wife under control."

Bernie rolled his eyes. "Good luck. She thinks she's a princess, but she's a royal pain in the ass."

I left the dining room and climbed the stairs to the Presidential Suite. Before I even made it to the suite, I heard a child crying.

I tapped on the door.

When no one answered, I knocked louder.

"Who is it?" came a male voice.

"It's Ann Rutherford, one of the owners of the hotel."

The door opened and a young man stared blearily at me. He was holding a crying toddler in his arms.

I studied him. He looked much younger than the man who performed on stage. Spiky brown hair rose on his head like unmowed grass. Behind his glasses, dark eyes glowered at me.

"Where's our private chef? We're hungry," he said. "We were told we'd have one."

"Cody, I don't know who told you that a private chef was available to you, but that's not true. You're welcome to order from the in-room-dining menu or even our regular menu. Of course, we'd love to have you join our other guests in the main dining room. Or, if it's available, you're welcome to book the small dining room for yourselves."

A tall, thin woman appeared wearing one of our white, terry cloth robes. A white towel was wrapped around her head.

"Are you our maid?" she asked, scowling at me.

I brushed an imaginary piece of lint off my black slacks. "No, I'm not. I'm Ann Rutherford, one of the owners of the hotel. I'm explaining your food options to Cody. We'll try to accommodate your wishes as best we can, but our chef is busy in the kitchen taking care of our guests. If you would like to order food off the menu and have it sent up to the room, we'll be glad to take care of that for you. We also can provide food options for your little one."

Cody's wife stamped her foot and pointed at finger at him. "I told you we should have gone to a bigger place—a place more used to stars."

"Now, Dele, this place comes highly recommended. We don't want to be noticed. Remember? We're here to have some private time to ourselves. That's what the doctor ordered."

She turned and walked out of the room. Cody looked at me and shrugged his shoulders as much as he could with a toddler who'd fallen asleep in his arms. "Women! What can you do?"

It took all my willpower to keep my mouth shut. I was glad Rhonda wasn't with me. She'd tell Cody exactly how to handle his fussy little wife.

"I'll be around the hotel for a while longer," I told him. "Let the kitchen know what you want, and they'll take care of it. One other thing. The Beach House Hotel is known for its discretion. So if you and your family are out of the suite and mixing with the guests, it shouldn't be a problem. We ask all of our guests to honor the privacy of others. That's why it's so popular among stars like yourself."

I left the couple and went back to the kitchen to inform Jean-Luc what I'd told them.

He shook his head. "She is a... Bah! Never mind! Thanks for your help, Annie. Now tell me about Rhonda. You were there when she had her baby?"

"Yes. You won't believe how it happened, Jean-Luc!"

"I heard all about it." He chuckled. "Rhonda does love being in the kitchen. Tell her I can't wait to have her back here with me. But no babies."

I smiled. Jean-Luc and Rhonda had had their battles—mostly over recipes—but they'd become fast friends.

CHAPTER ELEVEN

After dinner, Vaughn and I went to the community hospital and took the elevator up to the maternity floor. Vaughn carried a huge arrangement of pink roses, and I held onto a handful of balloons designed for welcoming a baby girl.

When we reached Rhonda's room, I cautiously knocked on the partially-closed door.

"Come in," called Rhonda.

Will opened the door. His eyes lit at the sight of us and a broad grin spread across his face. "Come on in. Rhonda's just finished feeding the baby."

"Annie! Vaughn! You should see how perfect this baby is. She weighed in at 7 pounds, 3 ounces." Rhonda opened the blanket around the baby so we could get a look at her."

Vaughn set down the flower arrangement on a side table and turned to Will. "Congratulations! You're going to find that a daughter has a talent for getting her way around you." He shook Will's hand. "I'm happy for you, man!"

"Guess what we're calling her," said Rhonda. "Of course everyone knows I was planning on a boy so we could name him after Will. So now we've decided to call her Willow. Get it?"

Observing the look of pride that filled Will's face, unexpected tears stung my eyes as I hugged him. He was such a wonderful man, and this little girl was such a delightful surprise.

"Willow? What a perfect name for her," I said. "Though, Rhonda, she's already proved she's got a mind of her own."

Will chuckled. "Like her mother."

I went over to Rhonda, gave her a hug, and studied the baby in her arms. "The entire staff sends their good wishes to you and the baby and Will. Jean-Luc is anxious to have you come back. But he says no babies in the kitchen."

Rhonda chortled. "God! He would've freaked if I'd had the baby in his kitchen. Is everything all right in yours, Annie?"

"It's fine. It's always been one of my favorite rooms in the house, and now, it'll be even more special."

Remembering what had taken place there, we smiled at each other.

"So what's going on at the hotel?" Rhonda asked. "Bernie sounded harried when I called."

While the two men talked, I told Rhonda the latest happenings with Cody and his wife. "But, remember, you're not to worry about anything at the hotel. It's more important for you to get settled in with the baby."

"Can I ask a favor of you?" she said. "Will you take Angela to see the house Reggie has picked out? I said I'd do that for him tomorrow, and now I can't."

"Of course. It will be fun to see it."

The baby started to cry.

I turned to Vaughn. "Maybe we'd better go. It's been a long day for Rhonda." I gave her a kiss on the cheek and hugged Will once more. "Congratulations to you both on a beautiful little girl."

"Wait! Don't leave!" said Rhonda. "You don't know Willow's middle name." She winked at me. "It's Ann. For you, Annie. Willow Ann Grayson."

Touched, I clasped a hand to my heart. "I love it. Thank you so much."

"Nice." Vaughn took hold of my free hand and squeezed it.

"See you guys later," I said, pleased at the honor Rhonda

and Will had bestowed on me.

As we left the hospital, I thought of the look of wonder on Will's features whenever he gazed at Willow. I wished I were able to give Vaughn a baby of our own and bring that same look to his face.

At home, we found Liz sitting in the family room in front of the television. She waved limply at us and turned back to her program.

She looked so forlorn I went and sat beside her. "What are you watching?" I asked, putting an arm around her shoulder.

She made a face. "It's just something stupid. I'm not really paying any attention to it." She leaned against me and emitted a quivering sigh. "I hate all that's happened."

"Me too. It hasn't been easy on you. And, with the care of Robbie, it won't be easy in the future. But you'll get through it."

Liz sat up. Tears glistened in her eyes. "After you left for the hotel tonight, I called Troy to see if we could get together. He said he was busy and then told me he was falling for someone else. I asked him if my having Robbie made a difference to him, and he grew quiet. When I pushed him for an answer, he said he wasn't ready for children." Tears spilled onto her cheeks. "What am I going to do, Mom? I'll end up a single mother." Her breath hiccupped. "With a child that isn't even mine."

I brushed a lock of hair away from her face. "I'll help you all I can, Liz."

"I love Robbie, I really do, but I never thought it would come to this."

"The fact remains you're his legal guardian. He's a wonderful boy. This afternoon it was very clear how much you love each other. Let things go forward in their own way. You've got a lot of support. We'll work together. Okay?"

She sniffled. "Why did Dad have to go and die?" she said, sounding more like a child than the young adult she was. But I understood. One phase of her life was unexpectedly over and another had begun.

"Why don't you get some rest?" I said. "Tomorrow is another busy day."

We said good night, and I went to join Vaughn in our bedroom.

When I opened the door, he was sitting in bed, reading a book. He looked up when I walked into the room. "What's going on with Liz?" he asked. "I sensed you two wanted to be alone."

I told him about Liz's conflicting feelings and the worries she had about losing her independence. "I can't blame her. She loves her brother, but as she says, she never thought it would end this way. Supposedly, Robert told Liz that he if it were his choice alone, he'd want me to have Robbie, but he couldn't ask me to do it. He said if she had any problems with him to come to me."

Vaughn patted the empty space beside him. "Have a seat."

I sat down and turned to him.

He took hold of one of my hands. "I've done a lot of thinking about this. You've mentioned on a couple of occasions that you wished we could have a child of our own. Maybe Robbie is the answer to our wishes. Would you ever consider adopting him? We could give him a stable, loving home with all the advantages. And that would free Liz to love him like a sister, not a child of hers."

Feeling my breath leave me in a rush of surprise, I fell back among the pillows, momentarily stunned by the idea. *Could I do it? Take in Robert's and Kandie's child—the same child whose appearance had caused me so much pain?*

"Ann? What do you think?"

I closed my eyes, battling my whirling emotions. When I opened them, I stared into Vaughn's handsome face. With great tenderness, I cupped his cheeks with my hands and gazed into his dark eyes. "I think you are the kindest, the most wonderful, most generous man I've ever known."

"Are you amenable to the idea. Is that it?"

"I think maybe I am. I've always wanted more children. As you say, it would be the best arrangement for both Robbie and Liz. And, I have to admit, I've already fallen for Robo Rob. Whenever he smiles at me and calls me 'Gammy,' it warms my heart."

"I thought so." Vaughn drew me into his arms. "I really love you, Ann. It may seem an awkward circumstance to others but it feels so right to me. In the morning, we'll see how Liz feels about this and take it from there." He gave me the crooked smile I loved so much. "Now, Gammy, come to bed with me."

Long after we'd made love, I lay in bed gazing up at the ceiling, thinking about all the ramifications of adopting Robbie. We were lucky enough to be able to afford help, but our busy lives would change materially. Neither Vaughn nor I would settle for less than being an active part of Robbie's life. And many couples our age were becoming first-time parents. From that standpoint, we were ahead of the game.

After a restless night, I awoke early. Careful not to wake Vaughn, I rolled out bed and quietly dressed. I needed time to myself before addressing the issue of Robbie and Liz.

I tiptoed through the house and slipped out the kitchen door to the back lawn and down to the dock. At the end of the dock, waves like tiny, shy, wet kisses, licked at the pilings supporting it. As I gazed out over the water, the rising sun behind my back spread a rosy glow across the sky that reflected onto the inlet's rippling surface in front of me. The soft breeze stirred the water forming different patterns of light. I raised my face to the breaking day and drew several deep breaths, waiting for peace to fill me.

Images of Robert smiling at me during our good times filled my mind. When I thought of the gift Robbie could be to us, my past anger at Robert melted away. His little boy might have a lot of his father in him, but I would see that only the best of my ex shone through. I thought of how the past and the future were magically becoming one, a reminder that life was not in our own hands. The peace I'd been seeking wrapped around me, a gentle cloak of assurance that all would be okay.

I drew another deep breath and turned as Vaughn approached.

"You all right?" he asked.

I smiled. "I'm fine."

And I was.

While Elena and Troy played with Robbie in the pool, Liz met with Vaughn and me in our bedroom. She sat in one of the overstuffed chairs alongside mine. Vaughn sat on the edge of the bed facing us.

I listened as he quietly explained to Liz what he and I had discussed about Robbie's future. He stopped when Liz burst into tears.

I leaned over and patted her back. "Are you all right? We didn't mean to upset you, sweetheart. We're just trying to do the right thing for everyone."

Tears streamed down her face. "No, no you don't understand. I can't believe you would do this for Robbie. For me." She clasped her hands together. "Does it make me an awful person for wanting this to happen?"

"Oh, sweetie, no! By offering to adopt Robbie, we hoped it would make you feel even closer to him as his big sister, not his mother. Does that make sense?"

"Yes. It feels right." She gazed over to Vaughn. "I know now why my mother loves you in a way she never loved my father. Thank you, Vaughn, for thinking of Robbie and me."

His cheeks colored with emotion. He simply nodded.

"Liz, if you want to proceed with this idea, Mike Torson, the lawyer who works for the hotel, can help us straighten things out. In the meantime, we'll keep going on as we were. I'm not going to ask Robbie to call me Mom. I'll remain 'Gammy' for the time being, and then we'll see."

"I want to go ahead with this," said Liz, tearing up again. "But I promise I won't be just any sister to Robbie. I'll be the best sister any little boy could have." She grabbed a tissue from the nearby box and dabbed at her eyes. "I suppose that someday he'll hear the whole story. I just hope he won't blame me for doing this."

"Liz, you, as well as Ann and I, are thinking of him and what's best for his future," said Vaughn in a deep calm voice. "But there's no reason you can't be there for him along the way."

"You're right," she said, nodding thoughtfully. "I can do that, and I will."

"Honey, we're a family. All of us," I said.

Liz turned to me. "I know Dad would be pleased that Robbie will have a home with you. It's a little weird. Are you sure you don't mind, Mom?"

"I've done a lot of thinking about the past and the future, and I'm happy to do this," I said honestly. "Especially with Vaughn's help. He's a wonderful father to his own children and will be great with Robbie."

Liz studied Vaughn. "Can we spend some time alone? I need to talk to you."

"Sure. Should we go for a little sail? That's a good way to relax."

Liz smiled. "Sounds good."

After they left, I stayed in the bedroom for a while, letting my emotions settle. As I prepared to leave the room, I looked out the window that overlooked the back lawn and saw Liz and Vaughn, the white sail of their boat billowing in the wind as if they were about to take flight. *Good for them*, I thought, pleased two of the most important people in my life were getting along.

I hurried to find Robbie.

Elena and Troy were sitting next to one another, talking, on the steps of the pool. Robbie sat on the step above them playing with his plastic boat.

"Gammy! Boat!"

I kicked off my shoes and sat on the edge of the pool by him. "Let's see the boat, Robbie."

"Mine," he said, holding it away from me.

"It's yours, but let's share. Shall we?"

"No!"

"Robbie..." I began.

"Okay," he said happily, waving it in front of my nose and pulling it away.

"That's about all the sharing he's going to do," laughed Elena, turning to me.

I smiled, aware of how Troy's eyes lingered on her. *So that's how things are,* I thought and turned to Robbie once more.

As the famous saying went, life was indeed a bunch of circles.

CHAPTER TWELVE

The hotel was alive with activity when I walked into the lobby. A number of guests were checking out, and a group of other guests had arrived early in hopes of being able to get into their rooms. A late winter storm up north had sent people scurrying south.

I slid behind the front desk to help Tim handle the rush. As he finished with the checkouts, he said, "What are we going to do with all these guests hanging around?"

"Let me speak to Ana about getting rooms ready, and then I'll get back to you."

I went to find Bernie. He was in his office talking to Ana.

"May I join you?" I asked, aware of the tension in the air.

They both nodded.

"What is the status of the rooms?" I asked Ana. "Can we move quickly to get a few of them cleaned before long? We have an unusually high number of guests trying to check in early."

"That's exactly what we've been discussing," Bernie said in a tight voice. "Apparently one of the housekeepers was unable to make it in this morning. We have to have a better system for staffing that department."

Ana held up her hand. "Lourdes is on her way. Her mother was taken ill. I tried to explain that to Bernhard."

"I see," I said. "Okay, we'll go with the two housekeepers who are here. Let's double-team rooms and get as many check-outs done as fast as we can before Lourdes gets here."

She rose. "I'll go help them right now."

After she left the office, Bernie shook his head. "This whole business of the staff being one happy family is driving me crazy. We have to be more professional, Ann."

I took a seat and faced him. "As much as we want to be professional—and we are—the reason The Beach House Hotel is a success is due in large part to the feeling of service and dedication any guest receives from our staff. The people who work for us are thought of as our hotel family—people who are willing to go above and beyond for us, each other, and our guests."

"I get your point, but it makes it difficult to manage them," protested Bernie.

I hesitated, trying to make my words sound right. "They need oversight, but not constant management. That's why we set up departments. Right?"

Bernie gave me a steady look. "Do you really need me then?"

"Oh yes, we definitely do. Among other things, we want your expertise with the financial end of things. We're growing so fast that what started out as a fairly simple operation has become more and more complicated. And things are changing within both Rhonda's family and mine. We need to know that, when we're away, the hotel is being well run."

"Good. I like it here and want to be able to help." He gave me a wry smile. "I guess I have to get used to the idea that this isn't New York."

Relieved, I returned his smile. "It certainly isn't."

As I rose, ready to go to my own office, Tim knocked on the door and stuck his head inside. "You both better come. There's a disaster in the pool. Cody Craig's little boy has pooped in it."

"Oh no! We'll have to close the pool, clean out the mess, and then shock it," I said, well aware of health code regulations.

"We need to close it for at least twenty-four hours to let the shock treatment work throughout the filtration system," added Bernie, exchanging a grim look with me.

Bernie and I followed Tim outside. Cody and his wife Adele were stretched out on lounge chairs. Cody was wearing a speedo-style swimsuit and Adele was wearing a bikini bottom and nothing on top. Their son was running around the pool deck with nothing on.

I approached them and spoke quietly to Cody. "I understand your son has pooped in the pool and that he wasn't wearing a swim diaper as we and our health codes require."

His wife lifted up on one elbow and curled her lip. "You Americans are so uptight. I let Jack run free without any clothing so he doesn't grow up to be ashamed of his body."

Her condescending tone of voice set my blood boiling. Considering I wanted to slap her face, I spoke as calmly as I could. "Because of his actions and yours, no one else will be able to use the pool for at least twenty-four hours."

She jumped to her feet so fast her boobs bounced. "Not use the pool? You're kidding! Cody, we're leaving and going to South Beach like I wanted."

He looked up at me and shrugged. "What can I do? She's got her mind made up."

As his wife stomped off, Cody said to me, "I'll pay for any damage. Just add it to my bill."

He went over to his son and picked him up. "C'mon, Jack. We're leaving."

Jack pounded on his father's shoulder. "No!"

Cody gave me a weak smile. "Typical two-year-old."

Shaking our heads, Bernie, Tim, and I watched him walk away.

"He's got two typical two-year-olds, not one," I grumped.

"She's a looker, though," said Tim.

I rolled my eyes at Tim and turned to Bernie. "You'd better call the health department. I'm sorry, I have to leave to do a favor for Rhonda."

"Don't worry, Ann. I'll see that we follow proper procedure including putting up signage for our other guests. It's a damn shame for them to suffer because of people like Cody and Adele Craig."

"How about offering our guests a free soda or a bottle of water or something refreshing for their inconvenience?"

Bernie smiled. "Good idea."

When I drove into Rhonda's driveway to pick up Angela, she was standing outside waiting for me. I waved and pulled to a stop.

She climbed into the passenger's seat and gave me a happy smile. "Thanks for your help, Ann. Mom said she asked you to show me the house Reggie wanted me to see. I want your input. One of my friends ended up in a house she doesn't like because of a number of things she hadn't considered—her kitchen cupboards are too limited, and there's no play area for her baby. That's the kind of input I'm looking for."

"I'm happy to help. It's such an exciting time for you." My gaze rested on her. The last year had brought about a lot of changes for her. "How are you doing with everything, Ange?"

"Reggie and I are doing fine. School work has been tough, though, and his parents even tougher."

"Hmmm. I thought they'd come around." His parents were insufferable snobs. They'd wanted their only son to marry someone else who wasn't interested in marrying him.

"Things were getting better between us until Reggie announced he was going into business with Will. But, honestly, neither of us wanted to live in New York and raise a child there. We'd hoped they would understand."

"When your baby comes along, they may soften up. It's amazing what a new baby can do to help a tense situation. Years ago, Liz became the saving grace for me in dealing with Robert's parents."

"I hope it works for us," said Angela.

"Do you know the sex of the baby?"

"No. Reggie and I opted not to find out. It's best that way. You know how my mother is. We told her to hold off on buying anything until we found out." She grinned. "Reggie wants a girl. I want a boy."

"We'll all be so excited to see that little one," I said. "No matter the sex, your baby and your new baby sister can play together."

"As Mom would say, 'who'd a thunk it?'"

We smiled at each other like the friends we'd become.

I took a turn inland from the coast.

We drove into a neighborhood shaded by tall palm trees. Colorful hedges of oleander and hibiscus defined many of the yards. An occasional tricycle or a stroller dotted a driveway.

We pulled up in front of a one-story, white-stucco house and got out. The real estate agent we'd promised to meet stepped out of her silver Lexus and approached us.

"Hello, I'm Lynn Scheffler." She smiled at Angela. "And you must be Mrs. DelMonte-Smythe."

Angela nodded and held out her hand. "And this is Ann Rutherford, a dear family friend. My mother couldn't come."

The agent smiled. "So I understand. She called to tell me. Congratulations on having a little sister."

Angela smiled. "Thanks. We're hoping she'll be friends with my baby."

After shaking hands with me, Lynn led us inside. She

stopped us in the front entry. "As you will see, some color choices might not be yours. But that is easily changed. It's the only reason I can think of that the house is still on the market. It's a gem of a house in a wonderful, young family neighborhood."

Standing in the front hallway with Angela, I mentally erased the light-purple walls that offended my eyes. My gaze traveled beyond the living room to sliding glass doors leading to a screened-in pool and spa. Walking past the small dining area, we entered a sizeable kitchen that overlooked a family room that also had access to the pool. Off the family room was a sizeable bathroom shared by two bedrooms.

The other side of the house contained a master bedroom suite, a large bathroom, and a nice-sized office.

I remained silent as Lynn pointed out various features. But I kept track of storage closets, kitchen cupboards and other features I'd spent a lot of time thinking about for the renovation of my home. Aside from the light-purple wall color in the main rooms—a color that missed by a mile—the house was, in my opinion, as much a gem as Lynn had indicated.

As Lynn left us to check on the status of the two-car garage, Angela clasped her hands and beamed at me. "I love it. What do you think?"

"It's a wonderful house, and it looks like a great neighborhood."

"Great," said Angela. "I'm going to tell Reggie to go ahead with the offer." She squeezed my hand with excitement. "I'm so happy you're here with me, Ann. You've been such a big supporter of Reggie and me."

I gave her a quick hug. "Love you."

"Yeah, love you, too."

As Lynn returned to her, her smile broadened. "What do you think?"

"My husband will give you a call," Angela said.

"Okay. I'll be waiting for it," said Lynn amiably. "But tell him not to wait. I have a showing this afternoon."

"You do? Well, then, we'll take it," said Angela.

"We'll have Reggie call right away," I amended, ignoring Angela's frown.

"That will be fine," said Lynn, giving me a knowing smile as she shook our hands. She and I both knew that rushing to accept the price wasn't how Reggie would want to buy the house.

As we left, Angela gave me a sheepish look. "Reggie told me not to buy the house outright, but I got so excited I couldn't help myself. It's perfect for us. A house of our own."

"It's going to be wonderful for you."

Angela chuckled. "I'm going to tell Mom I'm going to keep the inside walls purple. Play along with me. Okay?"

I grinned. "Deal."

At Rhonda's house, Rita Ramos, Elena's younger sister, greeted us with a finger to her lips. "Mrs. Grayson is resting and the baby is finally sleeping."

Rhonda's voice came through the intercom system box in the living room. "Rita? Is that Annie and Angela? Tell them to come on back."

At Rita's nod of approval, Angela and I moved quietly into the master wing of the house. When we entered the master bedroom, Rhonda smiled up at us from the king-sized bed she shared with Will. Willow lay in a cradle on the floor next to Rhonda.

I tiptoed over to the cradle. Wrapped in a lightweight, pink-gauze swaddle, Willow was sleeping peacefully. "She really is beautiful, you know," I said to Rhonda.

She grinned. "Don't I know it. Will is in love with her. All he wants to do is sit and stare at her. I didn't think he would even go into work. But with Rita here, we've got things under control, and he finally left." Rhonda turned her attention to Angela. "How did ya like the house?"

Angela shot me a quick glance and smiled at her mother. "I love it. Even the purple walls. Their color is going to be perfect with the new furniture I plan to order."

Rhonda sat up straighter in bed. I hid my smile as I watched Rhonda struggle to be supportive. "But ... but ..."

Angela and I looked at each other and laughed.

"No worries, Mom. Neither one of us liked the color."

"You two ... you're trouble!" said Rhonda, laughing heartily.

At the noise, the baby woke and cried.

"You, too, little one," said Rhonda, her voice so full of love it brought tears to my eyes.

When I walked into the lobby of the hotel, it was eerily quiet.

I shot a worried look at Julie, who was working the front desk. "Where is everyone?"

"Out at the beach party," she said. "Bernie organized it for our guests."

I hurried outside, past the empty pool deck and on out to the wooden deck at the edge of the beach where guests had gathered for what appeared to be a luncheon buffet.

Bernie saw me and waved me over. Behind the small, portable bar we sometimes brought out here, Tim was offering assorted drinks to our guests.

"Hi, Ann. After talking to a few of the guests, I realized we'd better do more than offer guests a bottle of water. They were pretty upset about the pool being closed on such a hot, sunny day. So Consuela and I came up with this idea. Okay with you?"

I smiled. "It's perfect. Goodwill is an important way we've helped build this business. Did you get rid of Cody Craig and his family?"

Bernie grimaced. "Yes, but they took all the towels and the terry robes. I wasn't sure what you'd want me to do about that."

A smile slid across my face. "I think we should charge him for that. Before he left, Cody said he'd pay for any damages. Rhonda and I learned long ago to let our guests know that any stolen items would be charged to them. So far, our policy has worked very well. Many of our guests are happy to purchase them because the robes and umbrellas have become status symbols."

"Good," said Bernie, giving me a sly look. "I already added it to his bill."

I laughed, liking Bernie more and more.

CHAPTER THIRTEEN

After checking reservations for the rest of the month, I quickly called our PR contact to discuss a new ad. The shoulder month of April was looking empty. We agreed on a promo for a spring package, and then I hurried home for a late lunch.

The house was quiet when I entered the kitchen. I searched for Vaughn and found him outside on the dock with Liz. Elena and Robbie were wading in the water near them. My heart filled with the sight of them, reminding me that this is how it would be going forward. My grown daughter and a toddler son. I couldn't help wondering if Vaughn and I had made a huge mistake. I heard Robbie's squeal of delight, and some of the tension that had gripped me with an iron hand loosened its fingers. This was an innocent little boy who needed our love.

I went down to greet them.

Vaughn looked up and lifted his hand in a quick wave. "I think I've converted Liz to sailing," he called out to me before going back to showing her how to tie different knots on an unused docking line.

I crossed over to where Elena and Robbie were digging at the sandy edge of the water.

"Hi, Gammy. Look!" He pointed to a mound of sand.

Elena shot me a subtle wink. "We're making a sand castle...of sorts. I wanted to help him, but he had a fit about it, so I stopped."

I laughed. "Good job!"

I remained a moment, watching Robbie scoop up sand and stack it carefully on the pile of sand in front of him. The way he concentrated reminded me of Robert.

"Any calls?" I said, addressing Elena.

"Someone named Chad called to say he'd be here a little later to talk to you about setting up the wireless network in the house."

"Good. I want Vaughn to be able to address those issues with him." Vaughn would be leaving for New York soon, and we wanted the work done before he left.

When I approached Liz, she gave me a wobbly smile. "Vaughn and I have been busy with the boat...and talking. I felt guilty for thinking of giving up Robbie, but I understand now that because we're all a family, it won't really be that way, that it's more like sharing responsibility for him."

"And also relieving you of the financial responsibility," amended Vaughn. "He'll always be your brother. You'll always have input in his life and will, I hope, always have a close bond with each other."

"Do you feel better now?" I asked Liz, sweeping a strand of hair away from the troubled expression on her face.

Her face brightened. "We called Mr. Torson. He's going to meet with us tomorrow."

"I'm glad it's settled. I think having us adopt Robbie is the best thing for everyone. But, Liz, I hope you appreciate Vaughn's kindness, his generosity...and mine."

"Oh, I do, I do," she said so quickly, Vaughn and I laughed. I knew if the situation were reversed, Robert would never have considered it. He just hadn't been that generous.

Later, as Vaughn and I were sitting on the lanai eating a light meal, Elena brought Robbie inside for a nap.

He ran over to me. "Look!" He lifted his little red plastic bucket up to me. I peered inside. A single broken shell—

mostly whole—sat at the bottom of it. "A shell? How pretty!"

Robbie gave me a satisfied smile. "Mine."

I cupped his face in my hands and kissed his cheek.

His blue eyes studied me.

"Sleep tight," I said, as Elena took hold of his hand and led him away.

Thoughtful, I watched him go.

"He seems to be making a good adjustment," Vaughn commented.

"Almost too good," I said. "It makes me wonder if he was as neglected as Liz once told me. When I first met him, he seemed unusually content to be by himself, as if he was used to it. Maybe he had to entertain himself because Kandie wouldn't."

"Could be. He's certainly getting a lot of attention here along with exciting new experiences."

Liz joined us. "What are you two talking about?"

"Robbie," I answered. "You mentioned once that Kandie didn't spend a lot of time with him, that he was a total brat with her."

"Yeah, that's true. I don't like to talk about it, but she pretty much did nothing around the house but watch television. That's why Dad wanted me there. I'd at least see that Robbie's diaper was changed and that he was fed regular meals. He loves being here. And I've noticed that after the first couple of days, he's never mentioned Kandie or Dad again."

"I'll talk to Barbara Holmes about it. If you remember, she's the psychologist Tina Marks used when she was staying with me."

Before our conversation could continue, Elena returned. "Do you mind if I do some personal errands while Robbie is down for his nap?"

"No problem. In fact, why don't you take the rest of the day off?" I said.

"I'm going to read a book in my room," said Liz. "I'll hear Robbie if he wakes up. I'll take care of him. I want to spend some quality time with him anyway."

"How about we go for a walk along the beach?" Vaughn said to me after taking the last bite of his salad. "I've missed our doing that and there's something I want to discuss with you."

"Okay. I've got the rest of the day off. Bernie's got things under control at the hotel and Dorothy is due to come in. She'll stay through the dinner hour to take care of the office."

"So Bernie is working out for you?"

I nodded. "He wants to feel like he has more control, so I'm leaving him alone more and more. It's a learning process for both of us."

"But?" Vaughn stared directly into my eyes. "The tone of your voice tells me you're not entirely happy with that."

"But The Beach House Hotel is still my baby and always will be," I admitted.

Vaughn lifted my hand and kissed the palm of it. "And now we have a baby of our own. I'm so glad I found someone like you, Ann, because I know you'll be the kind of mother Robbie needs even as you take care of the hotel." He features softened as he continued to gaze at me.

My heart filled at the look of love in his eyes.

The white sand felt soft and warm under my feet as I strolled hand-in-hand with Vaughn. We'd changed into bathing suits, and the afternoon sun warmed my shoulders even as an onshore breeze brought a whisper of coolness to us.

From a distance, I could see The Beach House Hotel sitting like a royal entity embracing the beach, the wings of the building like open arms.

"It really is beautiful, huh?" Vaughn said. He gazed down at me. "But not as beautiful as you."

I smiled up at him, forcing myself to recognize the words he spoke to me were real and not merely his lines for the television show in which he was famous.

"I've talked to my kids about Robbie," Vaughn said. "After explaining the situation to them, they're okay with my going ahead with the idea of adopting him. It means a lot to me to have their acceptance."

"And to me," I said, giving his hand an affectionate squeeze. "I'll be sure to send them a thank you for their support."

"It'll be good to talk to Mike Torson tomorrow. My understanding is that he's already been in touch with Syd Green, your divorce lawyer, to help us at his end to take care of all the paperwork and court filings."

"Syd is good. He'll help clear the way for us."

Vaughn pulled me to a stop. "I'm changing my will to include you and Robbie. I know it's a little premature in both cases, but should anything happen to me, I'd want you taken care of, along with my children."

The idea of losing Vaughn made my stomach clench.

He chuckled. "Get that stricken look off your face. Nothing's going to happen to me. It's just a precaution. That's all."

In defiance, a shiver danced across my shoulders. "You take very good care of yourself, hear?"

"Yes, Ma'am. I will. I'm looking forward to being married to you for a very long time." A sexy smile appeared on his face. "Maybe we can sneak in a little...nap...this afternoon if we hurry back."

I grinned. Vaughn was Vaughn, and I loved him.

#

Chad's truck was in our driveway when we returned to the house.

"Great," said Vaughn. He turned to me with a smile. "Wait until you see all the things I want to do with wireless."

I shook my head. "Okay, boys and toys. I get it. Have fun!"

When we walked into the kitchen, Chad was sitting at the table. Sheets of notebook paper were spread out in front of him. A coffee cup sat on his right. Liz sat opposite him.

Chad stood. "Hello, Ann. I'm here to do the work we talked about."

I shook his hand. "This is Vaughn Sanders. Actually, you'll be doing the work for him."

They shook hands and then I turned to Liz. "Robbie's still sleeping?"

"Yes. I just checked on him. I think he's worn out from all the digging in the sand."

We smiled at each other.

"As long as you're here, Mom, I thought I'd call Angela back. She and Reggie got the house and she wants me to see it."

"Okay, I'm off the rest of the day."

I left Vaughn and Chad going over plans in the kitchen and headed to Robbie's room. Quietly, I opened the door and peeked in. He was just beginning to stir. Watching him, I couldn't help thinking of past miscarriages. I'd wanted more children after Liz, but it had never happened.

Robbie sat up sleepily. "Izzie? Layna? Mommy?"

"Peek-a-boo!" I stepped forward.

His smile warmed my heart.

"I'm here, Robbie."

He held up his arms. "Up. Want up!"

I lifted him in my arms and nestled my cheek against the still-warm skin of his face.

He squirmed. "Down. Get down."

I laughed. "Hey, Mr. Up and Down Boy! You're not going anywhere without a fresh diaper."

We played a little counting game as I changed him. Afterward, I set him down and handed him the blue blanket we'd bought him and he took off, holding one corner of it to his mouth and trailing the rest behind him. I wondered if he'd be just as cute as a teenager.

I followed Robbie into the kitchen and lifted him into his highchair. "How about some milk?" I poured milk into his sippy cup, and after handing it to him, I placed a graham cracker— his favorite—on the tray. As he took a sip of milk and nibbled on his cracker, his eyes never left me.

I sat down beside him. "Did you get enough?"

He held out his hand. "More, Mommy."

Not sure I'd heard correctly, I froze. "What did you say?"

His solemn gaze remained on me, and I had the odd feeling he was testing me. "More, Mommy."

"Sure," I said, rising and turning my back so he wouldn't see my tears. His clear voice, that magical word, made everything seem right with me.

I turned back to Robbie. "I love you, son."

CHAPTER FOURTEEN

After offering Mike Torson a cup of coffee, which he happily accepted, Vaughn, Liz, and I sat at the kitchen table to get his legal advice regarding Robbie.

"As soon as I got the initial call from you, Ann, I phoned Syd Green in Boston. He's agreed to handle the filing of paperwork for us." He turned to Liz. "From the time of death when you were given guardianship of Robbie, a 30-day window was opened during which you were to sign an acceptance of appointment. I informed Syd that we wanted to make a change to that appointment. Technically we have to file an objection but, of course, we're making it clear to the judge involved that this is a family decision in Robbie's best interest."

At Liz's stricken look, I clasped her hand. "It isn't a real objection to you. It's just terminology."

Mike went on.

"I have some forms and other paperwork for the three of you to sign. We'll file all of it with the Probate and Family Court in the county where Robert and Kandie last lived. As far as adoption is concerned, my understanding is that Robbie will have had to live with you for six months before we can do anything concrete about it. But, again, the judge involved may deem that requirement unnecessary because it's all family-related. The important thing is to have these papers of appointment filed right away." He pinned each one of us with a steady gaze. "Is everyone in agreement as to what we plan to do?"

I nodded along with Vaughn and Liz.

He smiled. "Okay then, we'll move forward on this. And may I say, off the record, that I admire the three of you very much for making the future of this child so secure."

Tears stung my eyes. I'd never imagined starting a family over again, but my sympathy had gone out to Robbie. In my heart, he was already mine.

Liz and I left the kitchen arm-in-arm, while Vaughn stayed behind with Mike to go over matters of his will.

Liz and I found seats on the porch and sat a moment, sharing silence.

Elena and Robbie joined us, wearing bathing suits. "Swim lesson time," Elena announced.

"Hi, sweet boy!" I said, holding my arms out to Robbie.

Robbie ran over to me. "Look, Mommy! A turkle!" He held up a plastic turtle.

I laughed. "It's a turkle all right."

Liz looked over at me, her eyes wide. *Mommy?* She mouthed.

I grinned. "It started yesterday. I think he's heard you call me Mom so many times, he thought it was right."

A smile slid across Liz's face. "You're perfect together. I'm so glad he already loves you like that. It takes a lot of my worry away."

Troy walked into the room, wearing a bathing suit that set off his muscled torso. "Ready for another swim lesson, Robbie?"

I saw the eager expressions on both Liz and Elena's faces at his appearance, and I wondered how he'd handle the situation.

Liz spoke up. "Vaughn and my mother are adopting Robbie. We're working out the details now. I thought you both should know."

Elena glanced at me. "That's wonderful."

"So you're free to go back to school and all?" Troy asked.

Liz nodded. "He'll always be my special brother, and I'll always give him a lot of attention, but he'll have a much better lifestyle with Mom and Vaughn."

"That's nice. I'm happy for all of you." He turned to Elena with a warm smile that told its own story. "Ready to join me?"

I noticed Liz's hurt expression, but I said nothing as Troy and Elena moved to the pool with Robbie.

"That's the woman Troy is interested in?" Liz whispered. The features of her face drooped with disappointment.

"It would seem so," I responded.

Liz gave me a long look and got up. "Guess I'll go see what's happening with Ange. We're supposed to go furniture shopping today."

After she left the room, I walked out to the pool to check on Robbie's progress.

"Mommy! Look!" Robbie cried. He held onto the side of the pool and eagerly kicked his legs, splashing water everywhere.

"Good job!" I said, proud of how he was adapting to the water. "Elena, I'm heading to the hotel. Call if you need me for anything. And thank you, Troy, for making the time for this lesson."

He smiled at Elena and turned back to me. "No problem! I'll see you back at the hotel as soon as this lesson is over. I'm pretty busy for the rest of the day."

I said goodbye to Vaughn and Mike and headed out. On the short drive to the hotel, I thought of Liz. I was glad Vaughn and I could relieve her of the daily care of Robbie but knew she'd always be bound to him. And when she fell in love, her future husband would need to know about the little boy we'd all taken into our hearts.

When I arrived at the hotel, breakfast was over and lunch

preparations were underway. I grabbed my usual cup of coffee and headed into my office, which seemed especially empty without Rhonda's usual, exuberant presence. I picked up the phone to call her.

A knock on the door stopped me.

"Come in," I called.

Bernie entered the room, followed by his faithful dog, Trudy. "Have a minute?"

"Sure. What's up?"

Bernie took a seat and lifted Trudy into his lap. "What do you know about the Hassels?

"The Hassels who were supposed to have a wedding here?"

"Yes. I just got a call from a relative of theirs. A woman by the name of Annette Bauer, who lives in New York. Her daughter Babette is getting married, and she wants to have the wedding here. The Hassels are encouraging this because they feel bad they had to cancel."

"Is this family some kind of royalty too?" The last thing we needed was another wedding go sour on us at the last minute.

Bernie shook his head. "No. In fact, Annette made it plain that her budget is limited, that she's doing this as a favor to a distant cousin who's helped her in the past. She's been a widow for quite some time."

"What dates are we talking about?

A smile filled Bernie's face. "The last weekend in April. I know it's a rush situation, but it's a slow time for us."

I returned his smile. Even with a late Easter, we had a few weeks in April when little was happening before we were hosting a slew of weddings, including my own.

"Okay, let's have Sabine get in touch with her and then meet with us. Lorraine Grace at Wedding Perfection owes us a favor for rescuing her from the Hassel loss. Maybe she can help to make this a nice wedding for PR purposes."

"Great," said Bernie. "Annette is coming down this weekend to look at the property. I told her I'd show her around. I met her at several functions at my old hotel. She's very nice."

An intriguing trace of color appeared on his cheeks.

I hid a smile. "Sounds like a plan. Anything else?"

"Not at the moment." He left, and I phoned Rhonda.

"Annie? How are things going?" she said, picking up the call right away. "I should be back to work part-time by the end of the week. As much as I want to spend time with Willow, I miss the hotel. Give me the scoop on everything that's happening."

When I told her about the wedding and Bernie's reaction, she let out a whoop, "I knew it! Bernie has a soft side to him. Maybe if we handle it right, he'll fall in love with her."

"Rhonda, we are not, repeat not, going to play matchmaker with him. He's a grown man still recovering from his loss. Remember?"

"We'll see," said Rhonda, stubborn as always.

I couldn't help laughing. Rhonda was Rhonda. Poor Bernie was in trouble and didn't even know it.

Before I left to go home for the evening, Bernie and I met with Sabine.

"I've talked to Annette," Sabine reported. "Her daughter Babette is thrilled with the idea of a wedding at The Beach House Hotel and promises to cooperate with whatever we create. They both seem like very nice people. Annette told me quite frankly that this was being paid for, in part, by her cousin."

"I admire her honesty," I said. "Under those circumstances, it would be fun to put together a very nice wedding for them.

In return, maybe they would let us photograph it for a new brochure. It would be fun to have the brochure focus on the mother of the bride." I turned to Bernie. "You've met Annette. Is she photogenic?"

"Oh, yes. Very much so." There was something in the tone of his voice that led me to believe he truly admired her.

"Okay, then. Let's make this work. Tomorrow, after I drop Vaughn off at the airport, I'll get in touch with our ad agency."

I quickly ended the meeting, anxious to spend as much time with Vaughn as I could.

"Mommy!" cried Robbie when I walked onto the screened porch of the house. He and Elena were sitting on the floor, building something with wooden blocks.

"Hi!" I went over to him and swept him up in my arms. It still surprised me that we'd formed a bond so quickly, but I reveled in it. Maybe he realized how eager I was to see that he was loved. Or maybe, I thought honestly, I'd slipped into the role of Mommy because there was no one else to fill it. Either way, I was grateful for the chance to raise a child with Vaughn. It made our relationship so much deeper.

Vaughn and Liz walked up toward the house from the dock. Watching the easy chatting between them, I had another reason to be grateful. I stepped outside to greet them.

"Hi, Mom!" said Liz, running up to me and giving me a hug. "Guess what? Vaughn helped me with a deal for Kandie's van. Tomorrow, I trade it in for a second-hand SUV, a four-wheel drive that I can use to go back and forth from here to school."

"Wonderful!" I smiled at Vaughn. He was such a nice guy.

He put his arm around me. "You ready for my last night here for a while? I've got something special planned."

"Oh?" I felt my lips spread into a broad smile.

"Yeah. Go pack an overnight bag and let's head out."

"Where are we going?"

"Not far," he said, grinning like a naughty school boy.

Curious, I hurried inside to pack. When I entered our bedroom I noticed a small suitcase sitting by the door. I resisted the temptation to look inside and went into the bathroom to freshen up before changing my clothes.

Several minutes later, I snapped my small suitcase shut. I hoped I'd packed the right things. The sundress I now wore would do for both dressy or casual situations, and I was pretty sure Vaughn would love the sexy new peignoir I'd ordered online.

When I walked into the living room, Vaughn was sitting on the floor making appropriate noises with Robbie as they pushed plastic trucks around. I pulled out my iPhone from my purse and quickly snapped a photo of them.

Vaughn's eyes sparkled as he turned to me. The dark, silky curls I loved to twine my fingers through hung in a clump before his brow. "Wonder what my fans would think of me now."

I smiled. "They'd love you, like always. But not as much as me." He had no idea how handsome he was, how he'd touched my heart with his gentle playtime with Robbie.

Vaughn got to his feet and swung Robbie up in his arms. "Okay, fella. Time to turn you over to Liz." He gave him a kiss on the cheek and handed him over to Liz. "Here you go. You and Elena are in charge. Your mother and I will return tomorrow morning in time for breakfast. I've got a mid-morning flight."

I gave Robbie and Liz kisses and allowed Vaughn to tug me out of the room, pleased by his eagerness.

After we got settled in the car, I turned to him. "Where are we going?"

"The Palm Island Club. Remember our first visit?"

I smiled. In many respects, our relationship had begun after dining there. After dinner that night, we'd returned to my house for a walk on the beach. In the moonlight, with the movement of the water whispering to us, we'd promised each other to see where our relationship would take us. The Palm Island Club would always be special to me.

Vaughn parked his car in the small parking lot at the end of a cul de sac. At the nearby dock, a motor launch awaited guests. The Club sat on a small spit of land most easily reached by a short boat ride, which made a visit there even more fun.

We got out of the car, grabbed our bags, and walked onto the dock. A member of the club staff greeted us. "Welcome, Mr. Sanders. Good evening, Ms. Rutherford. May I help you into the boat?"

"Yes, thank you," I said, trying to ignore the gasps of pleasure from the people seated in the boat at the sight of Vaughn. I'd never get used to it, but this kind of attention didn't seem to faze him.

I found a place to sit on the port side of the boat, and Vaughn joined me. The boat's engine revved, and we pulled away from the dock. Vaughn held my hand as the boat sliced through the water leaving its wake behind. Several seagulls followed us, no doubt hoping our disturbing the water might produce food for them. I watched them lift up into the air and swoop down again like pieces of popping corn, their noisy cries muffled by the roar of the boat's engine.

Vaughn squeezed my hand and smiled at me, absently rubbing my engagement ring.

As I did so often, I wondered at all the changes he had produced in my life. Meeting Vaughn and falling in love with him was one of the most surprising and best things that had ever happened to me.

After the short ride, we approached the club's dock. After being helped onto it. I waited for Vaughn to join me. Before he could leave the boat, he was quickly surrounded by admirers. He managed to step onto the dock and paused long enough to sign a few autographs.

A staff member took our suitcases, and we headed up a path to the rustic main building.

"Mr. Sanders, wait!" came a cry behind us.

A middle-aged woman hurried toward us, waving a piece of paper. "Will you please sign an autograph for my friend?"

Vaughn stopped. "Sure. Should I make it out to anyone special?"

The woman clasped her hands. "Just say it's for Linda."

Vaughn scribbled something on a piece of paper and handed it back to her.

"Oh my! Thank you!"

"Aunt Linda, are you coming?" called one of the younger guests.

As she hurried away, Vaughn and I looked at each other and laughed. Lots of people apparently had so-called "friends" like hers.

"Well, Mr. Sanders," I said, taking hold of his hand. "It seems as if you have all kinds of fans here tonight. How are we ever going to have a peaceful dinner?"

"Ah, I've taken care of that. Come with me."

We bypassed the main building and walked down a path leading to a number of cabins tucked in among Australian pines, coconut palms, sea grapes, and other greenery.

"I've arranged for us to have a private meal in our cabin," Vaughn said.

"Nice," I said, relieved to have him to myself. Sharing Vaughn wasn't always easy, and on this, our last evening together for a while, I dreaded the thought of him leaving.

With their weathered-gray clapboard exteriors, the cabins presented a rustic image. But I knew from a previous tour of the property that they were anything but rustic inside.

We followed the bellman to the front door of the cabin closest to the beach. With a flourish, the bellman unlocked the door and held it open while we entered.

We walked into a main living area that held a couch, three over-stuffed chairs and accompanying tables and lighting. By the window looking to the beach, a marble-topped table was set for dinner for two. Orchids formed a floral centerpiece. Crystal wine glasses sparkled beside water goblets. Heavy silverware defined the settings placed atop plush, floral placemats.

"May I show you to your bedroom?" asked the bellman, exchanging a look with Vaughn that caught my attention.

Vaughn and I walked to the bedroom door and looked inside. Touched by the scene in front of me, I turned to Vaughn with tears. Red rose petals were sprinkled atop the lightweight blanket and on the fluffy pillows. The lights in the bedroom had been dimmed. Soft, soothing music flowed from the special wireless speaker on the bureau. A number of lit candles sat on tables, flickering an invitation for us to come inside.

"You arranged this?"

He nodded, sheepishly.

As the young bellman arranged our suitcases on racks, I gave Vaughn a quick kiss. "Thank you. It's wonderful."

The bellman tipped his head. "Dinner will be served anytime you call, Mr. Sanders."

Vaughn slipped him some money, and after the door closed behind him, Vaughn turned to me. "I want this to be special for us—away from your worries at the hotel and our duties as new parents."

"Then let's make it special," I said, giving him a saucy grin. He grinned, took my hand, and we went into the bedroom together.

Following the first course of lightly seared baby scallops tossed in a sweetened-lime dressing, the entrée was a mustard-and-crumb-crusted rack of lamb served with mint jelly and accompanied by a mélange of vegetables and oven-roasted potatoes. Though Vaughn was normally careful with his diet, it was fun to see him dig into a meal like this with enthusiasm. A crisp, green salad, to cleanse our palates, came next. A light, lemon sorbet with a raspberry sauce ended the meal.

After the servers had gone, taking all the remains from the meal with them, Vaughn turned to me. "Shall we go for a walk along the beach. There's enough moonlight to allow us to see."

"Yes, I need to move around after a meal like this." I got to my feet, eager to get outside. I went into the bedroom to get my sweater and sat down on the bed, still rumpled from our lovemaking.

"You all right?" said Vaughn, poking his head inside the room.

"Give me a minute to make a phone call. I need to make sure everything's all right with Robbie."

Vaughn frowned. "Is this how it's going to be moving forward?" There was an edge to his voice.

I looked up at him. "Pretty much."

The frown smoothed out. "Guess I'd forgotten what it's like. Ellen was the same way when our kids were small."

"It's hard to go back to that kind of life," I admitted. "But I can't do it any other way. We've made a commitment to Robbie, and I'm going to do my best with him."

"Do you think we've made a mistake by taking him on?" asked Vaughn. "In retrospect, it was an awfully hasty decision."

I rose and wrapped my arms around him. "No, I don't think it's a mistake. After a horrible accident that took his parents away, Robbie needed a new family with his sister, your children, and us. He's one of the luckiest little boys I know to be given an opportunity to have all the advantages he'll have living with all of us."

Vaughn tipped my chin and gazed down at me with a smile so full of love, my heart lifted.

"You're a very nice lady. Know that?"

I responded to his gentle kiss with gratefulness. We both knew taking on a toddler wasn't going to be easy. Furthermore, it was a challenge that would stay with us all our lives.

Vaughn gave me a love pat on the bum. "Hurry and make the call and then let's go. I'll wait for you outside."

Liz answered my call. "Hi, Mom! What's up?" There was a happy lilt to her words I was glad to hear.

"I'm calling to check on things. Did Robbie go to bed all right?"

"Yes, he's fine. Chad is here. He's dropping off supplies so he can do the work for Vaughn tomorrow. And, Mom, Elena and I had a good talk about Troy. They've known each other for a while, and now, it's really gotten serious between them. So Troy's not wanting to date me wasn't really about Robbie."

"Good. That makes me feel better about a lot of things. I've got to go. We'll be back tomorrow morning. Thanks for taking care of Robbie. Love you."

"Love you too." She lowered her voice to a whisper. "Chad is awfully cute, don't you think?"

I chuckled. "Goodbye, Liz."

After the walk on the beach, Vaughn and I turned out the lights in the cabin and headed into the bedroom. Earlier, our lovemaking had been lustily hurried. I needed a different kind of time with him.

I undressed and began to put on my new peignoir set—fluttery black shorts and a black silk camisole trimmed in pink lace.

Vaughn's gaze remained focused on me as I slid on the silky shorts and prepared to slide the top over my head.

He grinned playfully at me. "Whoa, woman! What do you think you're doing? I'll just have to take them off."

I laughed. "At least let me model them for you. They cost a bundle. Take a seat."

I slid the top on and then pretended to do a model strut in front of him, swinging my hips with every step.

"You're killing me!" He reached out, clasped my elbow, and pulled me onto his lap.

His lips came down on mine, gentle, yet demanding. I knew what we both wanted and was pleased when he helped me remove the camisole and lifted me on top of the bed. My heart pounded with anticipation as I waited for him to disrobe and join me. I saw how ready he was and opened my arms to him, well aware of the pleasure that awaited me.

Later, sated and lying next to him, I realized how much I'd come to enjoy him—not just sexually, but in the way we fit together, the way we talked after making love, and, afterward, the way we curled up together as we drifted off to sleep.

Tonight had proved to be as wonderful as the others.

CHAPTER FIFTEEN

Sadness filled me as I pulled up to the airport. Neither Vaughn nor I was sure when he'd be able to return. The short break from filming the soap usually meant extra hours of work, depending on the schedules of the other stars. I'd thought the time would come after we were married when I could go back and forth from Florida to New York with him. Now, with the added care of Robbie, along with my hotel business, that was much more unlikely.

"Come home soon," I said, giving him a kiss, which I hoped conveyed my feelings.

We broke apart, and he lifted my chin. "I'll be back as soon as I can. But you know what my life is like."

I did. His wasn't a simple job. It involved much more than the television show. He had commitments to charities and to his own children. I understood that. But it didn't make it any easier.

Vaughn got out of the car, gave me a wave of his hand, and then he was gone.

Sighing, telling myself to focus on the future, I left the airport and headed to the hotel.

As soon as I walked into my office, Dorothy knocked on the door and entered, waving a piece of paper at me.

"What's that?" I asked.

"A cease and desist order from the Neighborhood Community Board. Someone has complained about the noise from the hotel's sound system."

"What noise?" I asked, genuinely puzzled.

"The other evening, Bernie piped music out to our beachside deck for one of our new sunset cocktail parties. That's all I know. Here. Read this."

I took the paper from her, glanced through it, and went to find Bernie.

I knocked on the door to his office, and at his request to enter, I went inside.

"What's this about music at the hotel being too loud?" I asked him, taking a seat in one of the two chairs facing his desk.

He frowned. "Who's objecting? After we got our license from ASCAP, I started using wireless speakers to play music for our sunset cocktail hours right here on our own property. We don't play anything but soft, soothing music that isn't the least bit loud."

I could feel goosebumps race up and down my back. *Was Brock Goodwin up to his old tricks?*

"Have you received any calls on this?" I asked, handing him the notice.

Bernie shook his head. "None has been reported to me."

"No calls from someone named Brock Goodwin?"

"No. Why? Should I know him?"

"He's the president of the Gold Coast Neighborhood Association board and a real jerk. He's caused us a lot of trouble in the past. Let me know if he ever tries to speak to you about this or anything else."

"Okay." He studied the notice and turned to me with a frown. "What do you want to do about this?"

"I'm going to talk to Rhonda, and then I'll get back to you." I rose. "Thanks, Bernie. Everything still on for Annette Bauer's visit?"

He smiled. "She'll be in Friday morning. I've arranged for Tim to pick her up."

"Good." I hated loose ends, and after losing out on their business, I hoped the Hassels would be pleased with Annette's daughter's wedding. Too bad their own daughter had run off with another man before her own wedding here at the hotel, leaving us to cope with an unexpected cancellation.

Instead of going back to the office, I decided to pay Rhonda a visit. I'd missed her and I was dying to see little Willow again. I checked in with Dorothy and left the hotel.

On the drive, I thought about Bernie. He was very capable and learning to deal with a small upscale resort instead of a busy, commercial hotel in the city. I didn't want to lose him. With Rhonda's baby and Robbie's arrival in my life, neither Rhonda nor I could devote the kind of overtime we'd put into the operation in the past.

I parked my car in the driveway of Rhonda and Will's house and admired the well-tended landscaping, the peaceful setting. The beige, two-story house with a brown, tile roof was elegant in its simplicity. Sitting on the edge of a small lake a block inland from the Gulf, it enjoyed the best of both worlds.

Anxious to see how Rhonda was doing, I knocked on the door.

Rita opened the door. "Ah, Ann. It's so good to see you. Rhonda's in her sitting room upstairs. It hasn't been a good day."

Worry caused me to frown. "Oh? Is she all right?"

Rita shook her head. "Go see for yourself. She'll be glad you're here."

When I walked into the sitting room off her bedroom, I found Rhonda staring out the window, her cheeks moist with tears.

"Oh, honey," I cried, rushing over to her. "What's wrong?"

She looked up at me and sniffled. "Everything. I'm worried my milk supply isn't enough. All Willow wants to do is eat ... constantly. And, Annie, if I seemed fat before, I'm even fatter now." She poked at her stomach. "See this? It's as doughy as ... as ... the cinnamon rolls I make." She let out a little sob. "I'm a mess. A total ugly mess."

I took hold of her hands. "Look at me. You're beautiful, and you've just had a beautiful baby. It takes time to get back to normal."

Rhonda drew in a shaky breath. "It's those obnoxious movie stars. They pop out a baby and, presto, their stomachs are flatter than ever. There's no fuckin' way that's possible. I hate their twenty-four-hour trainers and everything about them."

I sat in the overstuffed chair opposite her and studied her. "Do you think some of this has to do with the post-partum blues? It would be natural to feel a little down and overwhelmed."

She shook her head. "No, that's not it. It's about Will."

"Will?"

Rhonda nodded. "All he does is pay attention to Willow. He's absolutely foolish over her." Fresh tears spilled from her eyes. "He ... he sometimes doesn't even seem to know I'm around. It's not ... like it ... used to be," she hiccupped between sobs.

I rose, went to her, and wrapped my arms around her. "Will adores you, Rhonda. I imagine he's still enthralled by the miracle that his love for you has produced. But you'll always be number one with him. He's told me more than once that he couldn't live without you. Have you seen how he looks at you?"

Rhonda dabbed at her eyes and gave me a hopeful look. "You think that's all it is? I remember how it was to lose Sal to all those young girls. I could never be like them."

"Oh, hon, what you really need is a little pampering. I'm going to call the spa right now and make arrangements for you to get a mani and a pedi. Then I'm going to call Malinda at Hair Designs for an appointment for you later this afternoon. Okay?"

"You'd do that for me?" Rhonda's face brightened. "Oh, it'll be so good to get out of the house and have some time to myself." She got to her feet with renewed energy. "Let's go into the nursery and take a look at Willow. She's the sweetest thing ever!"

I smiled. *This* Rhonda was so much better.

Before we left her room, I quickly punched in the spa's number at the hotel and spoke to Troy. He agreed to fit Rhonda into the schedule within the hour. And when I talked to Malinda, she agreed to stay late to take care of Rhonda's hair. I hung up and gave Rhonda the news.

"How can I go meet Malinda at six? That's dinner time."

"Rita can see that Will gets dinner. And with you gone, it will give him some quality time alone with Willow. It will be good for all of you."

"Right," said Rhonda, grinning. "And it'll give me the break I need."

As we walked toward the nursery, Rhonda touched her chest. "I'm sore. They make all kinds of organic creams now for nursing mothers, but it still can be a bit painful."

I clapped a hand on Rhonda's shoulder. "Do you think that maybe you're trying too hard?"

"Maybe. Rita thinks so too." She faced me. "I just want to be a good mother. You know?"

"You already are, Rhonda. Think of Angela. She's a wonderful young woman, and you raised her by yourself for a number of years."

Rhonda's lips curved. "I'm so glad I have you for a friend,

Annie. Know that?"

I knew all right. Without Rhonda, my life wouldn't be the same.

We tiptoed into Willow's room and stood a moment, gazing at the perfect little girl who was sleeping peacefully. She was, I thought, an exceptionally beautiful baby.

After a few moments, Rhonda urged me to follow her out of the room. "Let's go talk hotel."

She led me downstairs, into the kitchen. "Have a seat, Annie, and tell me all about what's happening at the hotel. It's killing me not to be in on everything."

I sat at the kitchen table and accepted the glass of lemony iced tea that Rita offered me.

Rhonda took a seat opposite me and leaned forward in eagerness. "Is Annette Bauer still coming? And what else is going on?"

I gave Rhonda an update on the Bauer wedding and then told her about the cease and desist order.

Rhonda slapped her hand on the table. "Are you thinking what I'm thinking, Annie? Is that rat-bastard Brock Goodwin behind this?"

"I honestly don't know. That's why I wanted to talk to you before we did anything about it. We've had only a few sunset cocktail parties, and Bernie wants to continue them. He says the guests enjoy them, and the music isn't loud at all. I wonder if being so close to the water makes the music seem louder than it is. You know how sound carries across water."

"Maybe. Or is it just Brock up to his old tricks? We haven't heard from him in some time."

"I'll have Dorothy do a little snooping before we react to it. In the meantime, should we go ahead with the parties for our guests?"

"Sure," said Rhonda. "It's just a request from ' the

neighborhood, isn't it? Are there any other problems in putting them on?"

"No. We have all the licensing taken care of with ASCAP. There are no huge speakers—just a couple of strategically placed wireless speakers using our in-house system."

"Well, then, we'll go ahead and see who's behind all this. If it's Brock Goodwin, I'm going to bust his balls one way or another. I promise."

I smiled. Rhonda was back on track.

Things were hopping when I walked into the hotel lobby. What had started as a private, birthday luncheon in the small dining room had overflowed onto the pool deck, where the birthday group dominated the area with celebratory drinks that they'd offered to everyone else there. I watched in fascination as guests who didn't know each other melded into congenial groups, chatting beside the pool like old friends. This scenario didn't always happen, but when it did, it was wonderful public relations for the hotel.

I left the scene and asked Bernie and Dorothy to join me in my office.

They came in and took the seats I offered them at the small conference table.

As soon as Dorothy sat down, Trudy placed her paws on the edge of the chair and whined to be picked up.

"I just love this dog," said Dorothy, lifting the dachshund onto her lap and giving her a hug, then chuckling when Trudy kissed her cheek.

Bernie and I exchanged amused looks. The dog had become a favorite of everyone who came into contact with her. Even cranky guests eventually succumbed to her charm.

I reached over and gave Trudy a pat on the head. As she

licked my hand, I wondered if Vaughn and I should consider a puppy for Robbie. Boys and dogs just seemed to go together.

"What's going on, Ann?" Dorothy said, bringing me back to the moment.

"Rhonda and I are wondering if Brock Goodwin is behind this notice. We want you, Dorothy, to see what you can find out for us. If it's not Brock, we need to know who we should address about this issue."

"I'll be glad to," said Dorothy. Behind the thick lenses of her glasses, her eyes shone with determination. "I'm not about to let that nincompoop Brock get away with anything."

Bernie's eyebrows rose like question marks.

I chuckled. "Dorothy, why don't you fill Bernie in on our so-called friend."

"He's never been a friend of ours. In fact, he's done everything to try and make this hotel fail." She pulled herself up straight in her chair and began talking so fast, with such anger, that Trudy jumped off her lap and went to sit by Bernie's chair.

When Dorothy was through, Bernie nodded thoughtfully. "I've had to deal with a few people like this before. Big frogs in a little pond is all they are."

"This guy is more like a gigantic jackass on a tiny farm," said Dorothy, and we all laughed.

I checked my watch, ready for some down time. The complainer about the music was a newcomer to the area. After Dorothy talked to him, he settled down and quickly accepted her offer to have dinner at The Beach House Hotel on us. In cases like this, we were happy to exchange a free meal for goodwill.

When I finally walked through the door of my house, I

found Elena in the kitchen, wiping Robbie's mouth from dinner. She smiled at me and set him down on the floor. "There's Mommy!"

"Hi!" Robbie shrieked, running into my outstretched arms.

I hugged him close and reminded myself to enjoy these moments. I knew from raising Liz that the time would come all too soon when he wouldn't feel this way.

"How's Robbie?" I asked, picking him up and bouncing him on my hip. "Did you have a fun day?"

Elena smiled. "Troy and I gave him another swim lesson. For a few moments, he swam underwater all by himself."

"You did?" I said to Robbie. "You're a little fish!"

"Fish," he said proudly. He squirmed to get down when Liz came into the room. "Izzie, fish." He tapped a finger on his chest and smiled up at her.

She ruffled his hair. "That's good, Robbie! Izzie is proud of you." She knelt to his level and gave him a hug.

Watching them, I thought of Robert. He would, I hoped, be pleased by all we were doing to make Robbie happy and his future secure. Elena took Robbie to play out on the back lawn. Liz followed me into my bedroom and sat while I changed my clothes.

"Chad was here again today. He asked me to go with him to Harvey's tonight. I told him I'd let him know. He's very nice, and I really like him, but what point is there in dating him? I'm leaving to go back to school in a few days."

I shrugged in a noncommittal way. I knew there was more to the story. "You've got a lot on your plate right now."

"On the other hand, I'll be back here in two months. That doesn't seem like a long time," said Liz. "And he seems like such a great guy. We clicked right away."

I pulled a T-shirt over my shoulders and turned to her. "And?"

"And I want to have a date for your wedding."

"Ahhh, so that's it. Well, like you said, Chad seems like a nice guy. He came highly recommended for his IT work. Maybe you should take him up on the date. Just don't lead him on if you're really not interested in him."

Liz got up and gave me a hug. "Thanks, Mom. That's what I needed to hear. I'll go call him now." Her eyes twinkled. "Because I'm really interested in him."

I smiled as she all but bounced out of the room in her haste.

CHAPTER SIXTEEN

When Rhonda walked into the office Friday afternoon, she glowed with health and happiness.

"You look wonderful," I gushed, pleased to see her like this. Her hair had been recolored, styled, and cut, and her nails shaped and painted.

"After our talk and getting some pampering like you suggested, I've been feeling more like myself." Color rose in her face. "And things with Will are...well, wonderful. Like old times. He says I'm the most beautiful mother he's ever seen. Nice, huh?"

"Nice," I said, giving her a quick hug. "You ready to get back to work?"

"The doctor is suggesting I wait another week or so. She thinks I should enjoy my time at home. She doesn't understand how left out I feel while you and Bernie are working together handling things here." She grinned. "Besides, I wanted to see Annette for myself. She and Bernie..."

I raised my hand. "Hold it! No matchmaking. Understand?"

"Aw, Annie, you're no fun!" Rhonda complained. "It's time for another romance around here."

I shook my head. No one told Rhonda "*no*".

"Is Annette here?" Rhonda asked.

"She arrived about an hour ago. I haven't met her yet." I checked my watch. "We're having a meeting with her in about fifteen minutes. Join us?"

"I wouldn't miss it for the world," said Rhonda with a smug smile that sent a warning through me.

I showed Rhonda the latest printouts I'd produced on reservations, and then we went over bookings for private parties and weddings. Locals were using us more and more for special occasions as well as for regular meals at lunch and dinner. It was important business for us, adding a steady influx of cash that helped stabilize us during slower times.

"How about your wedding, Annie? Have you settled on any plans?"

"I haven't had time to do more than decide I want a very small, private wedding on the beach. I was thinking of a sunset wedding."

Rhonda frowned. "You don't want something bigger, something fancier?"

I shook my head firmly. "You know how I feel about all the publicity that comes with Vaughn. This is one time I want for ourselves, without the whole world watching us."

"Okay, then. How about a fabulous, long honeymoon?" Rhonda smiled. "The honeymoon Will and I had in Tahiti was simply marvelous."

"You have forgotten I have Robbie now. I could never leave him for any length of time. Not until I'm sure he's really secure with us. It appears as if he is, but it's been almost too easy. I want to meet with Barbara Holmes to see what I need to do to help him. Then maybe, Vaughn and I could take a short honeymoon."

"You've got Elena ..." Rhonda began.

"I need her help, but I don't want to be the kind of mother who never spends time with her child. I gather that's pretty much how Kandie operated. As long as Vaughn and I agreed to make him ours, I want him to think of me as his mother, not someone making an appearance every now and then."

"Good for you, Annie. I understand." Rhonda rose. "Now, let's go meet Annette."

As we walked toward Bernie's office, we saw him talking to a tall blonde and a distinguished-looking gentleman.

"Is that her?" Rhonda said in a stage whisper. "And who is that man with her?"

I pulled Rhonda to a stop. "Remember, we're not playing matchmaker here."

"Okay, okay. It's just that maybe Bernie needs a little help ..." She stopped talking as we approached them.

"Here are the owners now," I heard Bernie say as Trudy ran over to greet us.

Smiling, I stopped to pat the dog on her head and then walked over to our guests, studying them. Conservatively dressed in a navy linen suit, Annette was statuesque. Simple, gold earrings sparkled at her ears. A pleasant smile added to her lovely features. In tan slacks and a navy blazer, the gray-haired man standing beside her matched Annette's height and looked as regal as she.

I offered my hand. "Hello. Welcome. I'm Ann Rutherford."

"And I'm Rhonda DelMonte Grayson," said Rhonda, extending her hand.

As we were exchanging handshakes, Bernie said, "This is Annette Bauer and her ... friend ... Maxwell Hoffman."

"I'm so pleased to meet you both," I said. "We're planning a very special wedding for Babette."

Annette's blue eyes sparkled. "I can't tell you how thrilled we are to be able to do this. Max is here to help me with things."

"Joseph Hassel is an old school buddy of mine. I promised him I'd oversee his piece of the arrangements."

Annette beamed at him. "He's been wonderful. Simply wonderful."

Beside me, I could feel Rhonda's body stiffen. "So, have you been together long?" she asked.

Annette's cheeks turned a pretty pink. "Oh, no ... I mean ..."

"I met Annette through my wife," Max said. "They've become good friends."

"Oh, that's wonderful!" Rhonda said with so much enthusiasm we all looked at her. She smiled. "I'm sure Bernie will take very good care of you. He's excellent at his job. Right, Annie?"

"Oh, yes," I said, as Rhonda cast matchmaker smiles from Annette to Bernie.

Bernie's eyes widened. He cleared his throat. "I've just explained that Sabine will be handling the details of the wedding and, if desired, Lorraine Grace at Wedding Perfection will be called in to assist."

Rhonda bobbed her head. "Of course, of course. But you're the general manager here, and that's really important."

"Yes, we're all here to help with the wedding," I said, wishing I could glue Rhonda's mouth shut. "And I'll be working with you, Annette, on the promo shots you've agreed to make for us."

"I understand that her cooperation means a reduction in your normal fees," said Max, stiffly.

"That was the agreement," Bernie said, quickly appeasing him.

"Good, because the Hassels will be paying for the wedding, both as a gift to the bride and her family and as an apology to you for their late cancellation. They are well aware many hotels would have insisted on complete payment and are grateful for your understanding."

"My daughter ..." Rhonda began.

"Your daughter is waiting for you at home," I said, anxious

to get Rhonda away from them.

"Oh, yes," said Rhonda. "I can't stay long, but I wanted to meet you. And Annette, you're going to be the perfect mother of the bride for our publicity. Maybe Bernie could be the father of the bride in the pictures. You'd make a great couple."

"The ad agency will work out the details of how the photos should be done," I said. "But Rhonda's right, Annette. You'll be lovely."

We said our good-byes and then I took Rhonda's elbow and led her away before she said another thing.

"Annie, I think it's gonna work," said Rhonda when we were out of earshot. "Did you see the way Annette and Bernie were looking at each other?"

"Yes, but I thought Bernie was going to have a heart attack when you mentioned being a great couple," I said.

We looked at each other, and suddenly laughter bubbled out of us, echoing around us with happy sounds.

When we caught our breaths, Rhonda said, "Annie, I know I'm right. Just wait and see."

I shook my head. Poor Bernie. Poor Annette. Rhonda wasn't through with them yet.

Mid-afternoon, I left to go home for a small break before returning for the dinner hour. A group of state senators had met all day at the hotel for special hush-hush meetings that were ending with a private dinner. My role with these groups was to act as hostess—overseeing service, handling any business request that arose. Service, privacy, and discretion had made The Beach House Hotel a favorite place for small important groups like this.

At home, I found Liz and Chad sitting around the pool with Troy and Elena. At Troy's feet and under his supervision,

Robbie splashed in the water.

"Ahhh, this is what goes on while I'm working at the hotel," I teased.

"Mommy! Look!" Robbie held onto the side of the pool and bobbed his face in the water. He lifted his face and, smiling, gazed up at me for approval.

"Robbie! That's wonderful! I'm so proud of you!" I knelt beside him and gave him a watery hug.

Troy smiled. "He's doing really well, Ann. I think being able to work with him every day is making a big difference. But don't worry. I'm about to return to the hotel. I've got three more appointments at the spa today."

"Sounds busy. Good. We need the business."

I chatted for a while longer and then went into my bedroom to rest for a few minutes before changing my clothes for the evening affair. After I slipped on a robe, I lowered myself into a chair, intent on calling Vaughn.

"Look!" cried Robbie, bursting into the room with a book.

"Oh, good! Let's read!" I drew him up onto my lap and opened the book.

Each page showing a farm animal had something for Robbie to touch and feel.

As I sat talking to Robbie about each animal and the sounds they make, I thought of the many times I'd done the same thing with Liz. Robbie seemed as bright as she. I tightened my arm around him. It felt good to be doing this. A lot of my friends might wonder at my willingness to start a family over again, but I realized now how much I'd missed by having only one child.

Liz came into the room and smiled at Robbie. "What are you and ... Mom ... Mommy doing?"

"Meow," said Robbie.

"We're learning about farm animals, aren't we, Robbie?"

He smiled. "Moo."

Liz and I exchanged pleased glances. "He's changed so much since he's been here. It has a lot to do with you, Mom."

"You think so? I can't spend as much time with him as I'd like and keep on top of the hotel operation too."

"Elena is good with him. That's got to make you feel better."

"Yes, but it's not the same. I can't believe all of this is happening with me at the same time Rhonda's given birth."

"And now Angela will have a baby. Her house is perfect for her and Reggie and their family." Liz gazed down at the floor. When she looked up, there was a wistfulness to her expression. "Everyone's lives seem so settled compared to mine."

"You have plans to finish your schooling and that won't be done for another year. Sounds pretty settled to me."

"I know. Working in DC, I learned that, without a degree, you can't get anywhere. But I don't want to end up all alone. Some of my friends would be furious with me for talking this way, but I want what you and Vaughn have, what Angela and Reggie have. You know?"

"I understand. I want that for you too, but not before you finish school. Vaughn told me you promised him you would."

"I figured I owed him that for paying for my last year." She fiddled with her hands. "I guess I'm still wishing Troy and Elena weren't together. He's so nice."

"What about Chad? He seems nice."

"Oh, he is. But he doesn't have time to do a lot of dating. He's busy setting up his own business. I guess that's why he hasn't asked me out again."

"I wouldn't be in too much of a rush. It's better to be alone than to be with someone you're not head-over-heels in love with." I gave her hands a squeeze. "And like you said, he's not your typical young man. He's building a business. Besides, you'll be going back to school in a couple of days. Why don't you take the rest of your time here to relax before facing the end of the school year and all that comes with it? You've been through a lot of emotional upheavals. It will be good for you to just chill."

"Yeah, I guess you're right. Thanks for listening." As she left the room, I thought of the recent turmoil in her life. Liz was much stronger than she knew.

I hurried into the hotel, mindful of being a little late. But Robbie had wanted to cuddle, and I couldn't refuse him.

Sabine met me at the door to the private dining room. "We're all set here. Jean-Luc needs fifteen minutes' notice to serve, but he's getting impatient."

"Okay. The cocktail party for them went all right?"

"No problems."

I clapped a hand on her back. "Thank you, Sabine. I don't know what we'd do without either you or Jean-Luc. Have you seen Bernie?"

A smile swept across her face. "He and Annette Bauer are having dinner together. He said it was to discuss the upcoming wedding, but if I'm not mistaken, I saw a definite spark between them."

"Rhonda is going to be thrilled," I said, turning to a group of men headed our way. "Good evening, gentlemen. We're ready for your dinner."

Sabine and I ushered them into the private dining room and waited while they got settled in their seats.

"Welcome to The Beach House Hotel," I said. "It's always a pleasure to have your group visit us. For dinner tonight, you've selected strip steaks with a mushroom, bordelaise sauce, carrot soufflé, garlic-roasted potatoes, a tossed green salad and apple pie."

"Perfect," said one of Florida's more robust state senators. "And plenty of wine. Right?"

I nodded. "As requested, we have a nice cabernet to accompany the meal. Enjoy, gentlemen. I'm here to offer my assistance. As always, conversations among you will be regarded as confidential."

"Good," said one of the men. "Because we've got a lot of messages for the governor and not all of them are nice."

Amid the laughter that followed, I asked the wine steward to pour their wine.

Timing was critical. Jean-Luc was a chef who insisted his food be served hot. While wine was being poured, the waitstaff served an *amuse bouche,* which was a tiny, one-bite pastry shell filled with lemon crème topped with a tiny sautéed bay scallop.

A few minutes later, the waitstaff carried in the main course. The salad course would follow.

I was pleased to see how eagerly the men attacked their meal. Rhonda and I had taken a chance when we'd approached Jean-Luc to work for us on a part-time basis. It was a stroke of luck that someone of his caliber had agreed to do it and was now our full-time chef.

I was about to leave the room when I heard a cry and turned back to see one of the men struggling to breathe.

"He's choking!" said one of my staff.

I ran over to him, stood behind him, and placed my arms around him with my fists in his solar plexus. With a surge of adrenaline, I squeezed three times with all my might.

"It's come out," said one of the men standing by. "You saved him!"

Only when I stood back, breathing heavily, did I realize

how big the man was, how nearly impossible it had been to get my arms all the way around him.

"Thank you," cried the senator I'd saved. "I don't know how you did it, but I'm so thankful you did."

"She may not be very big, but the lady has strength," said another of the men, clapping me on the back.

Smiling, I accepted their praise, unwilling to mention that my body had turned so weak I felt like I couldn't move.

"Are you sure you're okay? Shall I call 911, just to be safe?" I asked the senator.

"No, I don't need any more help. But thank you."

Before he left, I'd have him sign a release. We'd had training for ourselves and our staff in the Heimlich maneuver, hoping we'd never have to use it. Now, I was really glad we knew how to do it.

Sensing how weak I suddenly felt, Sabine moved to my side. "Please, enjoy the rest of the meal," she said in her French accent to the crowd around us.

As the group retook their seats, the shuffling noise of their chairs was satisfying. Once I was certain everything was under control, I headed to the kitchen. Everyone was hopping to Jean-Luc's orders. I walked through the kitchen to the main dining room. Hotel guests and other local guests filled most of the room.

Sabine soon joined me. "Maria has the waitstaff under control in the small dining room. I thought I'd better check on you and things here."

"Thanks." I headed over to where Bernie and Annette were sitting.

When he saw me, Bernie jumped to his feet. "Annette and I were discussing the wedding," he said quickly.

I smiled. "Great. And, Bernie, I think Rhonda's right. You should take part in the photo shoots for our promo piece on weddings. You photograph well and can make sure things are done properly."

Bernie nodded, maintaining a serious expression, but I noticed the corners of his lips twitching in an effort to keep from smiling.

The kitchen staff was closing down for the night, and Julie, Tim's assistant, was overseeing service to the few remaining guests in the lobby area when I left for home.

CHAPTER SEVENTEEN

All was quiet when I entered the house. I tiptoed through the living room into the wing of the house where Robbie and the girls were located. Liz's room was dark. A light seeped under the door of Elena's room. I opened the door to Robbie's room. In the dim light from the decorative nightlight on his bureau, I saw him sprawled on his stomach, sound asleep. I couldn't resist patting him on his back as I studied his face and the way his long eyelashes floated like butterfly wings against his cheeks.

I quietly made my way out of the room, and sighing with exhaustion, headed toward my bedroom in the other wing of the house. As I approached it, I chided myself for leaving a light on and then distinctly remembered I'd turned it off before leaving the house.

Heart pounding, I crept closer to the door. It was cracked open, and now, I could see movement behind it. Debating whether I should call the police, I paused.

"Aren't you going to come inside?" asked a voice I knew so well.

"Vaughn?" I rushed forward into his waiting arms. "What are you doing here? I was going to call you earlier, but got sidetracked."

"I'm home for a quick visit. I had a break in scheduling and decided to take advantage of it to surprise you."

I snuggled against his hard chest. "I'm so glad you did! We've all missed you."

He chuckled. "It hasn't been that long."

"Every day without you seems long," I said, inhaling the spicy aftershave and manly smell that was his alone.

His lips came down on mine. All the weariness I'd felt earlier disappeared in a surge of lusty energy. When we pulled apart, he took my hand. "Come to bed."

My body pulsing happily, I followed him over to it, eager to welcome him home.

Later, lying in his arms, we shared our days.

"Reggie was on my flight. He met his parents in New York before coming down here to Sabal and Angela. He's arranged to complete his final course from here, checking in online, and writing a huge paper. He's a nice kid and very excited about their baby."

"Are his parents more supportive now?"

Vaughn shook his head. "I asked him, but he didn't want to talk about it."

"Hopefully they'll come around."

Our talk continued, discussing events with Liz and Robbie. After we'd covered most of the details, I fell into a blissful sleep.

The next morning hands patted my face, awakening me with a start. I stared into Robbie's eyes. Rising on an elbow I frowned at him. "How'd you get here?"

He laughed. "Hi, Mommy!"

I checked the bedside clock. Six AM.

"Up, Mommy. Want up."

I debated for a moment and then decided I was too tired to fight it. I lifted him up onto the bed. He crawled over to Vaughn and patted him on the chest.

"Daddy?"

Vaughn opened his eyes and stared at him with bleary eyes.

"What's up, sport?"

"Wake up."

Vaughn pulled Robbie up into his arms, rolled over onto his side, and said, "Any chance he'll go back to sleep?"

I watched Robbie twitch restlessly between us. "Not a chance."

Vaughn groaned. "Okay, I'll get up with him."

"I will too," I said. "I don't want to waste a minute without you. This afternoon, I have to check on the photo shoot with Bernie and Annette, but I think Bernie and the staff can handle the rest."

"Bernie and Annette?"

As I filled Vaughn in on the details, a smile spread across his face. "Does Bernie know what Rhonda is like when she has her mind made up about something?"

I grinned. "He's about to find out."

We got out of bed and quickly dressed. Elena wasn't due to come on duty until seven thirty. I'd arranged it that way so I'd have some alone time with Robbie at seven when he usually woke up.

I carried Robbie back to his room and changed his diaper, making a game of whispers so we wouldn't wake the girls.

When we entered the kitchen, Vaughn was scrambling eggs. He turned to me with a smile. "Coffee's ready. Thought you and Robbie might like some eggs."

I put Robbie in his highchair and turned back to Vaughn. "Thanks! It's nice to have a guy like you around the house."

He pulled me into his arms for a quick kiss. "It's always good to be home."

"The eggs!"

He laughed. "Oh yeah."

While he went back to his cooking, I placed cereal on Robbie's tray and filled a sippy cup with milk for him. Then I poured myself a much-needed cup of coffee.

Sitting at the table beside Robbie's highchair, I watched Vaughn serve up the eggs. He'd once told me how he'd had to learn to cook after his wife died and how it had become a hobby of his—a hobby we all could enjoy.

As we sat eating breakfast, I wondered if this was how it was going to be after we were married. In my mind, we already were married; the ceremony would just make it official for everyone else. I reached over and patted his hand. "Love you."

"Love you too." He smiled. "So any more news on the wedding? It's still on for June seventh?"

I nodded. "Everything is reserved at the hotel. Sabine is handling all the details."

"Good. I want to make an honest woman of you." The megawatt smile he turned on me lit my insides with excitement. He was the sexiest man, and against all odds, he was mine.

After he finished his breakfast, Vaughn rose. "Guess I'll check the boat."

"Want to take Robbie with you? That'll give me time to take a shower."

"Sure."

"Put a life jacket on him," I said and hurried out of the room.

When I emerged from my bedroom, showered, and dressed for the day, the girls were up.

"Where's Robbie?" I asked.

"He's playing on the screened porch," said Liz. "Vaughn dropped him off inside and went to do a couple of errands. Something for the boat."

"One of you needs to be with Robbie," I said. "I don't trust him. He is now climbing out of his crib."

"Oh, Mom," sighed Liz. "He's fine." She rose and followed

me out to the porch. My eyes widened when I realized the door to the pool was open. "Oh my God! Where is he?"

I ran out the door and looked into the pool. He was bobbing up and down in the water, his feet kicking frantically as he circled in the middle of the pool. The look of panic on his face was frightening.

"Robbie, I'm coming!" I cried, jumping into the pool with my clothes on. I swam to the middle of the pool and took him in my arms, trying not to show my panic. "There, little swimmer. You're all right. You just need a little help."

As he started to cry, I walked back to the shallow end of the pool with him. Sitting down on the steps into the pool, I rocked him in my arms. "You're not to go near the pool without an adult. Hear me, Robbie?"

"Y-y-yes," he hiccupped.

Fighting back tears, I hugged him close to me, realizing how much I already loved this little boy. I'd be devastated to lose him.

"Mom! Mom! Is he all right?" As she joined us on the steps, Liz's eyes seemed extra wide in a face gone pale.

"He's fine. He's a very good swimmer." I smiled with encouragement at Robbie. Though I wanted to yank him out of the water and keep him safe with me forever, I fought for calm so he wouldn't be afraid of the water.

Elena stood by, wringing her hands. "I'm so, so sorry. I should have been with him."

I took Robbie's hand and led him out of the pool. Apparently unaware of the seriousness of the situation, he ran over to get his plastic turtle.

I turned to the girls. "Let this be a lesson to all of us. Doors need to be locked at all times. And he needs to be supervised. We're going to have to adjust his crib and install a few more locks on doors so he can't get out to the pool and the dock.

And we need to reinforce the idea that he needs an adult with him before he can go into the pool."

As Liz and Elena bobbed their heads, I noticed tears in each girl's eyes.

Trembling from the realization of what might have happened, I went into my bedroom to change.

When Vaughn came home from doing his errands, I told him what had happened. We worked together to adjust Robbie's crib and to install higher locks on some of the doors.

"I've forgotten what life with a toddler is like," Vaughn admitted. "I thought he was fine playing on the porch."

Later, when it was time for Robbie to go down for a nap, I rocked him a little longer than usual, loving the feel of his active, healthy body in my arms.

Rhonda called as Vaughn and I were having a late lunch. "Are you going to watch the photo shoot?"

"Yes. Do you want to join me?" I asked, knowing the answer.

"You betcha. I wouldn't miss seeing this budding romance blossom into true love. I saw how Bernie and Annette looked at each other."

I laughed. "I'll meet you at the hotel."

Annette was a stunning mother of the bride, I thought, surprised by her ease in front of the camera as she posed in a variety of places around the hotel. Bernie was less comfortable in front of the camera, but the shots of the two of them together told a story of their own.

"I knew it," whispered Rhonda as we watched them kiss in the background as a model dressed as a bride pretended to cut into one of our sous chef's wedding cake masterpieces.

"Nice touch," said the photographer. "Now let's have the

bride and groom stand between the two of you. Then, we'll move to the dining room for shots of Dad dancing with the bride and then dancing with Mom."

"The two of you together look wonderful," gushed Rhonda, clapping her hands.

Bernie stiffened at the smile Rhonda bestowed him and then relaxed when Annette took his hand to lead him into the dining room.

As I watched them go, I noticed how the touch of her hand, the shy smile on Annette's face, softened Bernie's normally rigid manner.

Rhonda gave me a smile and flung an arm around my shoulder. "Told ya."

I pushed her playfully. "Let's see how it goes. It's just a photo shoot."

Tim hurried over to us. "I just got a call from the governor's office. He wants to schedule a surprise here for his wife next weekend. I looked at the reservations. We're booked."

I turned to Rhonda. "Let's put him in the Presidential Suite with a special rate."

"Sounds good to me. We're not getting enough use out of it. Was it cleaned after the fiasco with that rock star?"

"It's ready to go."

"Okay," said Tim. "I'll put him there at the lower rate."

"And Tim? Please find out what the occasion is so we can make it special," I said. The governor of Georgia's stay last winter had brought us new business. Maybe this would too.

After he left, Rhonda said, "Why don't you go home to Vaughn? I'll stay here for a while. Rita said she'd call me if I need to come home."

"Okay, great."

Feeling like a child let out of school, I all but skipped down the front steps of the hotel.

#

Lounging beside me by the pool, Vaughn snored softly. The sound of him, the sight of him next to me, brought such unexpected joy. I loved that he used a break in the filming of his show to surprise me every chance he got. Toward the end of my rocky marriage to Robert, we'd avoided each other as much as we could. I vowed to see that didn't happen to Vaughn and me.

Vaughn opened his eyes and smiled. "Penny for your thoughts."

I grinned. "With inflation and all, you'll not get much. I ..."

Vaughn grabbed my hand. "Playing games are we?"

I laughed.

"Where is everyone else?" he asked, sitting up.

"The girls took Robbie to see Angela's house."

"Ahhh. We're alone?"

"For the moment."

He stood. "How about a swim in the pool?" A pool had always been a place for us to romp.

Smiling, I got to my feet and adjusted my raspberry-colored bikini. It had replaced the lime-green one Rhonda had insisted I buy when I'd first met her.

Vaughn dove into the water and turned to me with a devilish grin.

"Don't you dare splash me, Vaughn Sanders!" I normally had to go in slowly, step by step. Only for an emergency would I jump in.

I was halfway immersed in the water when Vaughn swam up to me and tugged on my foot.

Laughing, I slid into the water, and then I took off, swimming as fast as I could. Vaughn stayed right behind me. When I reached the end of the pool and turned around,

Vaughn was waiting to draw me into his arms. I glanced around to make sure we were free of paparazzi.

"We're safe," said Vaughn. "They expect us to be on hotel property at your house."

"Good. I don't want them to know about Robbie. Who knows what stories they'd come up with. We have to be sure nothing goes wrong with his adoption."

"Don't worry. It's going to be all right."

More relaxed now, I snuggled up next to Vaughn. He encircled me with his legs and arms. I felt his reaction to my closeness and loved that he was exceptionally virile for a man in his mid-forties.

"Let's go inside," he murmured with a throaty tone that promised of many things.

I hesitated. "I don't know when the girls and Robbie will be back."

Vaughn gave me one of his lazy, sexy grins. "Then we'd better hurry."

We exchanged conspiring looks and raced for the steps at the far end of the pool.

Later, I lay in bed next to Vaughn, pleasantly surprised how satisfying a "quickie" could be. Sated, I checked the bedside clock and rose. "I'll beat you to the shower."

"Go ahead. I'll join you in a minute. I need to get the message from the call I ignored earlier."

I was drying off when Vaughn came into the bathroom. "The call was from Sam Nichols, the show's director. He invited me to go on a fishing trip in Alaska in mid-May. Apparently fishing for king salmon is good at that time of year. I accepted. That doesn't mess up anything with our wedding does it?"

"It better not," I teased. It was going to be such a small affair that nothing much was being planned ahead of time.

"I won't let anything stand in the way of our being married. I promise." Vaughn patted my bare behind.

"Okay, that's a deal." I gave him a kiss that proved how serious we both were.

CHAPTER EIGHTEEN

All too soon it came time for Vaughn to leave. As I saw him off at the airport, I couldn't help feeling blue. I didn't know if he'd have time for another short trip home before his fishing expedition in Alaska, and though it was only two months away, our wedding suddenly seemed a long way off.

Two days later, Liz left for Boston in her SUV for the final months of the school year with a promise to call me from the road at regular intervals. With both Vaughn and Liz gone, I was glad for Robbie and Elena's company in what now seemed a too-big house.

Elena and I worked out a schedule so that, in exchange for covering for me when I was detained by unpredictably long days at the hotel, she was given evenings and days off as often as my schedule allowed. I was trying to arrange more-regular hours at the hotel, but the nature of the business made it difficult. When Rhonda and I had hired Bernie as general manager, neither one of us had envisioned our family situations coinciding quite the way or as quickly as they had.

The weekend approached quickly as we prepared for the governor's visit. Daniel and Carlotta Horne were popular figures in the state, and we wanted to give them VIP service with the hope that he'd spread the news throughout the South.

It was becoming more and more difficult to coordinate events with Rhonda, but the two of us stood on the front steps of the hotel to welcome their arrival late Friday afternoon.

Carlotta was the first to emerge from their private car—a large black sedan. Standing next to it, her diminutive height made her appear fragile, but every voter in the state knew of her strength, her determination to protect her husband from naysayers. Pretty, she smiled at us as she waited for her husband to unfold himself from the backseat and come around the car to join her. Two security people stood on either side, automatically surveying the area. We'd managed to eke out accommodations for them in a converted storage room that we'd set aside for such purposes.

Daniel Horne was every PR person's dream—tall and good-looking, he had a natural friendliness that drew people to him. Even those who didn't share his political views admitted they liked the man.

As Rhonda and I approached him, his smile was heartwarming. "So glad to finally see this place for myself. I've heard nothing but good reports about The Beach House Hotel and the two of you."

Rhonda and I recited our standard, "Welcome to The Beach House Hotel," grinning at the sound of our voices matching syllable by syllable.

He smiled. "Guess you've said this a few times, huh?"

"A few," I answered, and held my hand out. "I'm Ann Rutherford."

"And I'm Rhonda DelMonte Grayson," said Rhonda, shaking hands with Carlotta and turning to him. "We're sure glad to have you here."

"Are our rooms ready?" the governor asked me.

"Yes," I said, smiling at him. I knew he was asking if we'd taken care of his special requests. "We've made sure everything is in order, as always."

"Thanks," he said. "I really appreciate it."

Bernie approached, Trudy at his heels.

"Bernhard Bruner is our general manager," I said. "He will ensure your stay is every bit as wonderful as you wish."

Bernie shook hands and exchanged greetings with Daniel and Carlotta.

"And who is this adorable dog?" Carlotta said, bending over to pat Trudy's head. She laughed when Trudy looked up at her and wagged her tail. She smiled at Bernie. "I've always wanted a dog like this. What's her name?"

"Gertrude von Bruner," said Bernie. "But I call her Trudy."

"Perfect," Carlotta said, laughing when Trudy rolled onto her back for a tummy rub.

"Please come in," said Rhonda. "We've arranged a short tour. Then some refreshments will be delivered to your suite."

"Ahhh. Thank you," said Daniel. He took hold of Carlotta's elbow, and they followed Bernie inside. Rhonda and I stayed outside to talk to one of the security men to explain our privacy policy and to make sure they'd be as unobtrusive as possible.

Paul and Manny handled the suitcases, and one of the men traveling with the governor parked the car in the garage.

Rhonda and I hurried inside and up to the Presidential Suite, arriving moments before the governor and his wife were led there by Bernie.

I checked the floral arrangement we'd placed earlier on the center table in the small foyer. The small box wrapped in light blue paper and adorned with silver ribbon sat beside it, as the governor had requested.

They entered the suite. "Again, welcome to The Beach House Hotel. We're honored to have you here," I said.

"Yes," agreed Rhonda.

I moved toward the door. "We'll leave you now. Enjoy your stay."

"We will," said Carlotta, glancing with surprise at the flowers and the present sitting on the table.

As we noticed the loving looks exchanged between the two

of them, Rhonda, Bernie, and I quickly left.

"Wow," said Rhonda as we descended the stairway. "Looks like the governor is in for a great weekend."

I laughed, and even Bernie grinned.

"So, Bernie," Rhonda continued in her not-so-subtle way when we reached the bottom of the stairs and stood in the back hallway, "when is Annette coming back to the hotel?"

"She's going to arrive a few days ahead of the wedding to relax a bit before the festivities. I've put her in the bridal suite for that stay."

"Good idea," I said. "You're coordinating all the details of the wedding with Sabine?"

"Yes. It's going to be beautiful. Annette and her daughter are thrilled. Max Hoffman will act as father of the bride and will return the day before the wedding, along with a few of the other wedding guests. Some will stay here. Others, especially the younger people, are staying at a motel in town. A matter of cost."

"Perfect. We can't afford to give our rooms away."

"Yeah, we're giving them a lot for almost nothing, all for the sake of the new brochure," said Rhonda. "That's why it's so important for you, Bernie, to make sure Annette is happy with everything."

I reminded myself not to roll my eyes at Rhonda's continued efforts at matchmaking.

"Yes, of course," said Bernie.

Our conversation was interrupted by Tim.

"Bernie, I need to talk to you. There's a problem with the room for the governor's security people."

Rhonda started to follow Tim and Bernie. I held her back. "That's why we hired him. Remember?"

She grinned. "Oh, yeah. We've got to learn to let go of the smaller stuff. Right?"

I nodded. The hotel was our baby, but we now had new, real babies of our own—babies that needed our attention. My thoughts turned to Angela. "How are Angela and Reggie doing?"

"Good," said Rhonda. "Reggie is holding off on going back to school until the baby comes. He's able to do a lot of his school work from home. He'll have to go back for a couple of weeks toward the end."

"I'm so happy for you that they're going to be living here in town," I said, giving her a big smile. "I have no idea where Liz will end up after school."

"Reggie's parents sure aren't happy about the kids moving to Florida. I can't imagine how things are going to work out between them and Reggie, but he seems determined to go ahead with the idea of working with Will." She shot me a worried look. "Angela tried talking to Katherine about visiting them after the baby is born, but Katherine told her they'd probably be traveling. Angela doesn't want Reggie to know how hurt she is by Katherine, but she tells me."

I gave Rhonda a steady look. "Give all of them a chance to settle their emotions. It's been a very trying few months. Reggie loves Angela. He'll protect her. You can't."

Rhonda's face tightened with worry. "That's just it. I want to."

"What does Will say?"

"He told me to back off, to let Reggie handle it. But it isn't easy, especially now with Angela's baby due any day. I hope it's easy for her. Not like me having a baby on your kitchen floor."

"Willow is a very determined child," I said, unable to keep from smiling at the memory of the surprise she gave all of us.

"Tell me!" said Rhonda. She checked her watch. "Guess I'd better get back to her. See you later. I'll be back for the governor's surprise birthday party for his wife."

She left, and I went into the office to check the reservations schedule. Annette could share the bridal suite with her daughter until the day of the wedding, then other arrangements would have to be made.

I'd just finished moving a few guests around for that weekend when Jean-Luc knocked on the door and entered. He stood stiffly in front of me, obviously working to remain calm.

"Hi! What can I do for you?"

"You can tell Bernie that I'm in charge of the kitchen," he grumbled. "I will decide how I want the menu to read for the Bauer wedding."

"Is there a problem?"

"*Oui*. He wants to tell me how I should do things. Always. I won't take orders from anyone but you and Rhonda."

"Okay. I'll settle any misunderstanding. Thank you."

"*Merci*." He turned to go.

"Jean-Luc?"

He faced me.

"We really appreciate all you do. *Merci*."

At his smile, I relaxed. He was a valued member of our team and I would do anything to keep from losing him. Even if it upset Bernie.

Later, after talking to Bernie, I left the hotel to have a couple of hours with Robbie before returning to the hotel for the governor's dinner.

As I walked into my house, I could hear Robbie crying. I hurried through the kitchen and onto the porch to see what was happening.

Robbie was lying on the floor, kicking and screaming.

"What's going on?" I asked Elena.

She grimaced. "He wants to go into the pool. I told him no. It's almost time for his nap."

Robbie noticed me and let out a louder wail.

I knelt beside him. "Hi, Robbie."

He looked up at me. "Candy?"

I shook my head. "No, honey. No candy."

Robbie let out a high-pitched scream and kicked his feet, pounding the carpet in sturdy, steady beats.

I rose to my feet. "Guess we'd better let him work it out," I said calmly.

"I think he's pretty used to having his temper tantrums end with a bribe of candy."

"Well, that's not how we're going to work it here. Let him cry. As long as he's not hurt and he doesn't hurt anything around him, we'll let him get it out of his system."

A few minutes later, Robbie stopped crying and sat up. Seeing Elena and me sitting on one of the couches, he studied us.

"Are you done?" I asked quietly.

He got to his feet.

"Come here, honey. I'll give you a little hug."

He ran over to me and climbed onto my lap. Wrapping my arms around him, I drew him close to me. He rested his head against my chest.

"When Elena says no, she means it," I said quietly. "And me, too."

Robbie's body stiffened, and then, as I rubbed his back, he relaxed. "I love you, Robbie," I murmured, thinking back to the time he'd fallen into the pool. I'd been terrified of losing him.

He lifted his head. "Mommy?" He patted my arm, and I waited to hear what he'd say.

"Mine."

I chuckled quietly and exchanged smiles with Elena. He was a two-year-old all right.

"Elena? Want some time to yourself? I think I'll take Robbie with me to visit Angela. It might be good for both of us to spend time together away from the house."

"I'd love to be able to see my sister at Rhonda's. What time do you want me back here?"

"How about five o'clock? I'll need time to get ready for the dinner at the hotel."

Elena got to her feet. "Great. See you then."

She left, and I continued to hold Robbie on my lap until he finally wiggled to get down. We'd added another link to our growing relationship, but I realized I needed to spend more time with him.

When Reggie answered the door, a frown marred his youthful brow. "Hi, Ann. I'm glad you called. I'm worried about Angela."

"What's wrong?" I asked.

He shook his head. "She's going crazy unpacking and cleaning. I told her to slow down, but she says she wants everything ready for the baby. I can't get her to stop. Maybe you can."

He opened the door wider and indicated for Robbie and me to come inside.

The interior had changed a lot since I'd last seen it. The purple wall color was gone, replaced by a soft, warm écru. A beige couch stretched across an expanse of the living room, flanked by two soft-cushioned chairs covered in a beige and green tweed that reflected colors in the large Oriental rug that lay on the tile floor.

"She's in the kitchen," said Reggie.

Holding onto Robbie's hand, I followed Reggie into the kitchen, where we found Angela unpacking a box filled with kitchenware. "Hi, Ann! Hi, Robbie! It's starting to look like a home." She held up a frying pan. "I keep telling Reggie we need to have everything settled, because I'm not sure how much longer this baby is going to wait. The baby's dropped."

I studied her shape and realized how close to delivering she must be. Several boxes lay by her feet, and several more were stacked by the bookcase in the family room. "Why don't you take a rest while I help you?"

"Would you? We have a bunch of books that need to be placed on the bookshelf."

I held up an empty box. "Sure. Let's try it. Robbie can play with the box while I unpack the books."

"Thanks, Ann," said Reggie. "Now you sit down for a while, Ange, and take a break."

I set to work removing books from boxes and placing them on the bookshelf. Robbie crawled in and out of the box like a playful puppy. I'd just put the last of the books away when Robbie started fussing. I turned to pick him up and noticed the wide-eyed expression on Angela's face.

I shot to my feet. "What's wrong?"

"I think I had my first contraction," she said. "Reggie?"

He hurried to her side. "What? Is it the baby?"

"I think I'd better sit down."

I lifted Robbie into my arms. "Do you need me to do anything for you?" I asked Angela, unsure whether to stay or go.

"No, thanks. Reggie and I want to do this alone. Right, Reg?"

"I've got everything under control," said Reggie, looking a little green as he ushered Angela to a kitchen chair.

"Okay, call me if you need me. I'll leave the two of you to take care of things."

###

At home, I turned Robbie over to Elena, before heading back to the hotel. As soon as I walked into the lobby of the hotel, Rhonda rushed over to me and clasped my arm. Her eyes danced with excitement. "Angela called me. She's having her baby! Can you believe it? I'm about to become a grandmother." She paused. "A very young grandmother."

"It's so exciting. How far along is she? Is she at the hospital?"

Rhonda shook her head. "Not yet. Her contractions are still ten minutes apart, so she'll wait until they're closer. Ange says they come and go." Rhonda gave me a worried look. "Oh, Annie, I hope it doesn't drag on and on. I don't want her hurting. Besides, the suspense is killing me. They still don't know the sex of the baby."

I gave her a quick hug. "I'm sure she'll be fine. And Reggie will be right there to support her."

Rhonda smiled. "Angela told me Reggie's trying to do the breathing exercises along with her, but he keeps getting faint. She promised to call when she goes to the hospital."

Rhonda stood by the front entrance to greet the governor's guests as I hurried to the office. I'd just set down my things when my cell phone rang. I glanced at caller ID and picked it up.

"Hi, Angela! What's up?"

"Is my mother there? I can't reach her on her cell. I'm getting worried. I think I'm going to have the baby, then everything stops. They told us in the birthing class not to go to the hospital until the contractions were steady."

"Hold on, Angela. I'm going to get your mother." Continuing to reassure her, I rushed out of the office to find Rhonda.

She was talking to the mayor and his wife when I entered

the front hallway. Her eyes widened when I held up the phone and signaled her to join me.

I handed her my cell and went to speak to the mayor. "A family emergency. Let me show you where the group is assembling." I led them to the library where the governor's guests had gathered to surprise his wife.

As soon as I'd shown them into the room, I turned to find Rhonda.

She trotted over to me. "I'm sorry, Annie, but I've got to go. Angela is scared to death. I need to see her for myself. It sounds to me like she should go to the hospital and be checked out by the doctor."

"Go," I said, worried about Angela myself.

"I'll make it up to you. I promise," Rhonda called over her shoulder.

I spent the next half hour greeting guests as they arrived for the special event. Some guests, like the mayor, were local. A couple of others were staying in the hotel. Still others were staying at competitive properties. It was these guests that Rhonda and I wanted to impress. The Beach House Hotel was small, but every bit as able to provide them with an elegant setting, wonderful food, and excellent service.

At the exact scheduled time, the governor and his wife descended the stairway from the Presidential Suite into the lobby.

I smiled and stepped forward. "Good evening. It's my pleasure to offer you a drink in the library."

The governor turned to his wife. "That sounds like a lovely beginning to the evening. Shall we, Carlotta?"

Carlotta smiled at her husband. "Let's do it."

I led them to the library and stood by as the governor opened the door with a flourish.

Cries of *Happy Birthday!* rang in the air.

Carlotta's look of surprise gave way to a tearful smile.

Before stepping back, I checked to make sure Sabine and another staff member were set to handle the small crowd.

The governor placed a hand on my shoulder. "Good job. I think we got her on this one."

I smiled, taking a moment to glance at the diamond earrings I'd helped him select for his wife. It was typical of the specialized services we offered our guests.

CHAPTER NINETEEN

The evening passed in a blur of activity. I oversaw the dinner for the governor in the small, private dining room so that Sabine and Bernie could handle our regular dining service in the larger dining room. Several guests were celebrating wedding anniversary dinners, along with a small group honoring a mother and the second anniversary of her 39th birthday.

While I smiled and chatted and took care of things for the governor's group, I thought of Angela and Reggie. They'd fought hard to be together and to have this baby. I prayed everything was all right.

Later, after bidding farewell to the governor and his guests, I raced into the office to check my phone for messages. We'd made it a rule to keep cell phones out of the private dining room. I eagerly lifted my phone. There were two messages from Rhonda and one from Elena. Heart pounding at the thought of something wrong with Robbie, I punched in my home number and waited impatiently for Elena to pick up.

"Hi, Ann," Elena said into the phone. "Sorry to disturb you, but Robbie was crying for you. I got him calmed down, but he's really become attached to you. Maybe after losing his mother, he's worried about losing you too."

My heart clenched. "Is he okay now?"

"Yes. He's asleep and settled for the night, but I thought you ought to know about this. I'll probably be in bed when you come home. I think I might be coming down with a spring cold."

"Thanks." Concern made my mouth dry. "I'll check on him when I get home. Angela's baby is on its way, and I have to cover for Rhonda."

I clicked off the call with a sigh. My life sometimes seemed so demanding.

Rhonda answered on the first ring. "Annie, you've got to help me. I'm at the hospital with Angela and Reggie, but I can't stay. I have to go home to Willow. Will you come and sit here while I go feed Willow and then come back? I'm worried about Angela. I don't want to leave her alone."

"Sure. I'll get there as soon as I can." We ended the call, and I went to talk to Bernie. After he assured me everything was just fine at the hotel, I left for the hospital.

The small waiting room on the maternity floor was empty when I arrived. I walked down the corridor to the room assigned to Angela and peeked inside. Angela was lying on the bed. Reggie stood by one side of her, holding onto her hand while she grimaced in pain. A nurse stood next to the bed, coaching Angela.

Angela noticed me. "Did my mom leave?"

"Yes. She'll be back as soon as she feeds Willow."

"But I want her here!" said Angela between grunting breaths.

The nurse began to speak softly to Angela.

"If you need me, I'll be in the waiting room," I told Reggie. He gave me a weak smile. "Thanks."

I started to step away when Angela called to me. "Don't go! I want you to stay." Her smile was sweet. "You've been such a help to me from the beginning."

The nurse gave me a troubled look. "The doctor is on his way. When he comes, he'll want you to step outside."

My insides froze. "Is everything all right?"

The nurse's smile was practiced. She stepped away from Angela's bedside and spoke to me softly. "A C-section is a possibility. We'll see what he says."

As the doctor entered the room, the nurse hurried over to Angela.

I left quietly and returned to the waiting area. Too nervous to sit still, I paced the floor.

Reggie soon joined me, looking as if he was about to cry.

My heart pounded with dread. "What is it?"

"They can't get the baby to turn around, and now they're worried about the baby's heartbeat. They've taken Angela into the operating room for a C-section." He teetered on his feet.

I grabbed hold of his arm and led him to one of the couches. "Here. Have a seat. They'll let us know as soon as they can how things are going."

Reggie lowered himself onto the couch and held his head in his hands.

I patted his back. "It'll be all right. You'll see."

When he looked up at me, tears swam in his eyes. "I love Angela so much. If anything happens to her, I don't know what I'd do."

"She'll be fine. She's in good hands," I said, hiding my worry.

Rhonda burst into the waiting room, took one look at the two of us, and said, "Oh my God! What's wrong? The nurse told me you guys were in the waiting room. Is it Angela? The baby?"

She stumbled toward us, tears already streaming down her cheeks.

I stood and took hold of her. "Everything's going to be fine. She's having a C-section. We're waiting for news."

Reggie stood. Rhonda turned to give him a hug. "Oh,

honey. She'll be fine." She wrapped her arms around him in a bosomy hug. When I noticed his shoulders shaking, I left them to their privacy.

I was just returning from the coffee machine when Rhonda hurried down the hallway to me. "Ange is okay, and it's a boy! An eight-pounder! No wonder she needed some help." She clasped her hands in a prayerful pose. "I'm so relieved they're both okay."

Hugging her tightly, I said, "Me too."

She grabbed hold of my hand and tugged at me. "C'mon! Come see my grandson!"

We walked to the nursery window. Rhonda tapped on the glass. A nurse looked over at us and grinned before holding up a round-faced baby who I thought might resemble Reggie.

Reggie joined us at the window. "Angela is still in the recovery room, but she'll be out soon." He gazed through the window at the baby the nurse was showing us.

"Beautiful, isn't he?" he murmured, seemingly unaware that tears of joy were spilling onto his cheeks.

My heart filled at the sight. Angela had been right about him all along.

The next morning, before Robbie was awake, I called Bernie. "I'm not going to be able to make it in today. My nanny is sick and I need to spend time with Robbie. There are no special functions on the books. Will you be all right?"

"Yes. Annette is flying in this afternoon, but I'll take care of her. She decided to come in a couple of days early." I smiled at the ring of happiness in his voice.

"Okay. Call me if anything unexpected comes up. Thanks, Bernie. It means a lot to have you here."

I hung up and called Rhonda. "I'm not going into the hotel

today. Robbie needs me, and Elena is not feeling well."

"No problem. It's my day to be on call anyway. But, Annie, wait until you hear what Ange and Reggie are calling the baby! Evan William DelMonte-Smythe. Isn't it beautiful? The Evan is for Reggie's mother. Her maiden name was Evans. And William is for Will. You know how much Angie has come to love him. Adorable name, huh? If that doesn't win over Katherine Smythe, nothing will."

I laughed. It was as clever a way as any to try to smooth things over between Angela and her difficult mother-in-law. "Let's hope it works. Have the kids told Reggie's parents about the baby yet?"

"Yes," said Rhonda. "They're on their way down here as we speak. I just hope it doesn't turn out to be a bad thing."

"Me too." I looked up at the sight of Robbie padding toward me in wet diapers. "Here's Robbie. I'd better go. Congratulations to you and everyone else. I'll be in touch later."

I clicked off the call and lifted Robbie into my arms. "Hi, big boy. Ready to get your diaper changed?"

He patted my cheek. "Mommy."

"I'm here, Robbie. I'm here."

After changing Robbie's diaper, I sat with him in the kitchen while he ate his breakfast. As I sipped my coffee, I watched him attack his scrambled eggs with pleasure. Every few moments an expression crossed his face that reminded me of either Robert or Liz. *Strange how genetics plays such a big part in all of us,* I thought. I couldn't help wondering what a baby of Vaughn's and mine might have looked like. We'd never know, but we'd make the most of it with this little boy.

My cell phone rang. Liz.

"Hi, sweetie! How are you? I haven't heard from you in a while."

"Things are good. Very good, in fact. I've been talking to my counselor, and with all that's happened with Dad and Kandie, she's been able to find me more scholarship money for next year."

"Wonderful! As we've discussed so often, it's important for you to get your degree."

"Yeah, I really get it now, after realizing how it would be if I were ever left on my own to raise a family." She was silent for a moment. "How's Robbie?"

I watched him stare solemnly at me. "Why don't you ask him? I'll hold the phone up to his ear."

I lifted the phone to Robbie's ear. "Say hi to Izzie."

His face lit with pleasure. "Hi, Izzie! Hi! Hi! Hi!"

I took the phone back. "Did you get that?"

She sniffled. "I'm doing the right thing by allowing you to adopt him, aren't I?"

"Under the circumstances, yes. But, Liz, you'll always have a part to play in Robbie's life. You owe him that, don't you think?"

"Yeah. I want to be there for him no matter what happens."

"Good. Everyone, including your father, would be pleased with the decisions we all have made."

"I know Dad would be happy to have you involved. It's what he really wanted."

Robbie whined to get down.

"Hold on, Liz." I put Robbie down and then raced after him as he headed for the lanai. "Everything else okay?"

"Fine," Liz said. "By the way, Chad called me. Actually, we've been talking almost every night. It's amazing. I feel like I've known him forever."

"Oh?"

"He's coming to an electronic convention in Boston. We're going to meet up later this week."

"So this is serious?"

"Pretty much," Liz answered cryptically, not giving any more information.

"Okay, keep in touch. I'd better go. Your brother is heading for trouble."

Liz laughed. "Go get 'em, Mom!"

I clicked off the call and reached Robbie just as he was attempting to climb atop the table to get to a candle I'd forgotten to move safely out of the way.

I swiped him up into my arms and gave him a squeeze. "Okay, let's find something else to do. How about a swim in the pool?"

"Pool," he shouted happily.

Elena came out of her room as I was changing Robbie into his swimsuit. "How are you feeling?" I asked her.

"Pretty lousy," she admitted. "I think if I rest today, though, I'll be able to get back onto my schedule tomorrow."

"Don't worry. I've got him for today. I think we both needed this anyway. Just take care of yourself."

Little did I know how exhausted I'd be by the time Robbie was due for his afternoon nap. After I put him in his crib, I lay down in my bedroom. Thinking I'd just rest for a few minutes, I closed my eyes. An hour and a half later, I was startled awake by the sound of Robbie's cries through the baby monitor.

I sat up, trying to get my bearings. At his continued cries, I got to my feet and hurried to get him. When I entered the room, he was standing in his crib. His tear-streaked face lit up at the sight of me, and he held out his arms to me.

"Hi, Robbie," I crooned, lifting him into my arms and settling down in the rocking chair with him. As I hugged him to me, inhaling the little boy smell that was so typical of an active toddler, I realized I could never give him up. He'd become mine.

After I changed Robbie and gave him a snack, we headed to the hospital to see Angela and her baby, Evan.

In the hospital gift shop, we picked out a stuffed Teddy Bear for the baby, to go along with the baby monitor I'd wrapped and set aside a long time ago.

As we exited the elevator onto the maternity floor, I could hear Rhonda's voice and then the sound of laughter from down the hallway. Robbie looked around wide-eyed as we passed a number of rooms to reach the one assigned to Angela.

At our appearance, Angela beamed at us from the chair she was sitting in. "Hi, Ann! Come see my little boy."

The baby was asleep in Angela's arms. Rhonda and Will, holding Willow, stood by. Reggie sat on the edge of the bed, gazing at his wife and son with a look of awe on his face. It was a scene none of us had imagined a year ago.

Still holding onto Robbie, I peered at the baby. "He's beautiful, Angela," I said. "I'm so happy everything went well. How are you feeling?"

"I'm glad it's over. But Evan is so beautiful, it's all worth it."

"What did your parents say when you told them?" I asked Reggie.

Reggie grimaced. "My mother loved his name until I mentioned DelMonte-Smythe. Typical, huh?"

"When she sees this adorable little boy, she won't care," I said, attempting to put a happy spin on it. Even so, Rhonda and I exchanged knowing looks.

After kissing Willow on the cheek, I handed Angela the teddy bear. "Robbie and I picked this out for Evan."

"Mine!" shrieked Robbie, reaching for the toy.

"You have yours at home," I reminded him as he squirmed to get down.

"Hey, buddy!" said Reggie, taking him into his arms. He

swung Robbie up in the air, turning Robbie's whines into squeals of joy.

At that moment, Reggie's parents walked into the room.

"What do we have here?" said Katherine, frowning at our assembled group.

"Hi, Mom and Dad," said Reggie, going over to them, still holding Robbie. "Come see Evan." He smiled at his mother. "We named him for you."

Her features softened. "That's so sweet, dear."

He smiled. "It was Angela's idea."

Katherine darted a look of surprise at Angela. "Really? That's so ... so unexpected of you."

Angela smiled. "We thought it would be nice. You're his grandmother." She struggled to get out of the chair. Reggie gave her a hand.

"Would you like to hold him?" Angela asked Katherine.

Katherine's eyes swam with tears. "May I?" She took the baby into her arms. She smiled as she gazed down at the baby and turned to her husband. "He looks like you, Arthur."

As Arthur studied the baby, his body straightened. "I believe he does." He smiled at Reggie and then acknowledged Angela. "Congratulations to you both."

"Thank you. I'm glad you're here," said Angela.

"Me too," said Katherine, giving Angela a steady smile. "Arthur wasn't sure we should make the trip so soon, but I wanted to see my grandson."

Katherine moved toward Angela and gave her a kiss on the cheek.

"Thanks, Mom," said Reggie softly and the tension in the room evaporated.

I took the opportunity to say good-bye. "See you later. Much love to you all."

"Stay," said Robbie, tugging on my hand.

Before he could work himself into a temper tantrum, I swooped him up into my arms. As I left the room, I heard Katherine say, "Who was that child?"

"Ann's new little boy," said Rhonda. "It's a long story."

"Oh my! I can't keep up with the two of you," Katherine replied.

Rhonda laughed. "Don't even try!"

As I moved down the hallway, Katherine's reaction made me smile. Nobody could keep up with us. Our lives seemed to be filled with one surprise after the other.

CHAPTER TWENTY

I'd just put Robbie to bed that evening when Vaughn called. "Hi, Ann! Did I catch you at work?"

"Yes, but not at the hotel. At home. Elena wasn't feeling well, and Robbie was showing signs of needing time with me, so I stayed home today. And, believe me, spending the day with a toddler is a whole lot of work."

He chuckled. "Yeah, I bet. I've been busy too. I'd hoped to come home next weekend, but it looks like that isn't going to happen. And the weekend after that is the fishing trip in Alaska, so it looks like I won't see you for a while."

I bit back my disappointment. "I understand. Next weekend is the Bauer wedding, so I'll be tied up a lot of the time. But that doesn't mean I wouldn't love to have you here."

"Just a few weeks, then our wedding and a whole month off for me." His voice grew husky. "Just think what we can do then."

Anticipation curled through me. The thought of Vaughn spending a whole month with me was tantalizing.

We exchanged news and talked more about Robbie and the need for one of us to spend more time with him.

"I'll make an effort to do more things with him when I'm home," Vaughn said. "I've got to go now. I'll call you as often as I can. Can't wait until you're officially mine."

I smiled. Now that it was becoming a reality, I was getting more and more excited about our wedding plans coming to fruition. A small, informal wedding and a short honeymoon sounded perfect.

###

When I walked into the hotel's kitchen the next morning, Consuela was pulling a sheet pan of our famous breakfast rolls out of the oven.

"Smells delicious," I said, pouring myself a cup of coffee. "Anything new?"

Consuela smiled. "I think Bernie and his lady friend are getting along nicely."

"Lady friend? Do you mean Annette Bauer?"

She nodded. "*Si*. He is so happy."

I smiled. "Very interesting."

As I walked toward my office, I saw Annette and Bernie having coffee in the dining room and went over to them.

"Hi, there! You two are up early. What's happening?"

Bernie got to his feet. "We're discussing the wedding."

Annette smiled up at me. "Actually, we're discussing a lot of different things."

I accepted the chair at the table Bernie offered me and joined them.

"Did you know Bernie and I met several times in New York when he was dating his girlfriend?" Annette's eyes sparkled with mischief as she gazed from me to Bernie. "We liked each other then, but neither of us was free. Now we are."

"Yes, indeed," said Bernie formally, taking a seat once more. Though he acted as though nothing much was going on between them, the lingering, loving look he shot Annette gave him away.

Why, they're in love, I thought. Rhonda was going to be thrilled, though I suspected it had little to do with her matchmaking efforts—something Rhonda would never admit.

"Where's Trudy?"

"In my office, waiting for us to get her. She knows she's not allowed in the dining room," said Bernie.

"Such a darling dog," commented Annette, bringing a smile to Bernie's face.

"Is everything set for the wedding?" I asked Bernie.

He glanced at Annette. Color flooded his cheeks.

Annette clasped his hand and turned to me. "Bernie has been such a help. It's beautiful. Thank you so much."

"I'm so pleased. For both of you," I said, rising. "Guess I'd better get to my office. Annette, I know I'm leaving you in good hands."

Annette's cheeks flushed a pretty pink.

I was going over financial projections when Rhonda strode into the office, grinning. "Oh my God, Annie! I did it! I did it! Bernie and Annette were holding hands when I met them outside. I knew it! They're made for each other!"

I chuckled. No way was I going to burst her bubble. If she wanted to believe she had spread some sort of magic, I was going to let her.

Rhonda set down her purse and plopped into her desk chair. "Sorry to be so late, but as usual, Willow was hungry."

"No problem. How did everything go yesterday?"

"Things at the hotel were great. Tim is learning more and more about running a property like this from Bernie. He was a huge help." Her expression became somber. "And Ange is doing very well with her baby." She paused. "And Katherine."

"Oh?" I said, wondering at the tinge of sadness I heard in her voice.

"Yeah, the two of them are like...real buddies. I offered to go over and help Angela, but Angela said she didn't need me, that Katherine was going to help her. What's that all about? I'm her mother."

I rose and gave Rhonda a needed hug. "It's about trying to get along with a difficult mother-in-law. It will make a world of difference to Angela if she and Katherine can become friends. It's not about her not needing you."

Rhonda nodded thoughtfully. "Oh, yeah. Right. I hadn't thought of it that way. Good. I can live with that."

I smiled. "Of course. Now, what do you say? Should we give the go-ahead and buy some new spa products?"

Soon we were in discussion about hotel matters.

The hours slipped by, with Rhonda leaving to feed Willow and quickly returning to carry on business. Late afternoon, I took a break so I could spend some time with Robbie.

Later, when I returned to the hotel to help cover the dinner hour, Rhonda was already in the office.

"Annie, we've gotta talk," she said. "Will is upset with me for spending so much time at the hotel. He's right. The baby is a blessing we never expected. I want to spend more time with her. And you've already mentioned you should spend more time with Robbie. We need to do something about it. Like Will says, we hired Bernie to run the hotel for us, but we're not letting him do it."

My mouth turned dry. I sat at my desk, trying to fight the worry that seized me. I'd always thought of the hotel as our baby—Rhonda's and mine. I'd worked hard to make sure it was a success. How could I trust someone else to have that same sense of dedication?

"Let's talk to Bernie," said Rhonda. "Okay if I text him now?"

My blood turned into an icy river. Numb, I nodded. I'd promised Vaughn to have more time for him. I wanted to be a real part of Robbie's life. And after suffering the blow of losing her father, Liz needed my support.

Bernie entered the office, followed by faithful Trudy. The dog, used to me now, jumped up into my lap. I held tight to her and listened while Rhonda spoke.

"Bernie, we need to have you take on more responsibility so Annie and I can have more time with our families. What do you say?"

Bernie gave me a penetrating look. "Are you on board with this, Ann?"

I drew a deep breath, let it out slowly. My life was about to take another major turn whether I wanted it to or not.

"Good," said Bernie, "because I was about to tell you both that I've been offered a job in New York City. Annette thought I might want to consider it."

Stunned by the news, I gripped the arms of my chair. "Are you going to leave us?"

"Not now. I like it here." He raised a finger in warning. "But I've been waiting for you to recognize that I can do a lot more than you've allowed me to do. As general manager, I should be doing a lot of the work you are doing. I've mentioned it before. Now, maybe we can agree to let me do the job you've hired me for."

Rhonda and I exchanged looks of dismay.

"As owners, we need to know what you're doing and how things are going," I said.

"Of course. We can set up meetings on a regular basis. Maybe two or three times a week. And, Ann, while I am perfectly capable of handling the day-to-day business at the hotel, I cannot take the place of the two of you in making social contacts. The Beach House Hotel has succeeded in large part because the two of you represent the hotel."

"Yeah," said Rhonda. "Guests like it when we greet them."

"More than that," said Bernie, "your handling of special events with high-powered people has given them a sense of trust that their privacy will be protected—something many larger hotels are unable to control."

My mind spun. It would be wonderful not to be stuck

behind a desk all day. It might be fun just to look over reports someone else had prepared and make recommendations to others.

"What about staff? Do we have enough?" I asked him. "Tim is your assistant and can take on more work, I'm sure. We could make Julie front office manager and bring in people to assist her or you. We could hire a good bookkeeper too. What do you think?"

"Good idea, Annie," said Rhonda.

"How about letting me come back to you with my recommendations?" said Bernie, calmly, firmly. "You can review them, and then we can talk."

I swallowed hard. This is how it would be in the future. "Okay. I'm going to call my hospitality consultant in Boston to get some information about how other small, upscale hotels are organized and staffed. Then maybe we can amend your contract. You are willing to make a commitment to stay, aren't you?"

Bernie smiled. "Yes, indeed. Annette likes it here too."

"Oh? Do you mean you and Annette ..." Rhonda began.

At my glare, she stopped talking.

Bernie checked his watch and rose. "Thank you both so much for this opportunity. The Beach House Hotel is a stunning property that deserves all the attention I can give it. I promise you I'll do a good job."

Trudy jumped off my lap, and she and Bernie left the office.

"Well, what do ya know," said Rhonda, beaming at me. "Guess our timing is right. What would we have done if we lost Bernie?"

"I hate to even think of it," I said. "But it isn't going to be easy to hand things over to him. We've done everything ourselves."

"We've gotta try, Annie. We've gotta try."

CHAPTER TWENTY-ONE

As I told Vaughn about the change in my role at the hotel, tears stung my eyes. I felt like a young mother sending her only child off to kindergarten. The hotel had been, in so many ways, something I'd borne—a special creation Rhonda and I had produced even while facing huge obstacles.

"Don't worry, Ann," said Vaughn. "As Bernie indicated, you and Rhonda will still be needed at the hotel; you just won't be dealing with the daily grind. With your spending less time overseeing day-to-day operations at the hotel, think of what it might mean to both of us. I'd like you to spend more time with me in New York and travel with me to other locations around the world."

"What about Robbie?"

"He'll be with us when it's feasible, of course. Our home will continue to be with him in Sabal like we've agreed."

"It sounds good," I said, realizing how free my life could be away from my duties at the hotel.

We talked for a while longer, and then Vaughn said, "I've got to go. My transportation is here. Good luck with the wedding. I'll call you after our special filming."

As we hung up, I appreciated how easily Vaughn made me feel better about things that troubled me. I loved that about our relationship.

With the arrival of the first wedding guests, the hotel came alive with activity. Cheerful voices filled the rooms and on the patio around the pool.

I walked into Bernie's office for the first of our transitional meetings.

Bernie rose to greet me. "Where's Rhonda?"

"She'll be along. She's checking with Jean-Luc on the meals for the rehearsal dinner and the wedding luncheon."

A frown creased Bernie's brow.

"It's something she's always done," I said, aware of his unhappiness. "She and Jean-Luc work well together."

"I understand, but in the future, I'll handle that. I've already talked to Jean-Luc about the changes in management. We have an understanding that he's in charge of his kitchen and can handle things his way." He gave me an apologetic look. "It's best that way."

"You know how chefs are," I quickly said, eager to ease the situation.

"Yes, indeed," Bernie said with a touch of irritation in his voice.

I winked at him, and he laughed. "They're all the same. The good ones anyway."

Rhonda arrived, and we went over plans for the wedding. True to his word, Bernie had prepared schedules and other reports for us to look over. Staffing for the wedding included hiring two temps to act as bartenders and another couple of temps as dishwashers.

"We need to hire two part-time bartenders on a permanent basis," said Bernie. "After the wedding, I'd like to look into it. With the lunch and dinner business growing and the additional sunset promotions I've put in place, we need them to be available to properly serve our guests."

"How much is that going to cost?" I asked, forcing myself to loosen my grip on the arms of my chair.

Bernie smiled at me. "I knew you'd ask, so I drew up this

schedule of labor hours, payroll, and overtime we've paid and some projections that factor in the additional business our promotions are bringing in."

We discussed the particulars briefly for clarification while I weighed the pros and cons in my mind. As long as there would be a return on the investment, I'd leave it up to Bernie. It was only fair.

"Sounds good," said Rhonda, and I agreed.

By the time we left the meeting, I was on board with what Bernie had done and planned to do. The wedding was his first test of leadership, and he was handling it well. The look of pride on his face was telling. It was his confidence, more than anything else, that made me more comfortable with turning the bulk of managing the hotel over to him.

As we'd all agreed, Rhonda and I would be present during the wedding weekend. Bernie and Annette would continue to be photographed for the wedding brochure. We planned to send these new brochures to various outlets, including a couple of brides' magazines and online, wedding-planning websites.

Following our meeting, Rhonda invited me to her house for lunch. Suddenly aware of our freedom, I happily agreed. Though things could never return to the pre-hotel days, we were now available to have a more normal life.

As I relaxed on her patio, I gazed at Rhonda and wondered what would have happened to me if we hadn't met. Without the hotel, I might never have met Vaughn. I wished he weren't going to make the trip to Alaska. The journey in the wilderness seemed so dangerous, so far away.

On the day of Babette's wedding, I walked into the hotel and stood a moment admiring the colorful, fresh flowers that sat atop the round table in the front entry. In return for the mention in our wedding brochures, Floral Designs had done an outstanding job of providing flowers for the occasion.

The small, late-afternoon ceremony would take place on the side lawn of the property where shade, flowering plants, and lush landscaping provided an intimate setting and some protection from the warm, late-April temperatures.

I stepped out onto the lawn to check on the arrangements. Folding chairs covered in white cloth to which tropical flowers had been pinned were lined up on either side of a wide, white-cloth aisle runner for the bride to walk on. Max Hoffman would walk Babette down to the simple altar that had been built especially for the occasion. A local minister from the Presbyterian church had agreed to perform the ceremony.

"It sure looks pretty," said Rhonda, joining me. "Just think, maybe Willow will be married here one day." She elbowed me. "Or Liz. Angela tells me that Liz and Chad are pretty happy about his visit to Boston. She thinks he may be the one for Liz."

"Really?"

Rhonda grinned. "Maybe she'll up and get married, like Angela."

"I hope not," I said sincerely. When the time came for Liz to get married, I wanted to be a big part of the celebration— before, during and after.

"Well, one thing's for sure," said Rhonda. "Our lives are changing."

We moved aside for the photographers, who wanted a clear shot of the wedding venue.

As the time for the ceremony came closer, Rhonda and I moved to our usual greeting spot at the top of the front-entrance stairs of the hotel, greeting wedding guests and directing them outside.

Rhonda and I followed the last of the wedding guests through the hotel and out to the side lawn. Musical notes from the harpist we'd hired for the occasion danced in the air—light harbingers of the music that would bring people to their feet.

The wedding march began.

Babette, a striking blonde, walked toward us on the arm of Maxwell Hoffman. In a long, white, lacy dress and simple veil, she looked as angelic as the excited smile that spread across her face. Standing up in front, her fiancé, a nice young man from New York City, beamed at her with such love that tears stung my eyes.

A collective sigh filled the garden as Babette moved down the aisle. *There is something so wonderful about weddings,* I thought, thinking of my own. In a little over six weeks, I would again be a bride.

After the ceremony, the group moved into the main dining room. Lorraine Grace at Wedding Perfection had decorated the private alcove to resemble the outside garden, carrying out the theme of a tropical, destination wedding.

Continuing his role of father of the bride for our brochure, Bernie looked every bit the real part. Even Trudy wore a white bow around her neck. I noticed Bernie talking to Babette and smiled. She was nodding her head enthusiastically and glancing from her mother to him. Love was definitely in the air.

Once I was certain that everything was under control, I left the hotel, eager to spend some time with Robbie and to talk to my daughter.

Still wrapped up in the beauty of the wedding, I entered the house missing Vaughn so much it hurt.

Robbie ran toward me, shouting "Mommy!" and my attention was diverted. I swung him up in my arms and nestled him against me.

After a moment, he wiggled to get down.

Elena smiled at me. "I need to go to the mall. I thought Robbie might want to go with me. He likes seeing all the colors and shapes."

"Sure, that would be fine. And then you have the evening off. Right?"

She smiled. "Troy and I are going to the movies. Pretty lame, huh?"

"No, it sounds perfect."

Elena and Robbie left, and I wandered through the house, feeling restless and a little blue. When the phone rang, I eagerly picked it up.

"Hi, Liz! I was going to call you."

She laughed. "Beat you to it! What's going on? I heard that you and Rhonda aren't going to be at the hotel as much."

"Right." I explained the new routine to her.

"Wow! Are you going to be all right with that, Mom?"

"It's going to take some time to get used to it, but it's all for the best. I'll be able to spend more time with Vaughn and Robbie."

"Oh, good."

"So I understand you and Chad had a good time together in Boston," I said and waited for her response.

"Angela wasn't supposed to say anything about it. Well, I might as well tell you. I think I've found the man I'm going to marry."

At my surprised silence, Liz continued. "Don't worry, Mom. It isn't going to happen anytime soon. He's busy setting up his business, and he knows I want to finish school. So nothing is going to happen for at least another year."

"Are you guys really in love?"

"We're both pretty sure this is it, but we want to take things slowly. If things continue to go well, Chad mentioned getting engaged at Christmas. And Mom, when I come home this summer, I want to move in with him."

"But, Liz..."

"I need to be sure of this, Mom. I've never felt this way about anyone. But everything is happening so fast I want to know it's real. I don't want to make the same mistake Dad did."

Ahh, so that's it, I thought. Both Robert and I had made mistakes in the past. "Okay, Liz. You're an adult. I understand."

"Mom? I think I know what you and Vaughn have. It's magical, right?"

My lips curved at the thought. "Yes, sweetie, it feels that way. So tell me more about this young man you love so much."

I sat back in my chair and listened happily as my daughter told me all the reasons she thought Chad was special.

"And, Mom, we're going to make his business grow. His customers love him, and he's so good at his job. He'll do the labor, and I'll handle the marketing and all. A little like you and Dad, huh?"

"Uh, we'll have to talk about that later," I said, unwilling to burst her bubble of happiness. But if I had any say in it, her situation with Chad would be a lot different.

"Gotta go, Mom. Thanks so much for listening to me. Love you."

"Love you, too, Liz." As I hung up, I realized how much I'd missed talks like this with Liz and promised myself as I grew busier with Robbie, I'd still save precious time for Liz.

CHAPTER TWENTY-TWO

M y eyes flashed open. I lay in bed, aware of the perspiration that dotted my brow. The dream that still pumped fear through me faded in and out of my mind. It had been so scary, so frightening. In it, Vaughn was sitting all alone on a glacier amid tall mountains. I'd cried out to him over and over, but he'd ignored my pleas to come to me.

I sat up and wiped the sleep from my eyes. I knew it was a silly dream, but I couldn't shake off the sense of losing him. I checked my bedside clock. Four o'clock in the morning. Sinking back among the pillows, I forced myself to take calming breaths. Vaughn wasn't scheduled to leave for Alaska for another three hours. I'd call him then.

Unaware I'd fallen asleep again, I was startled by the ringing of the phone. Groggy, I picked up the receiver. "H..hello?"

"Hi, sweetheart! It's me. Sam Nichols and I are being picked up soon. I just wanted to say hello and good-bye. I can't wait for this trip to Alaska to begin. It's been a difficult few weeks and I need a break so that I'm rested for our wedding."

"Vaughn, I just had the most terrible dream. You'll be careful, won't you?"

"Of course. We'll be traveling with a seasoned pilot who's also a good guide. And the weather is supposed to be great. Don't worry. I wouldn't miss our wedding for anything."

The tension that had knotted my shoulders eased. "I can't wait. After shooting the Bauer wedding at the hotel, I'm excited to put some of my ideas together for our wedding. It's going to be so beautiful."

"You're going to be beautiful," Vaughn amended. "How's our little boy doing?"

"He's becoming such a 'cuddle bug.' I have to admit I love holding a little one again. The temper tantrum part I could miss."

We chuckled together, well aware that the one came with the other.

"I've got to go. I'll call you as often as I can, but I've been told some areas are out of phone range, so hang tight."

"Okay," I said, wishing I hadn't had that dream. I reassured myself that Vaughn was in good hands—Sam was an experienced fisherman and the pilot who'd serve as their guide was an excellent one.

"Ann? Don't worry. I'll bring back lots of salmon. See you soon."

We hung up, and I lay in bed a moment, telling myself not to worry foolishly. I'd recently seen a television program on the Antarctic that I now thought had prompted the dream. The mind, I knew, could conjure up all kinds of weird things. And my mind had become overactive as I tried to lessen my role at the hotel. Too much time on my hands, I realized.

I rose out of bed and tiptoed into the kitchen for a cup of coffee. Sitting at the table sipping my coffee, I thought of all I had to be thankful for. The babbling sounds of Robbie talking to himself came through the baby monitor, bringing a smile to my face.

When he began to fuss, I stood up and went to get him.

As I opened the door to his room, he looked up at me. "Mommy! Down!"

I laughed and went to him. He lifted his arms and I swept him up in my embrace. "Good morning, sweet boy!"

He snuggled against me. I thought as I had so many times

how unpredictable life was. I got him dressed for the day, and we went into the kitchen. Reminding myself that I didn't have to rush into the hotel, I sat with Robbie while he ate breakfast and played a word game with him. Elena had the day off, and it was just the two of us in the house. Outside, the sun spread lemony light on our surroundings, coating the tips of the ripples in the inlet's water with golden brightness.

A day to be outside, I told myself. I smiled at Robbie. "How would you like to go to the zoo?" I'd heard the zoo in Naples was nice.

"Zoooo?"

"We can see monkeys and other animals," I said, excited about the prospect of introducing him to something new.

Robbie clapped his hands together. "Ma-kee"

"Okay, that's what we'll do."

After breakfast, I packed a diaper bag with all the necessities, including water, juice, and snacks. I got Robbie loaded into his car seat and then struggled to heft his stroller into the back of my SUV.

Driving down the coast, I felt like a kid skipping school. I couldn't remember when I hadn't been worried about the hotel, the future, my life. I sang songs barely remembered from Liz's toddler days. When the words wouldn't come to my mind, I made them up.

Robbie caught my spirit and shrieked with glee as I laughed at the silliness of it all.

The small zoo was a treasure. Seeing animals up close in a comfortable setting delighted Robbie. He laughed and pointed and tried to sound out their names. The surprised look on his face when a giraffe came right up to us to get the food we were offering it brought laughs out of me and the people standing next to us. And, later, when Robbie saw a stuffed giraffe in the gift shop, there was no way we could leave without it.

During our drive back home, Robbie sat in a daze in his car seat, clutching the giraffe. As I caught glimpses of him in the rearview mirror, my heart filled. He was such a treasure. I felt foolish now for wondering if I'd be able to handle the fact that he was Robert's child by another woman. The fact that he was Liz's brother made him special.

At home, I gave Robbie his lunch and settled him down for a nap. On my way back to my bedroom, intending to lie down myself, I noticed Rhonda's car pulling into my driveway.

Smiling, I went to greet her. "Hi! Come on in. What are you doing on your free day?"

She grimaced. "That's just it—nothing. We gotta talk, Annie."

I ushered her into the kitchen. After serving us both some of Consuela's blackberry iced tea, I took a seat opposite her at the kitchen table.

"What's going on?"

"I went to the hotel to talk to Jean-Luc about a new recipe idea, and he..." her lip quivered... "and he told me not to worry about things like that anymore. He said he had everything under control." Tears filled her eyes. "It's my frickin' kitchen. Not his."

I reached across the table and squeezed her hand. "It used to be your kitchen—before we turned The Beach House into a hotel."

"Yeah, but Annie, even afterward, I was part of it. That's the agreement we made with Jean-Luc. Remember?"

"I do. But things have changed."

Rhonda sniffed. "Well, I want to change 'em back to what they were."

"I know how you feel," I said sympathetically. "But it's too late. When we began, it was just the two of us working like crazy, wondering if we'd make it. Look at all the changes since then."

"I know." Rhonda slumped in her chair. "You're right. But it hurt my feelings—Jean-Luc talkin' to me that way."

"Believe me, I understand how you feel," I said. "I've had a wonderful morning with Robbie, but I don't know if I can simply turn the hotel over to Bernie and the others. After being so much a part of the daily operation over the last two years, I need to know what's going on."

"That's not all that's bothering me," said Rhonda. "Will and I had our first real fight. He told me to let some of the hotel business go, to relax and enjoy what we had together. I agree Willow is a blessing. I love her, and I want to be the best mother I can to her, but that hotel is my baby too."

I drew a deep breath and struggled to sort through my own emotions. Deep down, I wanted to be able to tell Bernie to leave things like they were when he first came to the hotel, but I knew, for so many reasons, that was unrealistic.

Rhonda twisted her hands. "I know Will is right. I just needed to let off a little steam. Ya know?"

"Oh, hon, I do." I knew very well what Rhonda was going through because I was experiencing the same ups and downs of our changing lives.

The conversation turned to Angela and the baby. Pride filled Rhonda's face. "That Evan is a tough little guy. But big and strong as he is, his Aunt Willow is going to show him a thing or two. She's bright and active and determined to get her way. She's already spoiled. Can you believe it?"

"Better be careful," I teased.

Rhonda laughed. "I will. I don't want her to become a brat like a certain someone we once had to deal with. Any word from our famous actress, Tina? I've been thinking of her."

"Me too. Last time I talked to her she was going on location for her new movie. And remember, her problems were a very real cause of her behavior."

Rhonda stood. "You're right. I'd better get back to my little princess. It's time for her to be fed."

I rose and gave Rhonda a hug, wondering what was going to happen to the two of us.

Vaughn called from Alaska as I was sitting by the pool with Robbie. "Hello from the rugged north."

"Hi, sweetie? How was your flight?" I asked.

"Long, but well worth it. We flew over some pretty amazing stuff. I can't wait to get inland. The scenery there is supposed to be even more spectacular."

I smiled at the enthusiasm in his voice. Vaughn worked hard and deserved a nice break like this.

"What's happening on the home front?" he asked.

As I told him about Robbie's experience at the zoo, we laughed together. It felt so good to be able to share the small details of my day with him.

"And how are things at the hotel?" he asked.

"I'm guessing they're good. I haven't had any calls for help. It's not easy to let go. Rhonda's having trouble with it too."

"Probably a good idea to start slowly. Someday you might want to sell it."

My insides froze. He knew how important that hotel was to me. "Is that what you want me to do?" I asked in a deceptively quiet voice.

"Not necessarily. But you've got a nice business going. People in the industry are starting to notice."

As nausea twisted my stomach, I remained quiet.

"Ann? Are you there?"

"Yes," I answered. Then eager to change the subject, I said,

"Do you have all the proper gear with you? I imagine Alaska has plenty of stores to outfit fishermen."

Vaughn laughed. "You ought to see the hip boots I just bought. They're huge."

We talked about the fishing trip, then, at the signs of Robbie's restlessness, I told Vaughn I'd better go. "Love you. Talk to you soon."

"I'll call as often as I can, but phone service will be sketchy." He paused. "Ann, I'm sorry I mentioned selling the hotel. I know it upset you."

"It's all right," I said, though the idea still sickened me.

"Love you, Ann."

His melodious voice sang softly in my ears as he clicked off.. I sat a moment, wishing Vaughn was here beside me.

"Mommy?"

Robbie looked up at me from where he was sitting on the steps of the pool. The look of worry on his face startled me. I leaned over and cupped his cheek in my hand.

"It's okay, Robbie. Ready to get out?"

"Juice."

I helped him out of the pool, dried him off, and we headed into the kitchen for our afternoon snack.

Is this what my life will be like? I thought uneasily. I thought back to the days when Liz toddled around me. Even then I'd occupied myself with outside activities—volunteering at the library and working for Robert. I'd loved that life. Having Robbie didn't mean staying in the house with him all day. Elena was here to help me, and there were many worthwhile charitable projects to work on. My concern evaporated. I'd taken a chance joining forces with Rhonda. I would just let things evolve into another phase of my life. As long as I had Vaughn in it, I wouldn't worry.

CHAPTER TWENTY-THREE

As I drove through the gates of the hotel, I told myself to remain relatively quiet at the meeting Rhonda and I had scheduled with Bernie. We had to give him a chance. He'd signed an amended contract and was encouraging Annette to move in with him.

Rhonda met me in the office beforehand. Sitting there, going over the reports Bernie had prepared and emailed to us, it seemed like old times as we chatted about the list of upcoming events Bernie had described at the hotel.

"Lots of weddings," commented Rhonda. "But they're mostly local, which means we're not selling rooms to the wedding parties. What's up with that?"

"We'll have to make some suggestions about these events, but, Rhonda, we have to go easy."

"I know," she said grumpily.

I studied the numbers. They looked good. Food sales had picked up.

By the time our meeting was to begin, Rhonda and I had only a few questions to ask.

Bernie showed up at our office at the appointed time, and after exchanging greetings, we sat around the small conference table.

After we discussed the weekly sales and payroll, Rhonda mentioned the issues she had with the wedding events.

Bernie stiffened and then nodded. "You're right. We'll look into bringing in more destination weddings. I'll have a report for you next week."

The meeting concluded on a high note, and then we sat and talked for a few minutes.

"I understand Annette is moving in with you," said Rhonda to Bernie, a gleeful note in her voice nobody could miss.

He smiled. "She's going to be spending time with me here."

"You're a perfect pair," said Rhonda, grinning broadly at us both.

I chuckled. Rhonda still believed her efforts at matchmaking were what had brought Bernie and Annette together.

Bernie rose to go.

"Where's Trudy?" I asked.

"She's at home. Some of the guests complained about her. I'm not sure what I'm going to do. I'm looking for a pet sitter."

I cleared my throat. "I might be willing to take her for a few afternoons. She and Robbie got along beautifully when you visited us. I've been wondering if we should get a dog."

Bernie's eyes lit with pleasure. "That would be great if you could have her. You could see if you'd like a dog, and it will give me time to find a pet sitter until Annette gets here. She loves Trudy."

The look of excitement on Robbie's face when he saw the dog erased any doubts I had about my decision. Tail wagging, Trudy ran right up to him and stood by as he awkwardly patted her on the head. Elena and I looked at each other and smiled.

Trudy continued to trail after Robbie as he coaxed her into a game of tag. When he collapsed in a heap on the floor, she went over and sat beside him.

"Good idea, Ann," said Elena. "Robbie will go down for his nap without any fight."

"Ahhh, a method to this madness," I said, leaving the room to answer my phone.

I looked at the number, frowned at our lawyer's name and picked up the call. "Hello?"

"Ann, Mike Torson here. I would like it if you and Rhonda would come to my office to discuss a matter that has come to my attention."

My heart fell. "Is it another lawsuit?"

"I'd rather not go into details now. Can you join me at the office with Rhonda at, say, four o'clock?"

"Yes, but..."

"Great. See you then," Mike said and clicked off the call.

As soon as I hung up from him, Rhonda phoned me. "Did you just get a call from Mike Torson?"

"I'm meeting him at four o'clock this afternoon. Are you?"

"Yeah, but I'm worried. Do you think Tina's mother is trying to sue us again?"

"I don't know. It isn't like Mike to be so abrupt. I'm worried too."

As I waited outside Rhonda's house for her to join me, I studied the large, two-story home that she shared with Will and the baby. It couldn't match The Beach House in size, of course, but it was a beautiful home. Rhonda loved it.

She emerged through the front door and hurried over to my car.

Sliding into the passenger seat, she turned to me with a worried look. "Something tells me this meeting with Mike isn't going to be good."

"I've been wondering what is so big he couldn't tell us over the phone," I admitted, pulling out of the driveway.

Outside Mike's office, I parked the car, and then, giving

each other smiles of encouragement, we hurried inside the white-stucco building.

The receptionist looked up at us and smiled. "Ann? Rhonda? Mike asked me to put you in the small conference room. Please come this way."

Rhonda and I followed her into a room dominated by an oval mahogany table. We took seats on either side of the far end and waited for Mike to appear. We were lucky to have him represent us. Small in stature, he'd earned the nickname Tyson. Others forced to face him in an opposing situation often found themselves outwitted before they could recover. And he would, I was sure, protect us now.

After the receptionist had offered us water or coffee, which we turned down, she left.

In a matter of moments, Mike appeared. "Hello, Ann. Hello, Rhonda." He shook hands with us and then took a seat opposite us.

"Glad you could make it," he said.

"Okay, Mike. What's this all about?" Rhonda bluntly asked him.

He smiled at us. "This could be good news for the two of you. I received a phone call from a lawyer handling an inquiry from an investment group interested in possibly buying The Beach House Hotel."

My heart stuttered to a stop and then raced to catch up, leaving me feeling disoriented.

"Whoa! It's not for sale!" Rhonda turned from him to me. "Right, Annie?"

"Right," I said firmly. It was bad enough that both Rhonda and I were feeling pushed out of the hotel. Now, this.

"Are the two of you going to be able to keep up with the demands of the hotel? You both have had changes in your personal lives that make a big difference."

All my frustration burst out of me in snappish words. "Are you suggesting that because we're women and mothers we can't do the job of running the hotel?"

Mike blinked in surprise at the anger in my words. "No, that's not what I'm implying. Not at all," he said calmly. "As a matter of fact, it is for the opposite reason. You two have been so successful that others are interested. As I would advise any of my clients, I'm asking you to consider it."

"But it was my home," said Rhonda.

"And now it's a hotel." Mike turned to me. "Ann, I would suggest you talk it over with the hospitality consultant you know in Boston." He held up a hand to stop me from speaking. "Just to get feedback on what this might mean to you and the different approaches one might normally take. The decision is, and always will be, for the two of you to make."

Rhonda and I exchanged glances.

Remembering my earlier conversation with Vaughn, I said, "I suppose we can at least talk about it. But I have to be honest and tell you I'm frankly not interested. I'm even sometimes sorry we hired Bernie."

"Yeah," Rhonda agreed. "I like being part of everything."

Mike gave us each a thoughtful look. "This sometimes happens to people like you who have built something out of nothing. Why don't I tell the lawyer that it's a little premature, but that they can come back to us in a few months and see how you're feeling about it then?"

"Okay, that's fair," I said. "But I don't think I'll be changing my mind."

"Me too," said Rhonda. "Do you know what a dump that place was when Sal and I bought it?"

"Indeed I do," said Mike. "You've made it very special. Let's keep this interest of theirs quiet, and if and when the time comes, we'll have them sign a confidentiality agreement before exchanging any information. Before you consider doing anything, you might want to speak to your consultant about it."

"We're not going to even think about it now," said Rhonda. "Too much is happening too fast."

"I understand," said Mike.

"What is this group?" I asked. "Are they legit?"

Mike smiled. "Oh, definitely. It's very secure money. I wouldn't even bring this before you if it wasn't."

"Thank you," I said, forcing the words out of a mouth that had gone dry with tension. Like Rhonda had said, too much was happening too fast.

Mike chatted with us about an upcoming meeting he was attending at the hotel and, after social pleasantries were exchanged, Rhonda and I left his office.

Standing outside, Rhonda and I faced each other.

"How about a drink?" said Rhonda. "I've got a white wine chilling. Sound good?"

"Sounds wonderful."

Rhonda and I were in her upstairs sitting room. It was Rhonda's favorite spot in the house. She liked to spend quiet moments there. With our minds whirling with all kinds of scenarios, we needed this quiet moment together.

Willow sat in her infant seat on the carpet at our feet, kicking her feet and waving her hands in the air as if testing what her extremities could do. With her pretty features, straight brown hair, and bright brown eyes, she reminded me of a baby doll I once had. Her cheeks were round and rosy, a combination of good health and good eating. Already eight weeks old, she was, I thought, one of the cutest babies I'd ever seen.

While Rhonda sipped bubbling water, I enjoyed a glass of pinot grigio.

"What are we going to do, Annie? I never imagined selling the hotel."

"Me either. Why don't we put aside the idea for the time being? In the next couple of weeks, I'll put in a call to Roger Jamieson to see what consulting advice he has for us. We should at least know how something like this might work so we're not caught unaware."

"Okay, but I don't like it." Rhonda turned as Willow started to fuss.

"What's the matter, baby girl?" she crooned to Willow as she picked her up and rocked her in her arms.

Watching the two of them together, I thought what a miracle this baby was. *She was one lucky, little surprise.* Her parents adored her and would be able to give her a wonderful life. I was about to say so when Will walked into the room.

"Hi, hon," said Rhonda, her face alight with affection.

He gave Rhonda a kiss on the cheek and took the baby from her. Holding the baby up in front of him, he said, "And how's my *best girl*?"

He turned to me. "I can't wait to get home to Willow at night. I've never felt like this before."

My smile wavered when I saw the look of hurt on Rhonda's face.

"I'm sure you like to come home to both Rhonda and Willow," I said, hoping he'd catch my clue.

Ignoring me, he left the room with the baby.

Tears shone in Rhonda's eyes. "You see how it is? Will hardly even notices me anymore." She sniffed. "I thought it was just my fighting postpartum hormones, but I realize things have changed. *I* used to be the one he came home to at night."

"Maybe you just need to have some private time together—you and Will. Everything is revolving around the baby now, but that's not how it'll always be."

Rhonda let out a sigh that spoke volumes. "I feel lost. Everything has changed at home and at the hotel. What seemed so simple, so easy, so fun, now seems like a chore."

Concern rose in me. "Rhonda, maybe you need a break from all of it."

"Yeah, I think I do. My brother called me the other day to ask me to come for a visit. Richie and Margaret are too busy at the butcher shop to come here, and they want to see Willow. It should be nice this time of year at the Jersey shore—warming up and not too busy." As she straightened in her chair, a look of determination filled her face. "I'm going home to New Jersey. And I'm taking Willow with me."

"What about Will?" I couldn't help asking.

"He can decide for himself if he wants to make the trip. Like you said, I need a break. And God knows I'm not needed at the hotel." Her smile was weak. "Maybe you should take a trip too."

I shook my head. "I have no place to go. Not really." Sadly, it was all too true. "You go and have fun! I'll stay here and keep an eye on the hotel—whether Bernie and the others want me to or not."

"Go, girl!" said Rhonda, giving me a high five.

CHAPTER TWENTY-FOUR

I lay in bed, waiting for a phone call from Vaughn. With the four-hour time difference, it meant my staying up later than normal, hoping for a last call before they headed out of phone range.

The trill of the phone jolted me out of my half-awake state. Smiling, I reached for the phone.

"Hello, fisherman! How was your day?"

"Great," said Vaughn. "We all caught some nice king salmon and then Jim, our guide, fried some over the fire. Talk about delicious! Best I've ever had!"

I smiled at his enthusiasm.

"Ann, I've been thinking that we should take an Alaskan cruise to introduce you to some of the scenery up here."

"Sounds like fun."

He chuckled. "I can't wait to show you everything. How's Robbie?"

"Good. We've been doggy-sitting Trudy for a couple of afternoons. Robbie loves her so much I wonder if we should consider getting a little dachshund of our own. What do you say?"

"If they're all as cute and as smart as Trudy, I think it's a good idea. Every boy needs a dog. We had a lab for Ty and Nell, but I don't want a dog that big right now."

"Hmmm. I think I'll look into it further then."

We went on to other subjects, and much too soon it was time to say good-bye.

"I'll call when I can, but it's going to be a while. Love you,

Ann. You've made me so happy. I can't wait until you're completely mine."

"Love you too, Vaughn. More than you know." Unexpected tears stung my eyes. There were times when I didn't know how I'd ever survive without him. He made me feel so loved, so complete. I hung up feeling blue at the idea of not seeing or hearing from him for several days.

With both Vaughn and Rhonda away, days crept by. I kept busy doing things around the house, checking in at the hotel, and building a stronger relationship with Robbie.

One afternoon Angela called me. "Hi, Ann. I'd love to have you come to lunch. Reggie went back to school to finish up the last of his courses before graduation, and I need some good company."

"I'd love it," I said, pleased by the invitation. "What time do you want me there?"

"How about one. Evan should be down for a nap. That will give us a chance to talk."

"I'll be there," I said, cheered by her invitation.

Later, as I pulled up to Angela's house, I couldn't help thinking of Liz. It would be wonderful if she would live close by one day. If Chad's and her relationship continued the way it appeared to be going, it was a real possibility. As I climbed out of the car, Angela appeared at the front door and waved to me. Smiling, I went to meet her. "Hey, girl! You're looking great!"

She grinned. "Not like the movie stars who make it seem so easy, but I'm working on it."

"At four weeks postpartum, you're doing fine," I assured her. I placed an arm around Angela's shoulder and we went inside.

I paused. The house was spotless—everything in its proper place. "You've made the house so attractive. What did Katherine say when she saw it?"

Angela beamed. "My mother-in-law really liked it. Go figure."

"I'm glad you and Katherine seemed to get along when she and Arthur came to see the baby," I said, as I followed Angela into the kitchen.

"Me too," responded Angela. She indicated a chair for me at the kitchen table and then stood to face me. "But, Ann, it's not going to be an easy relationship. Katherine was excited about the baby, but both she and Reggie's father are still upset by the idea of our living here. Arthur said some very unkind things about Will. I'm glad my mother wasn't around to hear it. But Reggie likes and respects Will a lot. Will has a very good reputation and that goes a long way with my husband."

Angela tossed a salad in a wooden bowl and placed it and a basket of French bread on the table. "Bubbling water okay?"

At my nod, she retrieved a bottle of water out of the refrigerator, filled two glasses with ice, and poured some of the water into each glass.

"Everything looks wonderful," I said, impressed by her easy manner in the kitchen. It too was spotless and so tidy that one would hardly know a baby was in the house.

"Super simple, but I do love a nice salad," Angela said, taking a seat opposite me.

I took a bite of the salad she served me, and murmured, "Yummy!"

"Thanks." Her eyes shone. "I'm trying to make everything perfect so that Reggie and his parents have nothing to complain about."

Whoa! "How long are you going to be able to keep that up?" I asked in what I hoped was a pleasant, conversational voice even as I filled with dismay at the thought of such pressure.

Angela frowned. "What? You don't think I can do it?"

I reached over and squeezed her hand, and said gently, "I don't think you need to do it."

She gave me a quizzical look.

"Sweetie, you're wonderful as it is. Just do the best you can with you, the house, and the baby, and let the rest go."

Angela set down her fork. "Reggie doesn't know what it's like not to have a maid to pick up after him. It bothers him if things are too messy."

"So, you want to be his maid?" I loved this daughter-of-my-heart and hoped I wasn't being too outspoken.

A look of surprise crossed Angela's face. "Oh my Gawd! That's what I'm doing, isn't it? Becoming a maid on top of everything else."

"I'm not sure, but it sounds that way."

"Thanks, Ann. I appreciate your willingness to be so open with me. When you and Mom became partners, it was a good thing for both of us."

I blinked back the sting of tears. I'd been feeling so lost with Vaughn and Rhonda away that this connection with Angela meant more than a simple friendship.

"How's that baby of yours?" I asked on a brighter note.

A smile stretched across Angela's face. "He's such a good baby," she said, and then chuckled. "I think he knew he had to be good with Katherine around. That woman wants everything on a tight schedule. I've tried to keep it up, but sometimes it doesn't make sense."

"Right. Keep that in mind."

She nodded. "How are things with Robbie? He's such a cute little boy, but Liz has told me stories about how spoiled he was. I guess Kandie couldn't handle him. Is he changing with you?"

"He seems to be doing much better. He likes to know the rules, and though he fights them sometimes, he seems to understand when he's corrected." I grinned. "Actually, I adore him. He's funny and cuddly and bright. It's such a surprise to have a toddler again."

"I know how much it means to Liz to have you adopt him. She loves him, but would rather be his sister than his mother. I don't blame her. She told me she'll always feel a little guilty about it, but she is pretty sure her father would understand it's best for Robbie. I like her honesty."

"Me too," I said. It made me happy that Vaughn and I could give Robbie the gift of a good home and Liz, the gift of completing her education.

The baby's cry came through the baby monitor.

A smile lit Angela's face. "I'll go get Evan. I put him in one of the little outfits you gave him. I want you to see it on him."

While Angela went to get her baby, I put the dirty dishes in the sink, then stepped outside to the pool patio. *It's a wonderful house*, I thought, so pleased that Rhonda had Angela living near her. I hadn't mentioned Rhonda's difficulties to Angela and wouldn't.

Angela appeared, and I went inside to see the baby. He'd grown a lot since I'd last seen him over two weeks ago. Then, I'd thought he looked a lot like his father. Now, I could see a bit of Rhonda in him and knew she'd be pleased to hear it.

"He's adorable," I said, taking him from Angela. "And the outfit looks great on him." The white onesie was designed to look like a shirt, complete with blue bowtie. It was a bit cutesy, but it worked with Evan's broad chest and round tummy.

I held the baby while Angela prepared formula. Unlike her mother, Angela had problems nursing from the beginning. Her pediatrician finally said to try formula. That seemed to be working fine.

Angela and I chatted for a bit while she fed the baby, and then I bid her good-bye. Checking my watch, I decided to swing by the hotel and check a few numbers before going home to Robbie.

When I walked through the hotel kitchen to get to my office, Consuela stopped what she was doing and ran over to me. "Hi, Annie. So good to see you. I've missed you here these past few mornings."

I hugged her. "Rhonda and I are trying to let you and Bernie and the others carry on without us being here. But it's hard to let go."

"Rhonda's away?"

"Yes, she left a few days ago. She took the baby to see her brother Richie. You remember him, don't you?"

Consuela chuckled. "Of course. He's just like Rhonda."

We smiled at one another. Richie and Rhonda were like two peas in a pod—same looks, same wacky sense of humor, same big, loving hearts.

I grabbed a cup of coffee and carried it into the office. It had been awhile since I'd reviewed the schedule of events, and I wanted to see how I could help. We'd canceled our meeting with Bernie.

As I looked through the records, I saw that weddings continued to be the bulk of our events. I was pleased to see two new weddings scheduled for June, filling in a few Sundays.

A knock sounded at the door. Bernie stuck his head inside the office. "Can I speak to you, Ann?"

"Sure. C'mon in."

He came inside and took a seat. It seemed so odd to see him without Trudy at his feet. But she, dear dog, was visiting

Robbie at my house.

"What is it?" I asked after he was settled in his chair.

"We've had some people snooping around recently, taking photographs and even wandering the halls, peeking into guest rooms when the housekeepers have doors open. I don't know for sure, but I suspect they're looking at this property. Are you planning to sell it?"

"Nooo. Why?"

"If you are, I'm concerned about my job. I want to continue managing the hotel."

I leaned back in my chair. "Bernie, if we ever decide to sell the property, we'll be the first to tell you. But I think you understand that this hotel is more than a structure or a business; it's the heart and soul of Rhonda and me."

"Yes, I know. Thank you for being so honest with me."

"I always will be honest with you, which leads me to a very different issue. Vaughn and I are considering getting a dog like Trudy. Do you know of a good breeder in the area?"

A pained expression crossed Bernie's face. "I wasn't going to bring it up just yet, but would you consider keeping Trudy as yours? It turns out that Annette is allergic to both cats and dogs. She's been pretty miserable lately but didn't want to tell me. I finally had to ask her what was wrong and she confessed that it's Trudy. Annette loves Trudy; she just can't be around her for any length of time."

"Oh no! I'm so sorry to hear this, Bernie."

He looked down at the floor and then raised his face. His eyes were suspiciously watery. "Will you consider it? Taking Trudy? If you did, I could see her from time to time."

"Oh, Bernie, I don't even have to think about it. Trudy is perfect for us. She and Robbie love one another. And I promise we'll give her a good home."

Fighting emotion, he managed to say, "Okay, then. I'll

bring all her stuff to your house later today."

He left, and I picked up the phone to call Vaughn to tell him about our acquisition. His phone rang and rang. Disappointed, I left a message for him.

After reviewing financial reports, I went home appeased. There was no need for me to worry. Bernie was doing a good job of overseeing the hotel.

As I entered the house, Trudy ran to me, wagging her tail and letting out little yips of welcome. I leaned over and stroked her silky head. "Hey, little one. You're going to live here with us. What do you think of that?"

Trudy licked my hand, sat down on the kitchen floor and gazed up at me with what I could only describe as a doggy grin.

Laughing, I picked her up and hugged her to me.

When Robbie came running into the kitchen, Trudy wiggled to get down. I set her on the floor and the two of them ran in circles around me, filling the air with shrieks of glee and responding barks.

Elena came into the room. "Hi, Ann! What's all the commotion?"

I grinned. "It's these two. They love playing together."

"They've become such good friends, it's adorable."

"Trudy is about to become ours. It turns out that Bernie's woman friend is allergic to dogs. Sadly, Bernie has to give Trudy up."

Elena shook her head. "He must be heartbroken. Trudy is a real treasure."

Watching Robbie and Trudy play together, I was pleased her new home would be with us.

As I was changing into a bathing suit, Liz called. "Hi, Mom. I heard from the court. They want you and Vaughn to set a time to appear regarding Robbie's adoption. It's just a formality, but it's important."

"Okay. Vaughn is away, but when he comes back, we'll make those arrangements. If you don't mind, email me the information. Any other news?"

"As a matter of fact, there is. I'm going to spend the summer in Sabal working with Chad on growing his business. I'm glad I've been taking marketing courses because I've got some good ideas for him."

"Great, your room is ready for you anytime."

"Uh, Mom, the thing is I will be staying with Chad. Remember? We need to be sure of our relationship before moving forward with the idea of getting engaged."

"But, Liz ..."

"It's not all about the benefits of our friendship; it's about finding out what the other person will be like as both a business partner and a life partner. I've seen what a bad decision can do to a person and I don't want to end up like Dad—broken, broke and unhappy."

I held back a sigh. "You're an adult and can make your own choices ..."

"I know, Mom," said Liz, cutting off my remarks. "I hope you understand where I'm coming from. It's all happening fast, but I've never felt this way about anyone else."

"It will be wonderful to have you around."

"Yeah, I'm pretty excited about it. How's my baby brother?"

"Robbie is doing fine." I gave her the news about Trudy. "It's great to see them together. The two of them have already bonded."

"I bet," Liz said, laughing softly. "And how's Vaughn?"

"Having the time of his life. I miss him, of course, and can't wait to have him back home with me. Our wedding is so close."

"Speaking of your wedding, I ordered the casual dress you want me to wear. I love it! It fits perfectly."

"Oh, I'm glad," I said. "It's a simple ceremony, but I thought the dress was perfect for you."

After we'd chatted some more, I hung up. My thoughts returned to the wedding. As the time was drawing closer, I was becoming more and more anxious for the ceremony that would bind Vaughn and me together.

CHAPTER TWENTY-FIVE

Long after Robbie was safely tucked away in his crib for the night, I said goodnight to Elena and went into my bedroom to read. I changed into pajamas and climbed into bed eager to finish my book.

When I heard scratching at the door, I got up to check it out.

As I opened the door, Trudy marched into the room on her short, crooked legs, went over to the bed, and sat by it, giving me a steady look.

I walked over to her. "Really? You think you're coming into bed with me?"

Trudy wagged her tail so hard she almost tipped over.

I caught her in my arms and lifted her onto the bed. *What harm could a little cuddle time with her do?* I asked myself.

Climbing into the bed, I moved her aside and sat back on my pillow. The romance I was reading was a good one—a secret hung in the balance. I had to finish it before I could think about going to sleep. I was deep into the book when I realized I was clinging to the edge of the bed. Trudy was stretched out beside me, softly snoring.

I moved her over and resumed reading.

When I closed the book—happily ever after achieved—Trudy was still asleep beside me. I turned out the light and rolled onto my side. Trudy moved so that she was spooned against me. I trailed my hand down her sleek coat.

She made little puppy sounds in her sleep and moved closer.

###

The feel of something wet on my cheek jolted me awake. Startled, my eyes sleepily focused on a long dark nose, two bright eyes and a pink tongue. "Ugh. Good morning, Trudy."

I glanced at my bedside clock. Six AM.

"Better go back to sleep," I murmured, and rolled over.

Trudy climbed on top of my body and nudged my face with her cold nose.

I sat up. "Really?"

She wagged her tail and gave me a bright look.

I got out of bed, lifted her down and followed her to the kitchen door. "All right. Hold on. I'll get your leash."

Hoping nobody would see me, I stepped outside in my pajamas.

My next door neighbor, in jogging clothes, waved at me. "New dog, huh?"

I smiled and then hissed at Trudy to hurry up and do her business.

By the time Trudy had finished walking over every inch of our front yard to find the "perfect spot," I heard Robbie calling for me inside the house.

We hurried into the kitchen.

Tears spilling down his rosy cheeks, Robbie stood in the kitchen, holding onto his stuffed giraffe,

"I'm here, Robbie. I'm here."

I swept him up in my arms. I knew from talking to Barbara Holmes, the psychiatrist I'd used for Tina, and then Robbie, that he had a fear of being left alone as a result of losing his parents.

"You're all right, Robbie," I said, hugging him close.

Trudy whined at my feet.

"Down," said Robbie.

I set him down on the floor.

Robbie knelt beside Trudy and patted her on the head. "Here, Trudy. Here." He laid his head against hers, and she turned her face to give him a kiss.

Seeing their interaction, I was glad we'd taken in Trudy, even if, when sharing the bed with me, she was the biggest hog in the world.

As the next days passed, I was often reminded of the time when Liz was a toddler. Then, I'd been a very young mother who was trying her best to keep both her baby and husband happy while helping him build a business. Now, I was beginning to realize the benefit of having children at a much younger age. The difference between boys and girls was something else. Liz had liked to play quietly with her dolls and stuffed animals or try to read books by herself. Robbie wasn't the same quiet boy I'd first met in Boston. Now that he was comfortable in his new home, he was on his feet, running, climbing, and noisily "driving" cars and trucks, with Trudy at his heels.

Even though I was busy, I missed Vaughn. I tried calling him again and left a message on his cell, wishing him a good time and asking him to call when he could.

Rhonda phoned me one morning. "Hi, Annie. It's been so nice being with my brother's family, that I've decided to stay a few extra days. Will is going to join us. You don't mind holding down the fort?"

At the sound of the happy lilt in her voice, I smiled. "Not at all. But when you come back, I'm going to need your help to get ready for my wedding." A nervous flutter crossed my shoulders. I'd wanted a very casual wedding, but as I awaited word from Vaughn, I thought I might want to do things a little differently—more memorable.

#

One afternoon, as I was watching Robbie take swimming lessons from Troy, my cell rang. I jumped up to get it. It was Angela.

"Hi, sweetie! How are you?"

"Can you come over? Mom's gone, and I really need to talk to someone."

My heart stopped and sprinted ahead with concern. "Is everything all right?"

"Sorta," Angela said in a troubled tone that belied the word.

"Sure, hon. I'm on my way." I said goodbye to Robbie, Troy, and Elena and hurried to the kitchen door. Trudy trotted after me and gave me a hopeful look.

"No, Trudy. Stay."

Her ears drooped, and she dropped her head dramatically.

"Another time. Not now," I said and left the house.

As I pulled up to Angela's house, I wondered what was troubling her so much that she'd called me. But then, we were exceptionally close.

I got out of the car and went up to the front door.

Before I could knock, Angela opened the door.

I stared at her tear-streaked face with concern. "Honey, what is it?"

"I can't do this anymore." She took my arm and led me into the house. As I followed her through the living room to the kitchen, I noticed empty coke cans sitting on the living room table, pillows on the floor.

In the kitchen, dishes were stacked in the sink, several empty baby bottles lay atop the granite counter, and dirty pans sat on top of the stove.

"How long has this been going on?" I asked, surprised by the changes.

"For a couple of days," Angela said, sinking down into a kitchen chair. "Evan has decided to stay awake all night and sleep during the day when he isn't crying to be fed. Reggie is staying a few extra days in Boston to be with his buddies, and Mom is gone. What am I going to do? I'm so tired I can hardly see, and I can't keep cleaning the house all the time. Like you said, it's like I'm Reggie's maid." Her breath caught in a sob. "And he isn't even here."

"Oh, honey. I'm sorry." I wrapped her in my arms and hugged her shaking shoulders.

"I'm a terrible mother, huh?" she said between sobs.

"No. You're a very tired new mother. Why don't I send Elena over here to help you with Evan for a couple of days? She can make sure you catch up on your sleep. Then Reggie will be home to help you."

She lifted her wet face. "Would you? Could you?"

"Sure," I said. "Elena is a wonderful person. I'm sure she'll be willing to step in and help."

When I called Elena, she seemed genuinely happy to move into Angela's house for a couple of days.

I helped Angela clean up the kitchen and straighten up the house, then prepared to leave.

"Thanks so much, Ann. You're such a treasure," Angela said, giving me a hug.

"Love you," I said. "Now, I'd better go so Elena is free to come here."

We hugged goodbye, and I left feeling better about things. Angela was just tired and missed her mom.

With Elena at Angela's, my time was filled with taking care of Robbie and checking in with Bernie at the hotel from home. I realized my days of practically living at The Beach House

Hotel were over. I missed it. During those times when Robbie was napping or asleep at night, the house seemed too big, too quiet. And me, too lonely.

As Robbie was napping one afternoon, I settled on the couch to read a book. I was in a good part when the trill of my cell phone broke the silence, startling me.

I raced into the kitchen where I was charging the phone. I checked caller ID and eagerly picked up the call.

"Liz! How are you?"

"Mom, where are you?" she said, her voice wobbly.

"At home with Robbie. Why?"

"You need to turn on the television to the entertainment station. I'm catching a plane to Florida this afternoon."

"Why? What's going on? I thought you were going to drive home when your classes were over."

Liz let out a sob. "Turn on the television, Mom. I'm going to hang on while you do."

A picture of Vaughn flashed in my mind. Feeling as cold as a northern winter, I stumbled into the family room, clicked on the television, and turned to a news channel. A picture of Alaska was up on the screen, and an announcer said, "The plane carrying producer Sam Nichols, Vaughn Sanders, and their pilot guide was last seen leaving a small airstrip northwest of Denali National Park. Weather in that area is very unpredictable. On the day of their flight, a sudden snow storm came up. Since then, the weather has been unusually cold, rainy, and foggy, making a search for them difficult."

I dropped the phone on the floor and ran to the bathroom, where I emptied my stomach. The dream I'd had of Vaughn earlier came back to me. A throbbing worry pounded in my brain, making me feel as if I was going to get sick again. Tears rolled down my cheeks. *I should have begged him to stay home.*

When I was able to make my way back to the family room, I heard Liz screaming through the phone. "Mom! Mom! Are you all right?"

Feeling as if I had no strength left in me, I picked up the phone. "I'm here, Liz."

"I'll be there this evening. I've made arrangements with Tim to pick me up. Don't worry. They'll find Vaughn and the others. Love you, Mom. I've got to catch my flight."

She hung up, and I collapsed against the couch cushions. Deep, heart-breaking sobs echoed in the room around me.

"Ann?"

I caught my breath and turned.

Angela walked into the room. "Liz called me. She wants me to stay with you until she gets here. My mother is on her way too."

She sat on the couch beside me and I allowed her to pull me into her arms.

"Oh, Ann. I'm so sorry, I can't imagine how you feel. But I truly believe they'll find them. And, remember, Vaughn is tough."

I closed my eyes and willed myself to be strong. I told myself if I was strong, then Vaughn would be. I dabbed my eyes with a tissue Angela handed me and sat up. Drawing several deep, shaky breaths, I sifted through the reporter's information in my mind. A new thought occurred to me. If he was in a big tourist area, phone service might have been available.

I jumped to my feet. "My phone! Where's my phone!"

Angela picked up my cell from the floor and handed it to me.

I checked, but I hadn't missed a phone call or a message from Vaughn.

"What am I going to do?" I asked Angela, holding back a

sob with effort. "I can't just sit here and do nothing."

"Let's try to get in touch with Vaughn's company in New York to see what information they might have," Angela suggested.

"Good idea." I punched in the number for Roger Sloan, a producer of the show. I'd once vowed to never speak to Roger again for his malicious attempt to ruin Vaughn's reputation, but of all the people I could think of connected to the show, he was the best choice for information.

He picked up right away. "Hi, Ann. We're extremely concerned about Vaughn and Sam. Any word from Vaughn? Any guess as to what might have happened?"

Disappointment caught a sob in my throat. "No. I was hoping you had news of them for me."

"Sam called me a couple of days ago to say they were taking some extra time to fly north to check out a camp in a wildlife area. That's why we weren't concerned when he didn't call back like he said he would. We figured they had no phone service. We're trying to get through to the people at Denali Park."

My stomach churned. "Wildlife area? That sounds pretty dangerous."

"I know. I hate to think of a plane going down in a location like that. Listen, I have to go. I promise to call you if we get any news. I ask you to do the same for me. Okay?"

"Sure." Tears stung my eyes as I hung up. Any wildlife area in Alaska surely contained bears or heaven knew what.

"What's wrong?" asked Angela.

As I filled her in, I heard Robbie stirring.

"Guess I'd better get him up," I said.

"Want me to do it?" asked Angela.

I shook my head. "He's going through a phase where he wants to be sure I'm around."

She came with me as I walked to Robbie's room. When I opened the door, Trudy ran over to me for an ear scratch. Robbie liked her to sleep in his room when he went down for a nap.

"Mommy! I want down!" said Robbie, holding his arms out to me. He stared at Angela.

"Okay. Remember Angela? She's here to say hi to you."

He gave her a steady stare and then his lips curved into a smile that lit his face.

She laughed. "Robbie, you're such a charmer."

I changed his diaper and then Angela took Robbie's hand. "Come get a snack with me."

He turned around and looked at me.

"It's okay, Robbie. Mommy needs to lie down for a bit." Shock waves were flooding through my body, making me feel weak and nauseous.

I made it to my bedroom. There, I climbed under the covers fully clothed and attempted to stop the shivers that ran through me.

Angela knocked and came inside the room. "I've brought you some water, ginger ale, and a few saltines." She set them down on the nightstand next to me and then adjusted the blinds on the windows until the room was enveloped in a soothing, light gray.

"Is there anything else I can do for you? I'll take care of Robbie and Trudy."

"Thanks, honey. That's so sweet of you," I murmured, fighting fresh tears at her kindness.

She left, and I lay in bed, praying as hard as I'd ever had. Memories of Vaughn and me together assailed me in bittersweet waves—the sweetness tempered by the gut-wrenching idea of losing him.

CHAPTER TWENTY-SIX

I was awakened by the sound of Rhonda's voice. "Okay, where is Annie?" she said.

Fighting tears, I lay back against my pillow. Rhonda had left her family to come to me.

My bedroom door opened.

Seeing me awake, Rhonda rushed to my bedside and swept me up into a hug. "Annie, I heard about Vaughn's plane missing. I'm here for you. We'll hang on together until they find him. I'm sure he's okay. He's gotta be. I feel it."

"Aw, Rhonda, that's so sweet, but how can you be sure of such a thing?"

She gave me a steady look. "I sometimes have these feelings," she said seriously. "And I know he's alive. Trust me on this."

I let out a shaky sigh and mentally grabbed hold of this comforting thought. "If he's alive, then where is he? Do you have a feeling on that?"

She shook her head. "Nope. But they'll find him."

I gulped back a sob. "I don't think I can live without him, Rhonda. Vaughn is everything to me."

"I know how you feel, hon. Now, I want you to get up and have something to eat. We've gotta be ready when we get the news."

Energized by her enthusiastic confidence, I climbed out of bed and hugged her. "Thanks. I needed that."

We went into the kitchen and I looked around. "Where's Willow?"

"She's home with Will. We all came home together." She gave me a shy smile. "Will said he couldn't wait to have some time alone with me. Isn't that so sweet?"

I smiled. "So things are more or less back to normal between the two of you?"

Her cheeks grew pink. She bobbed her head. "Are they ever!"

I chuckled, pleased to see my dearest friend so happy. Surprised by the tears that filled my eyes and tumbled down my cheeks, I stumbled to a kitchen chair and sat down.

Rhonda sat down beside me and took hold of my hand. "When was the last time you ate, hon?"

I shrugged. What I'd eaten for breakfast and lunch had been thrown up.

Rhonda got to her feet. "Sugar and protein. That's what you need. How about some orange juice and a scrambled egg?"

"I'll try it, but my stomach is a mess of nerves."

Robbie and Angela appeared. Seeing me, Robbie ran over to me. "Mommy, up."

I lifted him into my lap and wrapped my arms around him. A shiver rippled across my shoulders at the realization that I might be raising this child alone.

Rhonda glanced over at me, reading my thoughts. "Don't even go there, Annie. Vaughn is coming home to you." She turned to Angela. "Any more news?"

Angela shook her head. "The dense fog is lifting. They're searching for them now."

Robbie twisted around in my lap and patted my cheek. "Love Mommy."

I forced a smile. "Mommy loves Robbie."

Sensing my sadness, he lay his head against my chest and wrapped his arms around me the best he could. His tender gesture brought the sting of tears to my eyes, but I refused to let them fall, even as Trudy looked up at me with inquisitive eyes and then lay at my feet.

"I've suggested that Robbie have a sleepover with me," said Angela. "He knows Elena is there, and I think he'd have a good time." Her voice rose with cheerful enticement.

"A sleepover? How fun!" I said with fake enthusiasm. I didn't think Robbie should be around me if I got bad news. It might bring up his parents' deaths and the memories we were trying to overcome.

My cell phone rang. I grabbed it.

"Mom? It's Liz. My flight's been delayed, so I'm not going to get there until late tonight. I'm sorry, but I'm there with you in spirit. No news yet?"

"No," I choked out. "Be safe, honey. I'll see you when you get here."

Rhonda gave me a questioning look when I hung up. "Liz's flight is delayed. She sounded frantic."

"She loves Vaughn too."

"Yes, they became close over spring break, dealing with Robbie and all." In my mind's eye, I could see them in the sailboat together, laughing and talking. Bile rose in my throat.

With Trudy in my lap, I sat in front of the television in the family room staring blankly at some goofy talk show, waiting for Liz to come home. I hadn't realized how missing one member of my family could make me sick with worry about another. I knew Robbie was safe, but I wanted Liz safely on the ground and with me.

Trudy sensed my unhappiness and kept looking up at me, then resting her head against my chest. I stroked her back, grateful for her comfort. Rhonda had gone home to feed Willow but promised to return. Will announced he would pick

Liz up at the airport no matter what time she got in—a gesture so sweet it had threatened to create more tears.

Memories of good times with Vaughn played over and over in my mind. After being so hurt by Robert, I hadn't wanted anything to do with another man—until I met Vaughn. Fame hadn't made him an egotistical jerk like so many other stars. Fame had given him confidence doing a job he found interesting and rewarding. It had brought its share of discomfort too. People recognized him wherever he went, which meant a lack of privacy I still found unsettling. Now, however, I hoped that same adoration from fans meant their prayers for his safety would join mine.

In the early morning hours, when at last I heard the sound of a car pulling into my driveway, I got up to greet Liz. Before I reached the kitchen, she'd opened the door and was rushing toward me.

"Mom! I'm so sorry!" she cried, giving me a hug. "No more news?"

I shook my head. "It's too dark for them to see. They'll search again in the morning. Thankfully, they have a lot more daylight in Alaska at this time of year than we do."

"Vaughn will be all right, won't he? He's strong and smart." Tears streamed down her cheeks. "I don't want to lose him too."

"We just have to hope that he and the others are all right, that it was simply a mechanical failure and they landed safely somewhere." Saying the words brought me no comfort. Life wasn't that simple.

Will, who'd been standing by silently, cleared his throat. "Is there anything I can do for the two of you? Rhonda will be back as soon as she can."

"Thanks, Will. Tell her to get a good night's sleep and we'll see her in the morning."

Will shook his head. "I'll tell her, but you know Rhonda, she'll want to be right here in case you need her."

I smiled. "I know. I'd feel the same way if the situation was reversed. Tell her I'm counting on her for breakfast."

He gave me a little salute and left.

Liz picked up Trudy and hugged her. "Can she sleep with me tonight?" Tears filled her eyes again. "Not that I'll do much sleeping. I'm so scared."

"Me too. But now that you're home, I guess we'd better at least lie down so we can face tomorrow. Robbie's at Angela's house for the night, but he needs to be with us."

The sun was just rising, painting the sky a soft pink, when I got out of bed and padded into the kitchen. Too exhausted to do much else, I fixed myself a cup of coffee and settled in a chair at the table. Staring out at the small sailboat tied up at our deck, I wondered if Vaughn would ever sail it again.

I heard a tapping at the door, and then Rhonda walked into the room.

"Hi, hon! How are you?" She gave me a hug. "I know it's early, but I couldn't stay away. I figured if you weren't up, I'd go ahead and fix a nice breakfast for you. You need to eat to keep up your strength." She stared at the blank screen of the television. "Oh my God! Haven't you heard? They've found the plane."

I jumped to my feet. "No! Where?"

Rhonda followed on my heels as I ran into the family room to turn on the big-screen TV.

An announcer was just ending a blurb on the news. "The plane is in an isolated area not easily accessed by vehicles. A helicopter is dropping searchers and rescue workers as close as possible to the wreckage site. They will hike to the plane to check for survivors. They've been unable to make contact with anyone there."

I stared at the silver spot sitting among what looked like a dense forest on the screen and closed my eyes. "He's dead!"

Rhonda placed a hand on my shoulder. "You can't think that way, Annie. He's alive until we know differently."

I collapsed onto the couch and held my head in my hands. An image of Vaughn smiling at me appeared in my head and quickly disappeared. I looked up at Rhonda with confusion. "I have no idea what it means, but I just saw Vaughn smiling at me."

"Oh, honey. That's good. That's very good," Rhonda said. "We can't do anything sitting here waiting for another announcement. Let's get some food in you."

"Okay. Then, I want to bring Robbie back here. He needs to be with us."

"I'll call Angela. You go get dressed for the day, and I'll start breakfast."

I left Rhonda and entered my bedroom. I sat down on the bed and leaned back against the pillows. Turning on my side, I clutched one of the pillows, wishing it was Vaughn. "Come home to me! *Please,* Vaughn, *please!*"

The image of the broken plane stayed frozen on my brain. Sobbing softly, I uttered another prayer for Vaughn's safety and those with him.

Rhonda tapped on the door. "How are you doing?"

"I'm going to take a shower," I answered, forcing myself to my feet to head into the bathroom.

Moments later, standing under a stream of warm water, I felt the tension in my body ease. I straightened as a new sense of purpose filled me. I was going to Alaska to be with Vaughn. The horrible waiting around for news in Florida was too painful.

I dressed and entered the kitchen, intent on telling Rhonda about my decision. Oblivious to the toast burning in the toaster oven behind her, she was staring at the television on the counter.

My stomach fell to my knees. "What's wrong?"

"They've reached the plane. Two of the people are dead."

"Oh my God! Have they identified the bodies?"

Rhonda turned to me. "Yes, the pilot and Sam Nichols are dead."

"Oh, that means..."

"And Vaughn is missing."

Trembling, too weak to stand, I sank into a chair. *Vaughn missing? How could he survive on his own? The weather, wildlife, the cold—it would be impossible!*

I shivered when I realized that the picture on the screen showed just remnants of what used to be a plane. Fire had damaged the wreckage. "Why would he go off on his own? Wouldn't it be better for him to stay with the plane?"

Rhonda sat down beside me. We stared at the screen. It showed men rooting around the area looking for clues.

"Now back to our regular programming," came a voice over the television. "We'll keep you posted on any updates. Sam Nichols was a highly respected person in the entertainment industry, along with Vaughn Sanders, the actor everyone loved."

I gripped Rhonda's arm. "He's talking about Vaughn as if he were dead."

"Yeah, I know. The bastard. Until we know for sure, he's alive. Right, Annie?"

Unable to answer, I simply nodded, hoping it was true.

CHAPTER TWENTY-SEVEN

After dutifully trying to eat breakfast and failing, I went into Liz's room to get Trudy. When I opened the door, the dog wagged her tail and then burrowed deeper under the covers. Liz stirred.

"Hi, Mom! Any news?"

I told her what I knew and lifted Trudy into my arms. "All we can do is pray and wait."

Liz raised her body up on one elbow. "Mom? I dreamed about him last night. I think he's going to be all right."

"I hope so," I said, wondering what my vision of Vaughn had meant—wishful thinking or a warning that he was already gone.

I was walking Trudy out in front of the house when Elena drove into the driveway with Robbie. Seeing me, his face lit with such excitement, my heart filled.

After Elena helped him out of the car seat and set him down on the ground, he ran toward me. "Hi, Mommy!"

Trudy barked and jumped up on me as I lifted Robbie into my arms. It seemed so crazy, this life of mine. Robert and Kandie were gone, Robbie was in my life, and Vaughn was missing. It was a crazy circle of circumstances. I prayed it wouldn't end with Vaughn's death.

Chatting about his sleepover, Robbie was unaware of the dire situation.

"How did he do?" I asked Elena, ushering her inside.

"He missed you, of course, but settled right down when we played our usual bedtime games." She put her hand on my elbow, pulling me to a stop.

"Ann, I'm so sorry about Vaughn. I wish there was something I could do to help."

"Thanks," I said. "Right now, we need to keep things on an even keel here. As soon as I find out that Vaughn is alive, I'm flying to Alaska. I'll need you here."

"Okay. You've got it."

I'd just finished making my bed when my cell phone rang. Seeing the number from New York, I snatched it up.

"Ann? This is Roger Sloan, just checking in with you. As I'm sure you know by now, Sam Nichols is dead. Have you heard anything at all about Vaughn? We know they're searching for him. If he's found alive, I'm sure you'll want to go to him. I have a private jet standing by for you. Keep in touch."

Touched to the core, I managed to get out a shaky, "Thank you." Roger Sloan had been cruel to Vaughn and me in the past. This was as nice a way as any to let me know he was sorry.

I hung up the phone and returned to the kitchen where Robbie was eating his breakfast. Rhonda gave me a questioning look.

When I finished telling her, she shook her head. "Amazing. Good for him."

We left Robbie with Elena and went into the family room. Liz was sitting in one of the lounge chairs, her eyes glued to the television. "They're going to give an update on the ten o'clock news."

Rhonda and I lowered ourselves into the couch next to each other. "I have a good feeling about this, Annie."

I smiled weakly. I needed more than a good feeling. I needed to know Vaughn was alive and well.

It seemed to take forever for the news report to go through

the major headlines of the day and instant weather report before continuing with news stories.

"And now for the update on the plane crash in Alaska. The plane carrying Vaughn Sanders crashed in a remote area of Alaska. Sam Nichols, the director of the soap opera, *The Sins of the Children*, in which Sanders stars, has been declared dead, along with the pilot of the plane. Vaughn Sanders has been missing ... excuse me, folks. My producer is handing me a note."

As the announcer read the note to himself, I held my breath.

"And here it is, the very latest news. Vaughn Sanders has been found alive. He's seriously injured, but he's alive. The rescue team is carrying him out on a stretcher now. He will be airlifted to the University of Washington Medical Center in Seattle."

I clapped a hand over my heart with relief. "Thank you, thank you," I whispered over and over again.

Rhonda jumped to her feet. "Yay! I knew it!" She pulled me up and did a little dance around me. Laughing, I joined her.

Liz grabbed hold of my hand.

The three of us were dancing in the middle of the room when Elena and Robbie rushed over to us.

"Vaughn is alive! Vaughn is alive!" I cried and swooped Robbie up into my arms.

"Wonderful," said Elena. Liz took hold of her arm, and the two of them danced together while Rhonda and I caught our breaths.

When they stopped, and Elena had been filled in with the news, she said to me, "Does this mean you're going to Seattle?"

"Yes. I've got to call Roger Sloan for the details. He has a private jet waiting for me."

"Do you want me to go with you?" asked Liz.

I shook my head. "No, thanks. I have no idea what I'll be facing and how long I'll be gone. It's best for you to finish up your school year. I promise I'll keep you updated."

"I'll handle everything with the hotel," said Rhonda. "Now, let's see about your packing."

My laugh was almost giddy. "First, let me call Roger."

Before I could punch in the numbers to call him, my cell phone rang. It was Roger.

"Guess you've heard the good news," he said without identifying himself. "I've called my guy in Miami. He'll pick you up in Sabal this afternoon at one o'clock. Be ready. I'll meet you in Seattle. We're going to make this work to our advantage. It's the most we can do to make something good come out of a lousy situation."

That was more like the Roger Sloan I knew, I thought. Still, I was grateful for the easy flight to get to Vaughn. He might be alive, but I still didn't know what I faced.

Flying in a private jet would have been the thrill of my lifetime if it were being made under different circumstances. As it was, I enjoyed the ability to stretch out, the availability of food and drink, and most of all, its cleanliness. But beneath all the appreciation was the urgent need to get to Seattle to see Vaughn. Being alive was one thing. Dealing with perhaps awful, permanent injuries was another.

As we flew into Seattle, I craned my neck to take in the majestic sight of Mt. Rainier. Tall and snow-capped, the mountain was very much a part of the scenery even after we landed. Roger met me, and we headed up I-5 to the University of Washington hospital where Roger had been told Vaughn was.

The closer I got to the hospital, the more nervous I became. Vaughn's condition was listed as serious.

When we arrived, Roger spoke to someone at the reception desk, and we were ushered into a back hall onto an elevator that took us to the surgical floor.

We found seats in the surgical waiting area. Restless, Roger left me to see what information he could find out. In moments, he came back. "Dr. Rathbone will meet with us shortly. They're working on Vaughn now."

I tried to swallow in a mouth gone dry. It sounded so ominous.

Moments later, a tall, gray-haired man in scrubs entered the waiting room. "Ann Rutherford?"

"Yes," I said, and rose.

"I'm Dr. Jason Rathbone. Won't you and Mr. Sloan come with me? We'll discuss Mr. Sanders' case there."

Roger and I exchanged glances and followed Dr. Rathbone into a small conference room off the waiting room.

Dr. Rathbone took a seat opposite us at the table. "Vaughn Sanders is one lucky man. He has a concussion, four fractured ribs, and his left arm is broken. His spleen was injured, but we were able to surgically repair the tear without removing it. He's going to be very sore for some time, but he's in remarkable shape and should recover nicely. When he's out of the recovery room, you can see him."

"Thank you, doctor," I said, brushing away the tears that were spilling down my cheeks.

The doctor smiled. "He'll be glad to see you. He mentioned your name several times. Any questions?"

"Will Vaughn have a full recovery?" I asked, knowing how unhappy he'd be as a long-term patient. And then, there was our wedding to consider.

"I see no reason he shouldn't recover well," said the doctor.

"When will he be able to travel?" Roger asked. "I've arranged for private transportation to Florida for Ann and him."

"Nice," said the doctor. "I would think he'd be able to make the trip in a day or two. He'll most likely heal best at home. As you know, we don't keep patients in the hospital any longer than we have to."

"Great," said Roger. "Thank you."

After the doctor left, Roger turned to me. "We'll set up a little news conference before we head to the airport."

At my frown, he hastily added. "Whenever Vaughn feels ready, that is. He has thousands of fans waiting to hear from him."

Trying to hide my dismay, I nodded. Apparently, that was showbiz.

An aide entered the waiting room awhile later. His gaze swept the room. "Ann Rutherford?"

I stood. "Yes."

"You can come with me to see your patient."

Roger stood and joined me as I followed the aide out of the room.

"Mr. Sanders has been taken to his room," said the aide. "I'll take you to him."

Roger and I followed the aide down a series of hallways into a wing of the hospital.

My heart leaped inside me when he stopped at a door and indicated for me to enter.

I took a deep breath, stepped into the private room, and choked back a gasp. The doctor hadn't mentioned how bruised Vaughn would be. His face looked like he'd been in a boxing match that he'd lost. A series of scratches marred his cheeks, adding to the effect.

"Hi, sweetheart," I said softly as I approached him.

He gazed at me sleepily and smiled. "I knew you'd come. Oh, God, Ann! It was terrible."

"Shhh," I whispered. "We'll talk later. Right now I want you to rest. You've been through so much." Tears rolled down my cheeks. "Thank God you're alive."

"Sam and Jim didn't make it. There was nothing I could do. Not with the way the plane landed and how badly they got hurt."

I took hold of his hand and squeezed it. "I know you, Vaughn Sanders. And if you could have done anything to save them, you would have."

"That's right, buddy," said Roger, joining us. "We're just glad you made it. When you feel better, I want to hear all about it. Others and I think you're some kind of hero to have survived on your own."

"I had to," said Vaughn in a drawl induced by the drugs they had given him. "Ann and I are going to be married soon. I wouldn't miss it for the world."

A chuckle bubbled out of me. God! He was the sweetest man I'd ever known.

Vaughn smiled. "I mean it, Ann. The whole time I was shivering in the cold, the memory of us together is what kept me warm inside. You saved me."

"No, darling. You saved yourself—for me."

CHAPTER TWENTY-EIGHT

When I went to see Vaughn the next morning, he was more alert. He and I exchanged several kisses, then I pulled a chair up to his bed and sat holding his good hand. After being so afraid I'd lost him, I never wanted to let go.

"How is everything back home?" he asked. "Liz called me earlier this morning. Guess I scared her and everyone else, huh?"

"Oh yes. You have a whole bunch of people back home cheering for your recovery. And, Vaughn, thousands of fans are waiting to hear from you. Before we go home, and when you're ready, Roger Sloan is holding a press conference for you." I couldn't hide the look of distaste I felt crossing my face. "Some kind of payback for the private jet service he's offered."

"He and I have discussed it. Apparently, this is the best exposure the soap has had in some time. They're writing some of it into next season's scripts."

At my look of disgust, Vaughn continued, "I don't mind. Not really, I'm just happy to be alive."

"Of course." Tears filled my eyes. "I don't know what I'd do if anything happened to you. You're so precious to me."

He looked away and then turned back to me. "We weren't scheduled to go on that flight. At the last minute, Sam wanted to try his hand at shooting some film at a wilderness camp he'd heard about. Jim was a little leery about the weather, but Sam was one of those guys who could talk anybody into anything, and soon we were on our way."

I squeezed Vaughn's hand. "What happened?"

"We went from clear skies to cloudy, and then the plane was completely enveloped in dense fog. The engine made a funny noise, and we were suddenly spinning in the air. Next thing I knew we were nose down and Jim was hollering for us to hang on. I'm not sure what happened next. I awoke to find the front of the plane crushed with Jim and Sam inside. I was lying beside the tail of the plane, hurting like hell."

"The doctor mentioned you had a concussion," I said.

"Yes, it took me a while to be able to size up the situation. After making sure there was nothing I could do for the others, I figured I should get away from the plane. I grabbed a couple of our sleeping bags, and I made it by foot to a small, cave-like space in the side of the mountain somewhere nearby. I knew it was a wildlife area and thought it might be dangerous to stay near the dead bodies." Vaughn stopped talking and gazed into the distance.

I stood and gave him a kiss. "I know it's hard for you to talk about it."

He shook his head. "No, I need to get it out." Tears filled his eyes. "Sam and Jim were crushed inside the plane. I've never seen anything like it. I tried to pry them out of there, but I couldn't. That's when I realized I'd broken my arm. I don't know how anybody would've been able to do it. Later, as the rescuers carried me out of there, I realized the plane had caught on fire. It must have happened during one of the times I blacked out, because I wasn't even aware of it happening."

"I'm sorry you had to go through this and sorry for Sam's and Jim's families. But, Vaughn, I'm so glad you were spared."

Vaughn's face displayed the misery he was obviously feeling. "Why, Ann? Why was I saved and they weren't?"

I shook my head. "I don't know. But you're still alive and we've been given a very precious gift."

Looking totally exhausted, he fell back against his pillow.

"I promised myself that if I got out alive and saw you again, I'd make every day count." His gaze rested on me. "We have to live well, be together, raise a little boy who needs us."

"Yes, Vaughn, we do. And I promise I'll always be there for you."

He blinked away tears. "Sorry to be such a crybaby, but that means everything to me."

"And to me," I said softly as his eyes closed.

I was still sitting beside Vaughn's bed when Ty and his fiancée, June, came into the room. I stood to greet them. Tall like his father, Ty had the same dark curls and strong features. Though I hadn't yet met him, I liked him right away. I'd also never met June Chang. We'd talked on the phone, and now, seeing her in person, I could understand why Ty was so attracted to her. Her sparkling dark eyes hinted of intelligence and a sense of fun. Her wide smile lit her delicate features, inviting friendship. I was thrilled to think these two would be part of my new family.

"Glad you could come," I said quietly.

Ty introduced me to June and we exchanged quick hugs.

Vaughn stirred and opened his eyes. At the sight of his son, a grin spread across his bruised face. Ty went over to Vaughn and gave him a gentle hug. June joined them.

"I think I'll give you all some time to yourselves," I said.

"You'll be back?" said Vaughn.

"I'm just going to get some coffee."

Downstairs in the cafeteria, I grabbed a croissant and a cup of coffee and sat at one of the tables. As I lifted out my cellphone from my purse, it rang. I smiled when I saw it was Rhonda and picked up the call.

"Hi, Annie. How's it going?" said Rhonda. "Is Vaughn

looking better today? They've announced there will be a press conference sometime tomorrow. Isn't that a little soon? Give me all the details."

I couldn't help smiling. "Vaughn is looking a lot better, but, Rhonda, he feels so guilty for not being able to help the other guys. The accident trapped them in the plane, and he couldn't get them out. I believe it's going to take him some time to work through all of this."

"You're bringing him home to heal, right?"

"As soon as the doctor gives us the go-ahead, we'll take a private jet back to Florida. That's why there's a news conference." I told her about the deal Roger Sloan had worked out.

"Roger's right, though," Rhonda said. "Vaughn has a lot of fans. They want to make sure he's all right. Guess he'll continue to be the star of the show for some time to come."

"Probably." I wasn't sure how I felt about that.

"Angela just walked into the room," said Rhonda. "She wants to say hello."

"Hi, Ann," said Angela. "I just want you to know that Reggie and I are ready to help you in any way. You know how I feel about Vaughn. He was a big supporter of my marriage to Reggie. We both appreciate that, and we love you too. Tell him to hurry home."

"Thanks," I said, fighting emotion. She was such a sweet girl.

After we hung up, I called Liz. "How are you doing, hon?"

"Good. Chad has been a good support for me. How is Vaughn doing? I talked to him this morning and he sounded a little out of it." Liz laughed. "He told me how much he loves you and me and Robbie and Trudy."

I smiled. "He's so grateful to be alive. We may be home tomorrow. I'll let you know as soon as I can when we'll arrive.

How is Robbie?"

"He misses you, but we're doing our best to keep him entertained. Chad and Troy have been playing with him in the pool."

I looked up as Ty and June entered the cafeteria. "I've got to go. Ty and June are here and I want to talk to them. I love you, Liz."

We hung up, and I waved Ty and June over to my table. Ty sat in a chair opposite me while June went to get them something to eat.

"What do you think?" I asked Ty.

Ty shook his head. "Dad looks awful, and he's feeling bad about the other guys." His eyes watered. "I'm so glad he made it out alive."

"It's been such a scare for all of us. I'm so glad you're here. I know it means the world to him, and I'm pleased to have the chance to meet June. She's wonderful."

His smile was so like Vaughn's my breath caught. "Yeah," he said, "I think so too."

June joined us carrying a tray of food. She placed the food in front of Ty and in the empty space in front of her chair and, after setting the tray on another table, sat down.

"Ann, I'm so glad to meet you, even if it isn't under the best of circumstances," she said. "I'd hoped you'd be able to fly out for the engagement party, but I understand how demanding a hotel can be. I worked as a front desk clerk at one of the big hotels downtown for one summer."

I smiled. "Rhonda and I have a small operation, but it's been more than a full-time job for both of us. Now, things are changing."

"We're excited to come to your wedding, aren't we, Ty?"

"Yeah. It's great to see Dad happy again after Mom died." He gave me a steady look. "I think Mom would've liked you."

I clapped a hand to my heart. "Thank you. That means a lot to me because Vaughn really loved your mother. She sounds like such a nice person."

"Yeah, she was. But so are you." Ty smiled at me and turned to June. "And so is this woman, who's going to be my wife."

I smiled at the adoring looks they gave one another. "Looks like it's going to be a year of weddings."

"Yes," said June. "We've finally decided on a date. We checked the Chinese calendar, and April 1st is an auspicious day for a wedding."

Ty laughed. "I know it's April Fool's Day but, hey, I'm no fool. If June says it's a good day for us, I'm game."

I chuckled. It was so like something Vaughn would say.

Ty looked at me. "I guess I'm getting a new brother, along with a new sister."

"I think you and June and Nell and Liz will all get along famously. And Robbie is a cute little boy who's learning to follow rules. It was your father who thought he should be ours. As you might know, he is my ex-husband's son, which makes it a little unusual, but we've all fallen in love with him."

"So sweet," said June. "Wait until you meet my family. I'm the youngest of three."

"I can't wait," I said sincerely. "I was raised by my grandmother and it was a pretty lonely existence. Having all this family is wonderful."

"And don't forget about Nell," said Ty. "She and Clint are serious."

"Is she planning on coming here to see your father?"

Ty shook his head. "She's going to meet you in Florida. While you were here in the cafeteria, she called Dad. That's what they arranged."

"Wonderful. We'd like to be able to get back to Florida as quickly as we can."

"We're not able to stay here," said June.

"Yeah, we're flying back tonight. Is there anything we can do for you?" said Ty.

"Your being here for your father is so appreciated."

June clasped my hand. "It's for you too, Ann."

"Thank you. I'm lucky to have found a family like this."

I left Ty and June in the cafeteria and headed back to Vaughn's room.

Roger Sloan was just leaving when I arrived. "We should be all set for tomorrow's press conference. I want you to take part in it, Ann."

I shook my head. "You know I don't like that kind of publicity. I'll cheer you on from the sidelines."

He gave me a steady look. "This is Vaughn's job and he needs your help. Understand?"

At his scolding tone, I flinched. For Vaughn, I'd do it. "Okay, I'll do my best."

After he entered the elevator, I went into the ladies' room and dabbed at my eyes. I hated being in the public eye.

When I returned to Vaughn's room, he gave me a thumbs-up sign. "Roger has arranged a morning flight for us. If Doctor Rathbone says it's all right for me to travel tomorrow, we'll do a quick press conference here at the hospital and be on our way. Nice, huh?"

I forced a smile. "Very nice. It will be wonderful to have you home. I understand Nell is going to meet us there."

"She wants to make sure her Dad is okay." His voice lilted with pleasure. This time, my smile was real. His kids loved him.

We chatted about things in Florida, and when Ty and June came to his room, I stood and explained that if I was going to be present at Vaughn's news conference, I needed to buy a new outfit. I'd come unprepared.

After a successful shopping trip to Nordstrom, I returned to the hospital to find Vaughn sound asleep. Ty was sitting beside Vaughn's bed, reading a book.

"Where's June?" I whispered to Ty.

He grinned. "Visiting a friend. She'll be back soon. And then, Ann, we have to head to the airport for our flight home. You don't mind, do you?"

"Of course not. I really appreciate your making the trip. I know how much it means to Vaughn, and to me."

"We'll arrive in Florida for the wedding on the sixth. Can't wait. It should be a good time for everyone. Especially now."

"I'm so excited..."

"Excited about what?" asked Vaughn, coming awake.

"Excited to think we're going to be married in three weeks."

He grinned. "Come here, babe."

Ty looked from me to him and got to his feet. "I'll give you guys some time alone."

Neither Vaughn nor I noticed when Ty left.

Lying next to Vaughn on the bed, I was careful not to hurt him. For some time, the spleen injury and broken ribs would be painful reminders of all he'd been through. His left arm was in a cast, and though it was awkward, he could move his arm and his fingers.

Tenderly, I touched the bruises on his face. A yellowish tinge was added to a few of the spots. The scratches and shallow cuts on his face had begun to heal. I couldn't imagine what a less-healthy man might look like after such an accident.

"I should be plenty healed by the wedding," Vaughn said, trailing a finger down my cheek. "Nothing's going to stop me from going ahead with it. I meant what I said. During some of my worst moments, I thought of you, Ann."

I struggled not to cry. "So many wonderful memories of us

together flooded my mind as I worried about you and waited for news. They were the longest days of my life."

At the sound of a knock at the door, I scrambled to my feet.

Dr. Rathbone walked into the room and smiled at me. "Guess everyone is feeling better."

"Thanks for all you've done for Vaughn. We can't wait to get him back home."

He nodded. "I don't see that as a problem. If all his vitals look good, you should be able to take that jet back to Florida tomorrow." He turned to Vaughn. "How are you doing, Mr. Mayor?"

Vaughn grinned. "Don't mean to be rude, but I'll be doing better at home. Hard to get a good sleep around here."

"Ahhh, we like it when our patients begin to complain. It means they're getting better. Now let's take a look at you."

I left them alone and stood outside the room. A young, red-haired nurse hurried over to me. "You're so lucky! Vaughn Sanders is such a doll! And super handsome."

"And so hot," said another nurse, a blonde, joining us. "Is he really as sexy as they say?"

I opened my mouth and closed it.

At my distress, the blonde apologized. "I'm sorry for asking you that. That wasn't very professional of me."

"Yeah, but we both want to know," kidded the red-haired nurse, laughing.

They left, and I couldn't help the sigh that escaped me.

After Ty and June left with promises to see us soon in Florida, Vaughn and I spent a couple of quiet hours together. I read a book while Vaughn either napped or watched television. We both watched, fascinated, as *The Sins of the Children* came on in the late afternoon. I'd forgotten how easily one could get caught up in the twisting plots of the show and how real the characters seemed after a while.

Later, as we ate supper in his room, we talked about it. "Yeah, I guess that's why it's hard for some people to imagine I have a real life—with you and Liz and Robbie and my kids."

"I guess that's why the news conference is so important to the show," I said, refusing to tell Vaughn about Roger's scorn at my lack of understanding.

"It shouldn't take long and then we'll be on our way to Florida."

I nodded, hoping I wouldn't disappoint him or Roger.

The next morning, I dressed with care. Studying myself in the mirror, I thought the turquoise knit dress was perfectly suitable for this occasion and would be useful in Florida as well. I brushed my hair, applied some light makeup to my face, and glossed my lips. Though I detested the idea of a press conference, I vowed to do my best for Vaughn.

When Roger saw me enter the conference room with Vaughn, he gave me a nod of approval.

A number of reporters, mostly female, and several cameramen had been admitted to the room. Seated or standing before us, they awaited Roger's introduction.

Roger cleared his throat. "Once in a while, a television hero becomes a real hero. We at *The Sins of the Children* are very fortunate to have Vaughn Sanders here with us today. Unfortunately, Sam Nichols, the director of the show, was not so lucky. Nor was their pilot. James Evans. We extend our deepest sympathies to both families."

He took a moment of silence and then, with a flourish of his arms, indicated Vaughn. "And now, to all our millions of loyal fans, I present my hero, Vaughn Sanders. Vaughn, tell us exactly what happened in Alaska."

Vaughn squirmed uncomfortably in the wheelchair the medical staff had insisted he use. With his arm in a cast and bruises on his face, he looked like a hero, but I know how he hated to be thought of that way.

Defying orders, Vaughn painfully rose to his feet. When the applause died down, he said, "I'm no hero, but I'm really glad to be alive." He gave a very brief summary of the accident, leaving out the gory details, and then announced, "As some of you know, I'm engaged to be married to a wonderful woman in three weeks, which is what kept me going. I keep my promises. I'm noted for that, even as mayor of my television town. Right, Roger?"

Laughter broke out. Vaughn held up a hand to stop it. "I want to say how sorry I am that Sam and Jim didn't make it. Sam has always been a wonderful influence behind the show, and Jim was a great guy—full of adventure and willing to take a risk to show off the state he loved so much. I've set up a fund to help his family. Jim left a wife and five beautiful children behind. Roger has prepared an information sheet on making donations. Please share that with your readers and audiences."

"Is that your bride-to-be?" asked a reporter, nodding his head at me.

Vaughn turned to me and smiled "Ann, come join me."

Reluctantly, I went to his side and shyly faced the group of reporters.

"Ann Rutherford is the woman I'm about to marry. Isn't she beautiful?" Vaughn's comments caught me off-guard.

Face hot, I rocked back on my heels.

"Ann, promise us you'll share some pictures of the wedding with us," said a female reporter. "Women everywhere will want to see them. If they can't have Vaughn, they will want to at least share in his big day. Vaughn is every woman's dream."

Other women in the audience clapped their approval. One young female reporter even whistled, causing laughter to break out.

I dearly wanted to tell everyone that our wedding was sacred, that it was asking too much of me for them to intrude in this way. But I realized that Vaughn was truly adored, that sharing him for a few moments after I and the others had almost lost him, was something I needed to do—I owed it to the world to be generous.

Forcing a smile, I said, "I'm sure we can find a way to share some of the details with Vaughn's fans. We all love him. Me, most of all."

"Are you going to get married at your gorgeous hotel?" a reporter asked.

"Yes, The Beach House Hotel is the perfect place for a wedding," I said, moving into PR mode.

"Vaughn, how do you feel about being married to a hotel mogul?" one of the male reporters said.

Vaughn and I looked at each other and laughed.

"Mogul?" I said. "Rhonda and I have a very special, small, intimate hotel. It's worthy of many things, but making us moguls isn't one of them."

"Ann's a very successful business woman," interjected Vaughn, "and that makes me proud."

"Any more questions?" said Roger. "We've passed out a statement on Vaughn's recollection of what happened. It would be very unfair to him to keep reliving that now."

"Do you plan to go on any more fishing trips in Alaska?" one reporter asked.

"I certainly wouldn't turn down the opportunity to do so again. It's a beautiful part of our country, and the eating is superb," said Vaughn. "Now, if you will excuse me, the doctors are signaling me that my time is up."

I took hold of Vaughn's good elbow as he lowered himself into the wheelchair. Quickly, ignoring the raised hands of other reporters, I wheeled him out of the room.

In a small room down the hall, I waited with Vaughn and Roger for the crowd to leave the conference room. We wanted the freedom to go to the airport without a whole lot of reporters following us.

"Good job, Ann," said Roger. "I think Vaughn's fans like you too, which is really important to the show."

Vaughn reached up and gave my hand a squeeze. "She's a gem. I told you she'd help us."

Roger smiled pleasantly. "I certainly hope Darlene and I will be invited to the wedding."

I put a mental foot down. "Actually, it's family only, but, when things are more settled, we'll hold a big party at the hotel and then, of course, you and Darlene will be invited."

Vaughn gave me a nod of approval. Neither one of us could quite forget the distress Roger and his infidelity to his wife had caused us. Even now, Lily Dorio was suing Roger for child support for her illegitimate child.

Roger's look of surprise was quickly replaced by a neutral expression of acceptance, which I noticed with relief.

A short time later, Vaughn and I were on our way to the airport, where a private jet awaited us. This time, knowing Vaughn was with me, I could hardly wait to enjoy the privileges of flying like this.

CHAPTER TWENTY-NINE

As Vaughn and I deplaned the jet at the Sabal airport, I noticed Liz, Robbie, Angela, and Rhonda clustered together inside the terminal waiting to greet us. Tears stung my eyes. This was my family. Three years ago, I hadn't even met them, except for Liz, of course.

We entered the terminal to a round of applause not only from the family but from people standing nearby who recognized Vaughn. He gamely waved with his good arm, but the cast on his left arm seemed to emphasize the fatigue that marred his still-bruised features. He walked gingerly, protecting the broken ribs and internal injuries still healing.

Liz gave him a gentle hug around his shoulder. "So glad to have you home."

He smiled. "Me too, sweetie."

Robbie held up his arms to be picked up. "Up, Daa."

Vaughn leaned over slightly, wincing, and ruffled Robbie's hair. "Sorry, buddy. Can't do any lifting, but you'll get a special super-boy hug when we get home."

As Vaughn straightened, Rhonda beamed at him. "Boy! You sure gave us a scare, Vaughn! You look wonderfully awful, if ya know what I mean."

He laughed. "Oh, yeah." He gave Angela a wink. "Lookin' good, Mama."

She smiled and pointed behind him. Nell ran toward him.

"Surprise!" she cried, hurrying carefully into his good, outstretched arm. Nestling against him, tears ran down her cheeks.

I reached out and patted her back, understanding her relief at seeing her father alive. She lifted her head and smiled at me. "Thanks, Ann. Ty told me how Dad's thoughts of you kept him alive."

I gave Vaughn a questioning look.

"It's true. What would I do without you?"

I sighed. I loved the guy so much.

"Okay, everybody," said Rhonda to our group. "The hotel's limo is awaiting us. Angela is our driver and I'm in charge."

"Of course, you are," I teased, giving Rhonda a little hug.

Liz helped me with my suitcase, and then we joined the others in the limo.

As Angela drove us through the streets of Sabal, I thought back to the first time I'd seen this charming, small town. I'd been so unhappy, so disillusioned about life and love. Today, with Vaughn and Liz and my new family beside me, I felt so very, very blessed for all I'd been given.

The sight of our house brought a smile to Vaughn's face. "Home, sweet home," he said, struggling to blink away tears.

I gave his hand a squeeze. "Sweetheart, you're home, safe, and sound. Thank God."

As Vaughn lay asleep in our bedroom and Robbie napped in his crib, I sat with Liz and Nell in the kitchen. It felt so good to have some girl-time with two of my favorite young women.

Nell gave me a worried look. "Ann, I hope you don't mind, but Clint is coming down to Florida tomorrow. He knows how important my father and you are to me, and he says it's time to meet you both." Her cheeks flushed prettily. "I'm pretty sure he's going to ask Dad for my hand in marriage."

"Oh, darling! How wonderful!" I exclaimed. "Liz has told me how nice he is."

Liz beamed at Nell. "Yeah, I told her Clint is the kind of guy all your friends wish had a whole lot of brothers. I felt that way too before I met Chad."

"Chad? Someone new?" Nell asked, placing her elbows on the table and giving Liz an impish grin.

It was Liz's turn to blush. "Chad is the hotel's IT guy. I met him here but didn't get to really know him until we spent several days together in Boston. He's the first guy I met who I can see myself with for the rest of my life. He's sweet and kind and..." she glanced at me and away..."and very, very sexy."

"Who's sexy?" said Vaughn, hobbling into the room.

"You are!" the three of us responded together, laughing as he faked stumbling back away from our adoration.

I rose. "Sit down, hon. What can I get you? A cup of coffee? Lemonade? Iced tea?"

"Lemonade sounds great," said Vaughn, carefully lowering himself into a chair opposite the two girls. "So what's going on?"

"I think our family might be growing," I prompted.

"My boyfriend, Clint, is coming here tomorrow for the weekend," said Nell. "He wants to meet you and Ann."

Vaughn cocked an eyebrow. "Is there something behind this meeting?"

Nell smiled. "I hope so. I love him, Dad. I really, really do."

"Hmmm, I see. And what about you, Liz? Are you going to help our family grow too?"

Liz clasped her hands. "Chad and I spent a few days together in Boston, and I've fallen hard for him. We've even talked about the future. I know it's early, but I've never felt this way about any other guy." Red color crept up her neck, into her cheeks and even onto the tips of her ears. "He loves me and I love him. We stayed up all night ..."

Vaughn raised a hand. "Don't tell me!"

"Vaughn," groused Liz. "We *talked* all night…

"Maybe the first night," teased Nell. "What about the second night?"

Liz sputtered for a moment and then burst into laughter. "God! Is this what it's like to have a sister?"

Amid our laughter, I glanced at Vaughn. He'd reached his hand across the table and both Liz and Nell had gripped it. A sigh of pleasure escaped me. *So this is what our family is going to be like.*

I heard Robbie's cry through the portable monitor and went to get him. Elena was taking the day off to give us the privacy we wanted…and needed.

After changing Robbie, I brought him into the kitchen and placed him in a chair next to Vaughn's good side.

Vaughn put an arm around Robbie and drew him close. "Are you going to learn a lot from your sisters and your brother." He looked at me and winked. "I can hardly wait."

Robbie pointed to the girls. "Sissies."

"Yes," I said. "Those are your sisters."

"So, Ann, is there anything I can help you with for the wedding?" Nell said. "Three weeks isn't that far away."

"While you're both here, you can go with me to pick out a dress. Now that we're going to allow pictures for the press, I need something a little different from what I'd picked out earlier."

"Uh, oh. Are we going all fancy?" Vaughn asked.

I shook my head. "No, we're sticking with a beach wedding like we planned. I just want something a little dressier to wear."

"Okay, whatever you say," Vaughn said and winked at me.

The girls looked at each other and sighed.

#

That evening when Chad came over, I studied him as he and Liz swam in the pool with Nell. Though he wore the rugged, handsome looks of a rough and tough outdoorsman, he had a gentle nature I liked. He wasn't afraid to speak up to Liz when she tried to order him around, but he listened and oftentimes did as she asked. I knew my daughter. She was a bright, young woman with lots of ideas that she sometimes imposed on others. I wanted her to be with someone who wouldn't let her get away with being in charge too often.

"What do you think?" Vaughn said quietly, indicating the two of them horsing around.

"I like him," I said. "It's the first time Liz has ever mentioned being in love. I think Clint is going to ask you for Nell's hand. How are you going to feel about that?"

"Old," he said, chuckling. "Seriously, Nell is ready for something like this. They've been going together for almost a year now. It's too bad I haven't met him before, but I can tell he makes Nell happy. And that's what matters to me."

I took hold of Vaughn's hand. "Now that we're bringing a little one into the family, it seems our other children are leaving us. Funny how this has all worked out."

"Yeah, but it feels right to me."

The next morning, the girls and I headed to the bridal shop. Rhonda and Angela agreed to join us there, and then we were all going out to lunch.

Elise Talbot welcomed us and invited us to take seats on the assorted cream-colored couches and settees. "We'll have Ann give us a fashion show out here," she said. "Help yourself to coffee, tea, and water, or if you prefer, I have a nice white wine. It's noon somewhere!"

"Oh, let's do it!" said Nell. "We have so much to celebrate!"

"Absolutely," said Rhonda. "My best friend is getting married to one of the two best men in the world!"

While Rhonda poured wine for everyone, Elise and I went to the back of the store to look at dresses. I didn't want a long, white, wedding gown, but I wanted something a little better than a normal dress. After discussing the pros and cons of a number of dresses, Elise and I selected three to show the others. She helped me into the first one—a simple A-line in pale pink; a number of cut-out flowers edged the hem.

Careful not to show how I felt about the dress, I went into the sitting room and twirled around.

"Very nice," said Nell.

"I don't like it," said Rhonda. "What's next?"

Smiling, I went back to change into dress number two.

When I stepped into the room, all chatter stopped.

"Don't try on anything else," said Rhonda. "This is the one."

"Yeah, Mom, it's perfect!" Liz said.

A sigh of relief left me. "Thank heaven, you like it. It's my favorite too. I think Vaughn is going to love it."

"Me too," said Nell. "But, Ann, he's so in love with you, he wouldn't really care what you wore."

I swooped down and gave her a kiss on the cheek. "Thank you, sweetheart. You've always supported the idea of Vaughn and me."

"What about me?" said Rhonda. "I've supported you too."

"And me," added Angela.

I smiled. "You all have." I gazed around the room at each of them, loving each one.

After changing back into my normal clothes, I joined the others in the sitting area and, relaxed on the couch now, took a sip of the wine. As the liquid slid down my throat, I thought how wonderful it was that we were all friends—mothers and daughters.

"Shall we go on to the hotel?" said Rhonda. "Angela and I have arranged a nice luncheon for us. It's kind of a bridal luncheon. I know it's early for that, but I realize Nell and Liz will be leaving on Sunday, and I wanted to make this time count."

I left the store with Elise's assurances that after a few tiny adjustments were made, the dress would be ready for the wedding.

At the hotel, Bernie greeted us with a wide smile. "Ann, I'm honored that you are going to be our special guest today." He turned to Rhonda. "We have the small dining room all set for you. And, Angela, I'm pleased to report that the flowers you ordered arrived in time."

Bernie led us to the dining room, where Sabine greeted us. "Come, enjoy yourselves."

We sat down at a table covered with green linen. A huge, low-rise arrangement of red anthuriums graced the center of the table.

"Oh, Angela! The flowers are beautiful," I said, pulling my chair up to the table. "I'm thinking of going with a tropical theme for the wedding. I thought I'd talk to Lorraine Grace at Wedding Perfection about it. Now that I've decided to go a little more formal, I'm getting more excited." I turned to Nell beside me. "Your father and I had decided to keep everything informal until I promised the press some pictures of our day. I think they would like to see something a little more elegant. It's a good way to promote the hotel."

"Besides, it's good practice for Nell and me, when our time comes. Right, Nell?"

"Liz, are you getting married?" asked Rhonda.

Liz laughed. "Not for a while. I've got another year of

school, and Chad wants to get his business up and running well, before thinking about it."

"Chad? The same hot IT guy we use at the hotel?" Rhonda blew Liz a kiss. "Honey, I had no idea it was so serious when I saw you last. The two of you are adorable together." She elbowed Angela. "Did you know about this?"

"Of course!" Angela said.

Following a lunch of jellied consommé, cold lobster salad and a lemon tart, served with a chilled pinot grigio, I bid everyone in the dining room good-bye, excused myself, and went back to the kitchen to thank Jean-Luc for a wonderful meal.

"You're welcome, Ann," Jean-Luc said, pleased. "We're all looking forward to seeing Vaughn. We're all happy to know he's safe."

"Thank you. We're very grateful he's home. I'd like to talk to you about my wedding supper. The press has asked for details and I thought this would be a good way to feature your cuisine and the hotel."

"Good idea. Let me come up with a few suggestions for you, *non*?"

"Wonderful. In the meantime, I'll talk to Vaughn about it, though you know he's not a fussy eater."

He chuckled. "Not fussy at all."

When I went into the office to check on a few things, I found Rhonda sitting at her desk.

"Hi, partner! What's up?"

"The girls went over to Angela's house, so I decided to come here. I miss the days of our running everything, but, when I think of going back to those long, hard days, I know I can't do it all over again. Not like that."

"I know what you mean. It seems to be working out. Bernie's doing a good job of running the place. Everything looks great, and our meal was spectacular."

Rhonda checked her watch. "I'd better get home to my little girl—the demanding little princess that she is." A look of adoration crossed Rhonda's face.

"I've got to get back home too. I need to check on Vaughn and Robbie."

As I was leaving the hotel, I paused to look back at the structure that meant so much to me. It was a beautiful building in a lush setting. But what made it special to our guests was the upscale feel of the place, the superior service. A sense of pride filled me at all we'd accomplished. We'd beat all odds to come this far.

When I arrived home, Elena was in the pool with Robbie. Vaughn was stretched out on a chaise lounge beside the pool, soaking up the sun. Seeing his bruised body, my heart stuttered. I went over to his chair and took a seat on the edge of it, needing to touch him, as if by the feel of his skin beneath mine, he was safe now and forever.

As I took hold of his hand, he opened his eyes and smiled at me. "Have fun getting ready for the wedding?"

"I think you're going to like what I chose for a dress."

"Not too fancy, I hope," he said.

"Just right," I answered, feeling like a new, young bride. *Had I ever been this excited to wed Robert?* I didn't think so.

Late that afternoon, Vaughn and I waited anxiously for Clint's arrival. Liz and Chad had gone with Nell to the airport to pick him up. It had been interesting to see how well Liz and Chad got along, anticipating what each other was about to say. I loved seeing a connection like that.

"You seem a little tense," I teased, gently rubbing Vaughn's back. "Is this going to be hard for you—meeting the man who's about to steal your adoring daughter away?"

He laughed. "That obvious, huh?"

"I'm glad you're protective of Nell, but she's a smart girl. I'm sure she's chosen well."

"I guess it's hard for me to realize that both of my children and Liz will soon be completely independent with families of their own. It makes me feel so old. My fiftieth birthday is not that far away."

"Vaughn, you look terrific, well ... maybe not so much at the moment ..."

Vaughn and I both laughed.

"Seriously, Vaughn, don't think of yourself as being old. After all, you're about to become a father to a two-year-old."

Vaughn gave me a steady look. "What have we heard about that, anyway? I want to have Robbie's adoption settled before the wedding."

I frowned. "I'll call Syd Green and have him follow up on it for us. He was going to try to arrange a telephone interview in lieu of our going to court in Massachusetts. We should have heard something by now."

"Okay. Robbie's been with us for almost five months. It's time to make it permanent."

With the arrival of Clint and the others, our conversation ended, but I made a mental note to call Syd first thing Monday morning.

Elena brought Robbie to me, and the four of us went outside to greet the man who had captured Nell's heart.

Clint Dawson's appearance was a surprise to me. Tall and thin, Clint appeared to be the opposite of Vaughn, whose broad shoulders, solid body and vibrant personality filled every room.

"We're so glad to have you here," I said, shaking hands with him and looking up into his bright green eyes.

"Thanks. I'm happy to meet the family at last," he said in a melodious voice. His handshake was firm, his self-confidence in place.

Even as he shook hands with Vaughn, I remained aware of the intelligence and kindness I saw there.

Nell smiled at me as if she knew what I was thinking.

My attention turned to Vaughn and Clint, who were sizing each other up.

"I thought maybe you'd like to take a look at my sailboat," said Vaughn in an obvious attempt to get Clint alone.

Nell rolled her eyes, and I hid my laughter.

After Clint had been introduced to Robbie and Elena, he and Vaughn headed down to the dock.

Liz sidled up to me and whispered, "Vaughn already showed Chad the boat."

I turned to her with surprise. "Really? All his paternal instincts must be in overdrive."

We smiled at each other, and I studied Chad. He, like Clint, seemed a great guy. I'd been impressed with him from the beginning.

Nell came over to me. "Ann? I know you've made Elena's room available to Clint but do you mind if he shares my room with me? Dad was a little funny about it earlier, but really..."

"Oh, honey, it's all right. Your father is fighting the idea that all of you kids are or soon will be totally on your own. It's sweet, really."

"I think Clint is going to ask permission to marry me." She chuckled. "It's going to happen anyway, so I hope Dad says yes."

"He will," I said. "Or we'll both have to speak to him."

Nell impulsively threw her arms around me. "I'm so glad

he found you."

"I'm the lucky one and I know it," I said, hugging her back.

When Vaughn and Clint returned to the house, both wore satisfied expressions. I winked at Nell.

"Clint likes my little day sailer," said Vaughn.

"I used to sail on the Chesapeake," he explained to me and turned to Nell. "Let's take a sail around the inlet. Vaughn said we could take it out."

"Maybe Chad and I could go with you?" offered Liz.

Chad nudged her.

Liz's face turned pink when she realized what was going on. "Maybe another day."

"Yeah, how about a swim in the pool?" said Chad, and they left us to get changed.

"Guess we'll go for a sail," said Nell, beaming at Clint.

Nell and Clint walked down to the dock, hand-in-hand.

Watching them go, I smiled.

"He seems like a great guy," said Vaughn, placing his good arm around me. "His family sounds great too. His parents have been married for forty years and seem like ordinary folks. Coming from the business I'm in, that's important to me."

"I like him," I said, "and if I'm not mistaken, we're about to gain another son."

He shook his head. "Probably should have bought a bigger house."

I laughed. "This one is just fine. If we're lucky, we'll have Liz right here in town with Chad."

"I've already warned Chad he'd better treat her well."

I liked this man who was acting like a protective father.

CHAPTER THIRTY

As Vaughn grilled some steaks with Chad and Clint, I fussed in the kitchen. Vaughn had requested my pan-fried potatoes seasoned with garlic and the zest of lemons. Liz was putting together a tossed green salad, and Nell was sitting at the kitchen table admiring the large diamond Clint had presented her on their sail.

"It's so beautiful," Nell declared. "And it was so romantic being on the water with the wind softly blowing around us. It made for a slow sail, but a great opportunity for a kiss or three. I'll never forget it."

I smiled and recalled Vaughn chartering a sailboat especially for his proposal to me. It had been such a sweet gesture.

"Maybe Chad and I won't wait," Liz said. "I'm the only one who's not engaged."

"Take your time, Liz. Chad's a good guy, but you have your schooling to finish," I said. "Besides, Christmas isn't that far off."

"What's this about Christmas?" said Nell.

"Chad and I are talking about getting engaged then," Liz explained.

"Nice," said Nell. "I haven't had much of a chance to really talk it over with you, but I like him, Liz. You look perfect together. No wonder Dad is getting all protective. Robbie will be the only kid left around here."

"Have you signed the adoption papers?" Liz asked.

"I'm calling Syd Green tomorrow to see what is holding up

the adoption. Don't worry, it'll all work out. Vaughn is anxious to have it settled."

The guys came in with the steaks.

We sat down to a late, family dinner while Elena read books to Robbie in his room. Looking around the table, I said, "I miss Ty and June. They should be here with us."

"They will be soon," said Vaughn. He lifted his wine glass. "Here's to weddings! All of them!"

At the meaningful look that Chad gave Liz, my lips curved with satisfaction. Liz might think it was too hard to wait to be officially engaged, but I wasn't worried about them. Chad's love for her was obvious.

After the main course was completed, I rose to check on Robbie. He was sitting in Elena's lap, his head bobbing with sleep. I lifted him out of her arms and carried him back to the dining room.

"Robbie is ready for bed. Everybody say good night to him."

"Night," said Liz, rising from her chair to give him a hug and a kiss.

I carried him over to Vaughn. "Give Daddy a kiss good night."

Robbie kissed his hand, then leaned over patted Vaughn's cheek. "Night."

"Give the others kisses too," I coached.

Robbie blew kisses to the others and laid his head against my chest. Walking back to the room with him, I filled with tenderness. As a young girl, I'd always wanted a big family. Robbie, lucky boy, already had one.

Sunday evening, with just the two of us plus Robbie and Trudy in the house, I lay on the couch exhausted. It had been a day of hellos and good-byes and laundry and getting the house back in order. To top it off, when he was told he wasn't going to the airport with Nell, Clint, and Liz, Robbie had put on a two-year-old's temper tantrum equal to the finest on Vaughn's soap opera.

"It's a good thing everybody is staying at the hotel for the wedding," said Vaughn. "It'll be easier on both of us."

"And how," I quickly agreed. I propped myself up on my elbow and smiled at Vaughn. He was stretched out on the couch. Trudy lay beside him, snoring softly.

"You ready for bed?" Vaughn wiggled his eyebrows suggestively, but he and I both knew playtime would be limited by his injuries.

When Elena showed up the next morning, I happily turned mommy duties over to her. I had an important phone call to make. I was put right through to Syd Green. "Ann, great to hear from you? How is Vaughn doing? Pretty scary stuff."

"It was terrifying, but Vaughn is making a good recovery. He's strong and healthy, which helps. It's sad, though, that he was the only one who survived. That's going to take a while longer for him to deal with."

"I can imagine," said Syd. "What can I do for you?"

I explained the situation with Robbie and that Vaughn and I basically had approval from the court but had no paperwork. "So we need to push that through."

"I'm sure it's a matter of its being overlooked or someone's dropping the ball. I'll get right on it through one of my contacts." He paused. "I must say I'm surprised by the turn of events, though I do believe Robert would be very happy you're raising his son. Through all of the bitterness of the divorce and what followed, I never heard him say anything bad about you as a mother."

"Thank you." I knew differently, but I wasn't about to share those times with him. They'd been said in anger after Robert had taken up with Kandie.

"On another note, how are things at The Beach House Hotel?" Syd asked.

I smiled. "We're doing well. Vaughn and I are going to be married there soon—a family-only celebration. But as part of the publicity following Vaughn's rescue, I've agreed to have a photographer take pictures for his fans. It should be good publicity for both the soap opera and the hotel."

He chuckled. "I love how you and Rhonda have a knack for making things work out well for the hotel. Are you sure you don't want to open another one?"

"With Rhonda's new baby and all that's happened to me, the thought of that is pretty chilling."

"Good for you, Ann. Keep those priorities. They're the ones that count. I'll be in touch with you regarding the paperwork for Robbie. It shouldn't be a problem."

My mind whirled as I hung up. Memories of Robert with Liz as a toddler assailed me. He'd never been the kind of father who played with his child, but he had watched me do it with a smile.

Vaughn was sitting in a chair on the dock when I went to find him. He looked up at me and smiled. "It's so peaceful, just staring out at the activity on the water."

"Are you all right? You were very restless in your sleep."

He sighed. "Another bad dream."

I leaned over and gave him a kiss. "I know how difficult this has been. Is there anything I can do for you?"

He shook his head. "Just get ready for that wedding of ours."

"I'm going to meet with Lorraine Grace at Wedding Perfection. I'd like her to decorate the small dining room.

With a photographer present for the press, we need to make this a little more formal than I'd planned."

"Fine by me. Whatever you want. Did you get in touch with Syd?"

"Yes, and he doesn't think there should be any problem with the adoption paperwork. He'll get right back to us."

"Good," said Vaughn. "Go and have fun with Lorraine."

I was heading back to the house when my cell phone rang. I checked the number and

frowned. No caller ID. I went to delete it and paused. Very few people had my cell number.

"Hello?"

"Ann? It's Tina. I heard about Vaughn. How is he? How are you?"

"Hi, sweetheart! We're doing okay. Vaughn was injured pretty badly, but he's healing well. However, the death of the other two men was quite traumatic for him and is very sad for us."

"Yeah, I heard he set up a fund for the pilot's family. I'm contributing to it."

"How nice. And how are you?"

"My new agent is terrific about finding great parts for me. I finished the movie I told you about earlier. It should be out in a few months. I've heard noises about an Oscar nod, but you know how those things go. We never can be too sure about them."

"Tina, that's wonderful! I'm so proud of you!" I said, truly happy for her. I couldn't resist adding, "What does your mother think of that?"

"I have no idea," said Tina. "We haven't spoken in months. It's been the happiest and most peaceful time of my life. None of this would've happened if I hadn't come to The Beach House Hotel. I tell people about it all the time."

"Thanks, we can always use more guests, though things are going well. Vaughn and I are going to be married on the beach at the hotel in a couple of weeks. It would be nice if you could join us."

"I'd love to. You know I'd be there if I could, but I don't think I can get there. I'm starting another film in ten days. But, Ann, I'll be there in spirit. It'll be like you and me together again, listening to the sounds around us. Coming from me, it may sound corny, but bless you, Ann, for all you did to help me."

My heart warmed. Tina had been so demanding, so difficult, so needy when I'd first met her. She'd come a long way since then. "I said it then, and I'll say it now, you'll always have a place in my heart."

"I know. Love you. I gotta go. I'll be checking up on you."

As she hung up, I heard the tears in Tina's voice. I blinked back tears of my own. So many stories had taken place at the hotel. Hers was one of the best.

Lorraine was thrilled to be able to help me with the wedding dinner. She had a few other ideas with which I eagerly agreed. Now that new plans were evolving, my excitement grew. I'd been content to simply join hands on the beach and announce our marriage. But now, with added ceremony, it would be even more special.

I left her and, on a whim, decided to stop by Rhonda's house to share the news. When I arrived, Rita greeted me with a smile.

"Hi! Is Rhonda here?" I asked her.

She nodded. "On the porch with Willow."

I walked through the living room, and onto the screened-in porch. Rhonda was sitting in a wicker rocking chair with

Willow, who was asleep in Rhonda's arms.

"Hi! Wait until you hear the latest news on my wedding!" I exclaimed, lowering myself into a couch nearby. I clasped my hands in excitement. "It's going to be so beautiful!"

I was halfway through the details when I noticed that the smile on Rhonda's face hadn't changed—as if it were frozen in place. Concerned, I stopped. "What's the matter?"

Tears rolled down Rhonda's cheeks. "I'm pregnant."

"Wha-a-at! How did that happen?" I choked out a laugh. "I mean I know how, but when? I mean ... never mind." I rose and gave her a hug. "Are you okay?"

She shrugged. "Oh, Annie, I'm just so unsure about it all. Willow's not even four months old. I wasn't even thinking about another baby. They tell ya that as long as you're nursing, you're fine, and with me being so down after Willow's birth, there wasn't that much going on, if you know what I mean."

"What does Will think about it?"

Rhonda made a face. "He's totally thrilled. I swear he's beginning to strut around the house like a frickin' rooster."

At the image of tall, gentle Will acting that way, I couldn't help smiling. "Oh, Rhonda, I'm happy for you both."

"Gawd! What's Reggie's mother going to say now?" said Rhonda, sniffing.

"She'll probably think you're lucky," I said. "I have a feeling a good night kiss is the most she gets."

Rhonda and I looked at each other and burst out laughing.

Willow stirred in her sleep. Rhonda rose. "Let me give her to Rita and then I want to hear all about those plans."

Rhonda returned to the porch with two glasses of Consuela's berry iced tea. She handed me one and sat down beside me on the couch with the other.

I described what Lorraine and I had come up with.

"Beautiful, Annie, and you'll be such a classy bride. And

you and Vaughn together? Wow! How's he doing?"

"It's going to take him a while to settle in his mind why he was the only one who survived. But he set up the family fund for the pilot, and that's making him feel better. By the way, Tina called me."

Rhonda leaned forward. "Ohhh? What is she up to?"

I filled Rhonda in on the conversation and how Tina credited coming to the hotel as a factor in changing her life.

"You're the one who really helped her, Annie, but I'm glad to know some of our guests have really benefitted from staying with us. How's the romance with Bernie coming along? If I say so myself, I had a lot to do with that one."

I grinned. Rhonda's matchmaking efforts hadn't really been needed, but I wasn't going to tell her that. She loved the idea that, because of her, Annette was moving to Florida to be with Bernie. I made a mental note to include them in the wedding, along with a few other members of our hotel family. Jean-Luc and Sabine would be busy inside before and after the ceremony, but they'd already promised to be present for the exchange of vows.

I left Rhonda's house feeling very conflicted. I was happy to think of Rhonda's and Will's exciting news but worried about the responsibilities that would be left to me. No matter how much day-to-day help our staff was, the tone of the hotel was dictated to them by us and our actions. And that meant overseeing the project.

CHAPTER THIRTY-ONE

Syd Green called a few days later to say that everything was set for Robbie's adoption. In lieu of appearing in court, a telephone interview was being granted, along with a visit by a local social worker to confirm that our home was appropriate. "It's just a matter of protocol," Syd explained when I protested. "My guess is that they will forego that."

Vaughn had no problem with any of it when I told him. "Just so it's all legal," he said, waving away my concerns.

That same afternoon, Mike Torson called. "Ann, we have to meet. We have a strong interest again on the part of the same prospective buyers of the hotel. They want to meet with you to discuss it. It's something you, Rhonda, and I need to talk about. I've come up with a couple of ideas—alternatives you may want to consider. I've had only preliminary, superficial discussions with them and have not disclosed any information, of course, without your permission."

"But, Mike..." I began and stopped. *What harm would it do to talk about such a thing? Roger Jamieson, our consultant in Boston had suggested we keep an open mind to the idea. And at the moment, I had no idea how we could continue in our usual pattern.*" All right. I'll call Rhonda and see if we can set up a time to meet with you."

"How about four this afternoon?" Mike said, making it impossible for me to put it off.

"Okay, if Rhonda agrees, we'll be there. I'll let you know."

I hung up even more conflicted than I was before. Working with lawyers had always brought some pain with it. And the idea of selling the hotel was already very painful.

Rhonda hesitated and then agreed to go to the meeting.

At the appointed time, I picked her up. We drove toward Mike's office in silence. I was about to ask Rhonda what she was thinking when she said, "It's my home, Annie."

"It must be difficult for you to think of selling," I said. "I still don't like the idea. The hotel means so much to me."

Rhonda turned to me. "Will thinks it's a good idea. It really pissed me off when he said it, but he may be right."

"Let's see if this whole idea is real or not," I said, feeling trapped by our circumstances.

We waited in a small conference room for Mike to appear. He entered the room, carrying a large number of documents.

After exchanging greetings, he sat down opposite us. "I'm glad you were willing to come to this meeting today. After learning who this buyer is, I've spent some time investigating them. Of course, I haven't gone beyond that. Without your permission to do so, I wouldn't. But I have drawn up a list of things we need to discuss in order to decide if we want to pursue this."

"Who is this buyer?" I asked, suspicious already.

"It's a group out of Massachusetts. Peabody, Lowell and Logan. Have you heard of them?"

"Actually, I have," I said. "We bid on a job for them and lost. Robert was furious."

"Then you know they have a good reputation. I checked their portfolio online. They own a number of small, boutique hotels, mostly out west and in Hawaii. I'm sure your prime location in Florida is one of the reasons they're interested in The Beach House Hotel."

"What about their finances?" said Rhonda. "Can they pay?

Because if we decide to sell, it's going to cost them big time."

"From all I can ascertain, their financial stability is there. Even a big purchase like you envision should be no problem for them. Of course, until we start exchanging information with them, we don't have the right to actual numbers. This leads me to a matter of great concern. If you're interested at all in pursuing this, we need to have a CA—or confidentiality agreement— in place. If word got out about your contemplating selling the hotel, it would attract the vultures of the industry to walk the property."

"And it might hurt our business," I said. "People might get the mistaken idea that we are in trouble. And if that word got out as the reason we wanted to sell, it could bring the perceived value down."

"I agree," said Mike. "We want to proceed carefully. Before I go any further with this, are the two of you interested in selling?"

Rhonda and I looked at each other.

"Can we talk about it?" Rhonda said. "This is a huge thing for us to think about."

"Yes. We've put our hearts and souls into it. I'd hate to think someone would come in and ruin it."

Mike smiled. "I thought you might feel that way, so I've come up with a few alternative scenarios to think about."

An hour later, Rhonda and I left Mike's office with a whole lot more to think about.

When I drew up to the front of my house, I stopped the car and took a good look at it. It was beautiful—the nicest I'd ever had—thanks to Vaughn. But it was so much more than a structure; it was the place where I knew I was loved, knew I was needed.

I pulled into the driveway and got out. Stepping into the kitchen, I heard the sound of running feet, and then Robbie appeared. "Mommy!" He threw his arms around my legs and smiled up at me.

My spirits lifted. I pulled him up into my arms and laughed as Trudy stood at my feet and barked for attention.

Vaughn came into the kitchen and smiled at me. "Guess the welcoming committee got to you first."

"Always room for one more," I said. "What's up?"

"Liz called. She's taken the last exam for the semester and will be heading home. She's decided to stop in DC to visit Nell. The girls are going to shop together for different dresses for the wedding."

"I'm so glad they get along. And happy Liz has agreed to go back to school in the fall to finish her last year."

"How was your meeting with Mike?" Vaughn asked.

"Interesting. Very interesting. Let's go out on the porch and I'll tell you all about it."

I settled Robbie on the carpet in front of us and placed several toys around him. While he played with them, I told Vaughn about the basic ideas Mike had presented to us.

"So you're actually thinking of selling the hotel?" Vaughn asked.

"Only with certain conditions in place," I said and blinked rapidly to cover the threat of tears.

Vaughn noticed and frowned. "How does Rhonda feel about this?"

"I think she realizes she can't continue her work there, except on a consulting basis. Not with two babies—two babies she never dared to dream she'd have after all this time." I drew a deep breath. "We both feel very lucky for the lives we have, for so many reasons."

Vaughn studied me and nodded thoughtfully. "If this turns

out the way you both want, I'll be happy with your decision. I've wanted you with me many times—many times you've been tied to the hotel. Without your having that constant responsibility, there's a lot we can see and do together, even with Robbie."

A new excitement filled me. Maybe Rhonda and I could pull off the deal we wanted. It was worth a try. If not, we'd find another way to make it all work.

Vaughn agreed to go with me to Elise Talbot's bridal shop for her help in choosing an outfit for him for the wedding. His willingness to try on a number of things touched my heart. He made a game of it, twirling in front of us.

After we'd selected the right things, we left to go to another store to find a similar outfit for Robbie.

We'd just returned home when we got a call from someone in the Family Court in Massachusetts. The woman asked me all kinds of questions about Robbie's care, the facilities we have and then asked to speak to Vaughn.

I listened as he patiently answered questions. "This is a decision we all made some time ago. We want the paperwork signed and filed now."

He listened and then said, "Thank you. Thank you so much. We will give him a wonderful home and the best life we can."

He hung up the call and turned to me. His eyes watered. "Robbie's ours. She apologized for the delay and said they weren't even going to pursue a home inspection, that they'd already received approval from a social worker who is a friend of Elena's. The delay has been one of those things that got caught in the system. As she said, this decision is a no-brainer from every aspect."

We hugged and tiptoed into Robbie's room, where Elena

had put him down for a nap. He was asleep on his back, clutching the stuffed giraffe I'd bought him at the zoo.

Looking down at him, I could easily see how much he'd grown. With all the swimming and other activities that kept him busy most days, his legs had grown longer and stronger, and his body had filled out. He was a darling little boy who would become a handsome man.

My thoughts flew to Robert. It seemed so odd that his last gift to Liz and me would be something so precious. Had he had a premonition that he was going to die, like Liz had once felt? Was that why he'd told her he wanted me to help raise his son? We'd never know.

CHAPTER THIRTY-TWO

R honda and I sat in the office at The Beach House Hotel as if great plans weren't waiting in the wings. I checked over the sales figures and she checked over the reservations.

"Looks like our summer might not be so bad," Rhonda said.

"It helps that we're coming up with special events. And with Sabine in charge of working with Lorraine Grace from Wedding Perfection to do weddings here at the hotel, it's becoming one of the top places for small, destination weddings."

Rhonda turned to me with a smile. "Having your wedding filmed here will give the hotel a big boost. You and Vaughn Sanders. Who would've thunk it a few years ago, huh?"

I laughed. "Not me. Amazing how things work out."

Rhonda grew serious. "Are you gonna be all right if we can get the deal we want on the hotel?"

"I think so. No, I know so. Let's call Mike and see if he has any news for us. He was supposed to talk to the group and get some feedback from the ideas we're proposing." As I picked up the office phone to call him, my cell rang.

I checked caller ID and smiled. "Great minds think alike, Mike. I was getting ready to call you. Rhonda's here with me. I'm putting you on my speaker. Any news?"

"I was able to talk to one of the lead guys in the investor group. They're signing a CA today, so the confidentiality issue is resolved. Their interest in the property has been very hush-hush so far, and he's promised to keep it that way. He's agreed in principle to the idea of your retaining a minority ownership for two years while you act as consultants to the business for continuity and so the quality of guest service and the facilities are not impaired. They've also agreed to a re-purchase option, which we can talk about later. I'm about to call Will to let him know what documents he needs to prepare for them. They'll also need payroll records, forecasts and the like. I suggest you bring Bernie in on this now."

"Have they agreed to keep Bernie general manager, like we wanted?" Rhonda asked.

"That hasn't been discussed, but it's on my list to take care of as things get rolling."

Hearing the conversation, it all became too real. I excused myself and quickly left the office so Rhonda wouldn't see my distress. I bypassed the kitchen and went out through a back entrance onto the side lawn. The beautiful garden there had become a favorite place for weddings and wedding photographs. I sat on a white, wrought-iron bench and took deep, calming breaths. It was time for another major change in my life. *I could do this, couldn't I?*

Rhonda walked toward me. "Annie? Are you all right?"

I patted the seat next to me. "It just hit me hard for a moment. But I'm okay."

Rhonda sat beside me. "It'll be all right, Annie. It isn't like we are simply walking away. We're gradually letting it go. Like seeing our daughters go off on their own. Ya know?"

"Yes, but it doesn't hurt any less." I threaded my fingers through hers. "When I first met you, I was so scared of the future. Now, see where I am. It's the best time of my life."

"Okay, that does it. No more regrets. The future will, no doubt, hold a lot more surprises." She patted her stomach. "This time, I'm sure it's a boy."

So much more than business partners, we smiled at each other.

I squeezed her hand and let it go before I rose. "Guess we'd better tell Bernie all about it."

Together we walked into the hotel.

Once Bernie got over his shock and knew we wanted him to stay on for the next two years, he settled into business mode. "It's important that our guests don't suspect this. We can't have people walking the property over and over again. I'll be glad to be the one to arrange the timing of their inspections as they complete their due diligence."

When we'd finished talking about that and other details, I said, "I hope you and Annette plan to attend my wedding and the dinner afterward. Tim and Dorothy are invited too, so we need to staff the hotel accordingly."

He smiled. "I already took care of it. Annette can't wait."

Rhonda elbowed him. "Say, Bernie, when are you and Annette tying the knot?"

His cheeks turned bright pink. "She just moved in. We're still getting used to one another."

"Don't wait too long," said Rhonda. "It's the best. Right, Annie?"

"It's going to feel very good," I admitted, hiding my amusement over Bernie's discomfort. He might not realize it, but between Rhonda and Annette, his days of being a bachelor were limited.

The day before the wedding, Vaughn and I stood on the front steps of the hotel, waiting to greet Ty and June. They, along with Nell and Clint, were staying at the hotel for the long weekend.

The limo pulled into the front circle.

Vaughn and I looked at each other and, chuckling, raced down the steps to greet them.

June stepped out of the limo, looking fresh and happy. She gave us a shy smile. Ty emerged behind her and gave us a little salute so like his father's that I couldn't help smiling. While I embraced June, Ty hugged his father and stepped back to inspect him.

"You're looking much better, Dad," said Ty.

Vaughn smiled. "Thanks. Feeling better too." He gave June a hug. "Welcome to Florida."

"And welcome to The Beach House Hotel," I said. "We'll show you around, and then we'll take you to our house. We want you to meet Robbie and Liz. Nell and Clint are already there."

As we toured the hotel, I was once more reminded of how beautiful it was. It pained me to know that I'd eventually lose control of it, but then when I looked at the family around me, I knew how lucky I was.

"It's really gorgeous," said June as we stood in the garden outside. She smiled at Ty. "Maybe this is where we should get married."

"I thought you wanted Hawaii," he said.

"I've changed my mind," said June.

"If you're serious, we'll talk about it." I winked at her. "I'm sure I can give you a special rate."

June laughed. "That ought to make my father happy. We'll see. My mother has her heart set on Hawaii."

We left the hotel and drove to our house.

"Come inside and meet the rest of the family," said Vaughn, ushering them inside.

When we entered the kitchen, Liz and Chad were sitting at the table in their bathing suits, sipping glasses of lemonade. They jumped to their feet.

Smiling, Liz approached Ty. "You're my new brother? I'm Liz." She gave him a quick hug and turned to June. "And you must be June. I've heard nothing but good things about you. I'm happy for you both and especially pleased that you're about to become my new sister. I've always wanted a large family."

"It won't be official until April of next year," June said. "But I can't wait until you and Nell are my sisters. I only have brothers."

"Meet Chad Bowen. He's my boyfriend," said Liz, turning to Chad.

"Hopefully more than that one day," he said agreeably before shaking hands with Ty and then, with June.

Elena appeared with Robbie and Trudy. Introductions were made. While Trudy was being spoiled by June, Ty and Robbie faced each other.

"My brudder?" said Robbie, giving me a questioning look.

"Yes," I said, "Ty is your brother—your big brother."

Robbie's gaze traveled way up to Ty's face. "Big."

"Can you say Ty," I prompted.

Robbie shook his head and pointed to Ty. "No, big."

Ty laughed good-naturedly. "Okay, buddy, you can call me big."

Satisfied, Robbie looked at June and turned to me. "Sissie?"

"Sure," I said, laughing. "Hope you don't mind, June. But you're one of the sisters already."

"Mind? I love it," she said, lowering herself to give Robbie a hug.

"Where are Nell and Clint?" I asked.

"They're outside in the pool," Elena said. "I'll tell them you're gathered here."

"Don't bother. We can all go out there. It's such a beautiful day." Though the sun was hot, an onshore breeze was keeping the temperature relatively cool for the sixth of June.

I ushered Ty and June out through the porch onto the pool deck. As soon as they saw us, Nell and Clint got out of the pool to greet them.

After everybody was comfortably seated, Vaughn said, "Anybody ready for a glass of wine? It's almost five o'clock, and we've waited a long time for this celebration. Right, sweetheart?"

I smiled at him. "A *very* long time."

I joined in the laughter that followed.

That night, after Robbie was in bed and the six kids had left for a night on the town, Vaughn and I stretched out on chaise lounges side-by-side near the pool. The lights in the pool cast a blue glow in the water, illuminating our faces in the dark. Above us, stars twinkled in the inky sky.

I sighed with pleasure and smiled at Vaughn. "It doesn't seem that long ago that we met, does it? So much has happened since then. I'm very grateful that you're alive."

Vaughn took hold of my hand and squeezed it. "Me too. I love you so much."

My throat thickened. I doubted Vaughn would ever really know all the things he meant to me. "I love you too. If it's possible for two people to become one, you're the better half of me."

His smile changed to a sexy one I knew well. "Good thing I'm feeling much better. I know tomorrow is our wedding, but like we said earlier, we've already begun celebrating. And I know the best way to do it."

"The kids ..."

"Don't worry, I can be real fast," he said, leering at me.

I laughed. "No way. C'mon, we'd better get started."

In our bedroom, we quickly undressed. Though Vaughn was feeling much better, I knew we'd have to be careful of his ribs and the tender spot where his spleen was.

Vaughn lay on his right side. "Come here."

I nestled up against him, loving the feel of his skin next to mine as he lowered his lips to mine.

Later, I marveled at the easy way we'd accommodated each other. Our wedding may be tomorrow, but we wouldn't need any extra practice to officially consummate the marriage.

CHAPTER THIRTY-THREE

I awoke and lay in bed gazing up at the ceiling. This was about to become one of the happiest days of my life. I glanced over at Vaughn beside me and thought, as I had so many times, how lucky I was to have found such a wonderful man.

Vaughn opened his eyes and smiled at me. "Scared?"

I shook my head. "Not at all. You?"

"No way." He kissed me and got out of bed. "While you girls are using the spa and doing your things, the guys and I are going sailing this morning. I've chartered the same boat I used for our engagement."

"Just be sure you're back in plenty of time to get ready for the ceremony. Remember, the photographer you chose will be taking pictures for your fans."

"Yeah, sometimes that gets to be a nuisance," grumbled Vaughn.

"I know, but I'm sure but their prayers helped keep you safe. That's why I agreed to have him take photographs."

While Vaughn showered and dressed, I put on a robe and padded out to the kitchen. Liz was already up. "Hi, Mom! Happy wedding day!"

"Thanks, sweetheart. Did you kids have a good time last night?"

"Yes, I really like Ty and June. It was good to get to know them a little better. And Nell and Clint are great. I love the idea of having so many brothers and sisters."

I grabbed a cup of coffee and sat at the kitchen table

opposite her. "And what about that little brother? It's official, you know."

"I got the notification. He's so lucky. I wouldn't have been able to give him the kind of home he has with you. I'll always be grateful to you and Vaughn. And, Mom, thinking back to our conversation, I'm sure this is exactly what Dad wanted."

"Well, it's worked out well for all of us. I always wanted more children, you know."

"Angela told me about Rhonda's new baby. What a surprise, huh?"

"Oh yes. But now that she's gotten used to the idea, she's thrilled. It's amazing what changes the last three years have brought." I studied her. "You seem very happy with Chad. I hope it works out. But, if it doesn't, don't worry. You're a wonderful woman with a bright future ahead of you."

"Thanks. I'm pretty sure about Chad, though. Nell likes him a whole lot, and he got along with everyone last night."

"Good. Those are good signs."

Vaughn walked into the kitchen. "Girl talk?"

I smiled. "How about coffee and a hot breakfast before you guys go sailing?"

"Actually, I'm going to pick up Chad. We'll have breakfast with Ty and Clint at the hotel."

"All right, my darling. I'll see you this afternoon."

I stood and went into Vaughn's embrace. "Be ready, bride. I'm going to make you mine today and forever."

"You two," declared Liz. "Do you ever stop with all the mushy stuff?"

Vaughn and I laughed.

"Wait and see," I said. "You'll be talking like us someday."

I sat in the Bridal Suite with Liz, Nell, and June. Though

I'd chosen not to have any attendants, it meant a great deal to have them with me. They'd get dressed with me and would go out to the beach before me.

As we were about to get dressed for the wedding, Rhonda and Angela came in. Wearing a gold caftan, and looking more rested than she had recently, Rhonda swooped me into a warm hug. "Oh, Annie! I'm so happy for you! You and Vaughn together are the best!"

She faced the girls. "I'm here to help Ann get dressed." She lifted a gaily wrapped package from her gold purse. "First things first. Vaughn wanted you to have this."

The girls gathered around me as I tore off the light blue wrapping. Inside was a long, blue velvet box.

I opened it and gasped with pleasure.

"Oh my God! It's gorgeous, Annie!" said Rhonda.

When I lifted out the diamond bracelet, a note fell to the floor. I picked it up and read it aloud: *Hugs and kisses for you. Love you always, Vaughn.*

"Oh, so sweet!" said Nell.

"Look," said June. "The gold X's are separated by two round diamonds. It does look like the symbols for hugs and kisses."

"Some guy he is," said Angela.

"And he's going to be my father," announced Liz proudly. "He sure has good taste."

Giggling with the others, I attempted to put the bracelet on.

"Here, allow me," said Rhonda. She fastened it around my left wrist and stepped back. "Oh, honey, it looks so good on you."

The girls put on their sundresses and left with Angela to head out to the beach, leaving Rhonda and me alone.

Almost reverently, I lifted my wedding dress out of its protective cloth bag and slipped it on. The knee-length, princess, A-line, chiffon dress was classic with its simple one-shoulder design. But I'd chosen the dress for its color. It appeared white until the light hit it. Then it became clear that the fabric was the palest of blues. Vaughn liked me in blue and I was pretty sure he was going to like me in this. The color against my tanned skin was perfect.

I slipped simple diamond earrings through my ear lobes. They and the bracelet were all the jewelry I needed. Malinda at Hair Designs had styled my dark hair to fall simply to my shoulders. Her assistant had helped me with my eye makeup.

As I slowly twirled in front of her, Rhonda's eyes filled. "Beautiful. Simply beautiful." She grabbed a tissue and dabbed at her eyes. "Oh my! It isn't just hormones. It's true, Annie. You are lovely."

"Thanks. Is the photographer ready?" I asked.

"I'll go check. See you in a few." Rhonda blew me a kiss and left.

Sabine entered with the photographer. "He knows he gets just a few shots here and then after the ceremony itself. We'll give him a few minutes and then you'll head out to the beach. Vaughn is waiting for you there."

My heart leaped in my chest. After all the turmoil to reach this point, it seemed so surreal.

Sabine smiled at me. "It's going to be beautiful—like you."

I did my best to smile and turn this way and that to satisfy the photographer, and then he was gone.

I clutched my hands together and said a quick prayer of thanks. Then, following Sabine, I moved outside toward the man I would love for the rest of my life.

Louise Atherton, a friend of Dorothy's and a justice-of-the-peace, had agreed to marry us. When Vaughn and I had met with her, we liked her very much.

Now, she and Vaughn stood on the sand in the shade of a palm tree that edged the hotel's property. Our wedding guests formed a protective circle around the spot to give us the privacy we sought on the beach.

The late afternoon sun had mellowed to a comfortable temperature, and a soft breeze caressed my dress in a sweeping motion, giving me the impression of floating. Like the guests and Vaughn, my feet were bare as I moved toward Vaughn.

In a pair of formal, black Bermuda shorts and wearing a white tux shirt offset by an aqua-blue bowtie, he looked adorable. When I got closer, I saw the tears in his eyes.

As I moved beside him, he whispered, "Ann, you're beautiful."

I smiled up at him, and then became lost in the magical moments of our pledging our love to one another. The exchange of rings was almost comical as Vaughn nervously pulled out the wrong ring from his pants pocket and tried to put the ring I had for him on my finger and it fell onto the sand. He picked it up and pulled the right ring—a smaller band— out of his pocket and slipped the diamond and platinum wedding ring on my finger.

After Vaughn had received his ring and the final vows made, Louise announced, "You may kiss the bride."

The round of applause that followed brought my entire surroundings into focus.

"Me too," said Robbie, running over to us. "Up. I want up."

"It's real, Ann," said Vaughn, holding onto Robbie and kissing me again.

I sighed happily. "At last."

Vaughn turned to the group. "We now ask you to join us at the water's edge. It's how I first knew Ann was special, and that someday we'd be together."

"Remember, I had to give you a nudge," said Nell, to a round of laughter.

"And I did my part too," said Rhonda. "I'm sorta a matchmaker myself. Right, Bernie and Annette?"

Observing the way those two were beaming at one another, I wondered if maybe Rhonda was better at it than I'd thought.

Vaughn directed us to the water's edge. We stood in a line and held hands.

"Hey! Wait for me!" came a cry behind us.

I turned to see Tina Marks running toward us. "Sorry, I'm late. But I couldn't miss this special day for anything."

I grabbed hold of her hand and pulled her into a joyful hug. "Come join us."

Vaughn asked our guests for a moment of silence to give thanks for being together.

I took a moment to observe the people standing with us. My appreciation for each one washed over them like the ripples at their feet.

I gazed up at Vaughn.

He smiled down at me with such tenderness, I felt my lips quiver.

My new life had started with The Beach House Hotel. I didn't know what the future held, but wherever I went, I would carry this place, this moment with me forever.

# # #

Thank you for reading *Dinner at The Beach House Hotel.* If you enjoyed this book, please help other readers discover it by leaving a review on Amazon, Bookbub, Goodreads, or your favorite site. It's such a nice thing to do.

The other books in The Beach House Hotel Series: *Breakfast at The Beach House Hotel, Lunch at The Beach House Hotel, Christmas at The Beach House Hotel, Margaritas at The Beach House Hotel,* and *Dessert at The Beach House Hotel,* are available on all sites.

Books 7 and 8, *Coffee at The Beach House Hotel* and *High Tea at The Beach House Hotel,* will be released in 2023 and 2024, respectively.

Enjoy an excerpt from my book, *Christmas at The Beach House Hotel-* (Book 4 in The Beach House Hotel Series.)

CHAPTER ONE

My cell phone rang. *Rhonda.* Staring out my kitchen window at the palm fronds rustling in the sea breeze like impatient children wanting to run and play, I picked up the call from my best friend in Sabal, Florida.

"Hey, Mrs. Grayson! How's it going? Those two little ones driving you crazy?"

Rhonda laughed. "Annie, I swear Willow is teaching Drew every one of her 'terrible two' tricks, but she's so sweet with him, I don't mind."

I couldn't help chuckling. Willow was two and a half, and Drew, thirteen months younger, was fascinated with his big sister and tried to mimic her whenever possible. They were darling together, but a real handful.

"Listen, Annie; we gotta talk. This mess at The Beach House Hotel can't go on like it is. I just got a call from Stephanie Willis from Connecticut. She was furious because, for the second year in a row, they couldn't get a reservation for Columbus Day weekend. She and Randolph have always been loyal guests of the hotel. What in the hell is going on?"

I let out a sigh of exasperation. "I'm not surprised a bit by this latest news. Ever since we sold it, The Beach House Hotel has deteriorated from the elegant, discreet, seaside resort we created to a commercial enterprise that is all about dollars, not class." The sale, almost two years ago, to the investment group of Peabody, Lowell, and Logan had turned out to be a big disappointment to both of us.

"Yeah," said Rhonda. "All the finer touches we provided our guests, making the hotel a first-class operation, are gone. No complimentary items in the room, no morning newspapers, no treats available to them. And last Christmas was a freakin' nightmare—cheap decorations, no bonuses for the staff, no community Christmas Party, none of our usual holiday fun. No wonder our return guests no longer feel a part of our family, the wedding bookings have cratered, and the locals are staying away from the restaurant."

"I'm tired of this kind of thing continuing to happen," I snapped. "We've tried talking to the new owners about our deep concerns, and it's done absolutely no good. I don't know what else we can do about it."

"I do," growled Rhonda. "We can take back the hotel. We have that contractual right, remember? That hotel was my home; we built it into something unique, and those SOBs are turning it into an ordinary, chain-style hotel where no one gives a damn about our guests."

"Take it back? Do you mean it?" Excitement surged through me in tantalizing waves. God! I'd missed running the hotel with Rhonda. Though our contract specified that we'd retain a minority interest in the business and would act as consultants, the new owners had scoffed at every suggestion we'd made. They'd even indicated in sometimes not so subtle ways that we should go home and take care of our families.

I felt a huge grin spread across my face. *It would feel so good to get rid of them!*

"It won't be easy, but, Annie, we gotta do it! Are you in?"

"Oh, yes," I said with growing determination. "It's time to stop this nonsense. Things have gone from bad to worse after Aubrey Lowell took over the management of the hotel."

"Yeah, what a little punk! Let's get rid of him and all the others!" Rhonda's voice changed, became tentative. "Will Vaughn be okay with your doing this? I think Will might fight me on this, but honestly, Annie, after staying at home for two years with the babies and with him thinking he's the biggest stud around, I'm afraid I'll get pregnant again. And at my age, it isn't as easy as it was when I had Angela. I love my babies, but I'm too old to have more."

I held back a laugh. Rhonda was in her mid-forties and her husband, Will, ten years older. But Will was so taken with the idea of having kids in his fifties that, given a choice, he would have many more.

"So, what about Vaughn?" Rhonda persisted. "Can you convince him it's the right thing for you to do?"

I hesitated, knowing he wouldn't be thrilled. Vaughn loved having me spend time with him in New York while he filmed *The Sins of the Children*, the soap opera he'd starred in for several years. But I missed the hotel's work environment and interacting with our guests. Fresh resolve rose in me. "Vaughn and I will work it out. The hotel is my baby as much as yours. Let's do it!"

"All right! Before I chicken out, I'll call Mike Torson right now."

"Let me know what we need to do next." I ended the call hoping Rhonda and I weren't making a big mistake. Together, we'd made a few.

After I hung up, I couldn't contain my excitement. Raising my arms in the air, I did a little dance across the kitchen floor.

"Me, too, Mommy!" cried Robbie. He jumped off his chair and grabbed hold of my hands. Laughing, I twirled in circles with him. As I looked down into his shining brown eyes, my heart surged with love for him. At almost five, he was a darling little boy with dark hair, a sturdy body, and a sweet nature. Liz was still the best sister any little boy could have, but at the time his parents, my ex, Robert, and Kandie, were killed in an automobile accident, she'd been unable to offer Robbie a secure home. Vaughn and I had been so right to adopt him.

As if my thoughts about my daughter had prompted it, my phone rang. Still chuckling from our crazy dance, I picked up the call from Liz. "Hi, sweetheart! How are you?"

"I'm busy with Chad's business, but I need to talk to you about my wedding. I'm not sure Chad and I want it at The Beach House Hotel—not with the way things are being handled there. Would your feelings be hurt if we changed our mind and tried to hold it at the Ritz?"

The Ritz? Telling myself not to overreact, I drew a deep breath. "What if I told you Rhonda and I are going to try to take back the hotel?"

"Really? Mom, that would be great! The Beach House Hotel is not the same kind of place it used to be. If you buy it back and make it the way it was when you and Rhonda ran it, I'd be thrilled to have the wedding there."

"Don't say a word to anyone else about this. We just made the decision today, and I haven't even had a chance to discuss it with Vaughn."

"Oh ..." Liz let the word drift into silence.

"I think I can get him to agree on this," I said, not at all certain I could.

"For what it's worth, I think it's important for you and Rhonda to do this on many levels. Vaughn is pretty used to having you around, though." Liz paused. "Good luck with everything. Here comes a call on the customer line. Gotta go."

I couldn't help the frown I felt form as I ended the call. Maybe I was being too optimistic about making our new plan work. I had my family to consider.

My cell rang again. I checked caller ID. *Mike Torson.*

"Hello, Mike. How are you?"

"I'm fine, thanks. I just got off the phone with Rhonda. Are you in agreement with her to exercise your right to buy back the hotel?"

"You bet," I answered, fired up again. "Under the new owners' direction, the hotel has really gone downhill."

"Even though it is within your right to do so under the contract you signed with them, you understand there will be resistance, don't you?"

"Yes, probably because they are more intent on making money than giving the guests an unforgettable experience." I couldn't hide the distaste in my voice.

"Well, yes, there's that. Also, they won't want anything to mar their reputation, so we have to be very discreet in how we pursue this," Mike said in his usual calm manner.

"I understand, but Rhonda and I want the chance to make things right. We invested the money from the sale, so we should be able to handle the purchase of it."

"You have the right to buy the hotel at a fair price, but we're going to need people on our side to do property inspections and an appraisal. The investors will have valuations done on their own, which will, no doubt, be substantially different from ours."

My stomach twisted. Peabody, Lowell, and Logan was an investment group from Boston that played hardball. Though Mike Torson was a clever and persistent lawyer, the battle might get nasty.

"I understand," I repeated, though I was certain there would be unpleasant surprises.

"Shall I begin to prepare?"

"I'll reconfirm with Rhonda, and we'll get back to you tomorrow. But, yes, this is what we want." I didn't mention that neither Rhonda nor I had discussed it with our spouses.

I hung up from the call and checked my watch. Vaughn was flying in from New York that evening, and I had approximately two hours to prepare my case.

After quickly calling Rhonda to give her an update, I checked on Robbie, who was happily splashing in the pool with Elena Ramos, our young, trusted nanny. I waved to them and then went into the bathroom to take a shower. Might as well look my best.

As warm water sluiced over my body, I felt my shoulders relax and my mind open. Vaughn was a good man, a kind man, who'd been happy to have me at his beck and call these past two years. I'd been more than pleased to do that because, even after two years of marriage, I was still crazy about him. Anticipating the intimate moments ahead with Vaughn, my fingers trailed my body. He was such a good lover—generous and giving.

After rehearsing my approach to Vaughn on the plan Rhonda and I had come up with, I got out of the shower and dressed in a blue blouse that Vaughn had once said matched the color of my eyes. I brushed my straight, dark hair until it lay smoothly inches above my shoulders. Giving myself a critical look in the mirror, I thought maybe I didn't look too bad. Vaughn sometimes teased me about being a hot babe, but I wasn't that. I smiled at the memory, though, and slipped diamond earrings into my earlobes. It would be so good to have him home.

When I walked out onto the lanai, Robbie called to me from the pool. "Look, Mommy!" He stood on the edge of the deep end of the pool, made sure I was looking, and then jumped into the water.

"Good job!" I called to him as he bobbed to the surface. At age two and new to the house, he'd almost drowned in the pool. Now, two and a half years later, he swam like a little fish.

"You sure you don't mind staying with Robbie while I pick up Vaughn at the airport?" I said to Elena.

She stood and faced me. Her dark eyes sparkled, and a smile lit her pretty face, framed by thick, straight hair that she wore in a ponytail most days. Over the last couple of years, she'd become like another daughter to me. And with Elena dating the boy Liz was once infatuated with, it seemed like family when we all got together. I couldn't imagine not having her around.

"I don't mind at all," said Elena. "Troy is due here for Robbie's swim lesson. Afterwards, Robbie can come with us when we go out for hamburgers."

"Sounds great. He loves to be with the two of you." I gave Robbie a quick hug, not minding that I got a little wet, patted the silky head of Trudy, our black and tan dachshund, and headed for the garage.

On the way to the airport in Ft. Myers, my body hummed with anticipation. With Vaughn gone so much of the time, each homecoming seemed special. I still found it amazing that of all the women he could have chosen after his first wife died, he'd married me. With Robert, my ex, pulling the old stunt of leaving me for the younger, voluptuous receptionist in our office, my self-confidence had been destroyed. But the relationship between Vaughn and me had a depth of tenderness and commitment I'd never known. I treasured him. I treasured us together.

As agreed, I waited in the baggage claim area for Vaughn to arrive. Hearing a commotion, I looked up. Vaughn was stepping off the escalator into a small crowd of people who'd recognized him, even with his doing his best to hide beneath a Yankees baseball cap. Some were holding up pieces of paper for him to autograph. He obliged a few and then quickly made his way toward me.

As he neared, I took a moment to study his tall, broad-shouldered form. His black curls and snapping brown eyes, familiar to fans across the country, looked wonderful, especially when a happy grin crossed his face when our eyes met.

I hurried forward to greet him.

People stepped back as he swung me up in his arms, heedless of the curious onlookers. In the past, I might have frozen with embarrassment, but I'd learned to live with the attention he got. I didn't necessarily like it, but I managed.

"Hi, darling! Glad you're home!" I murmured into his ear.

He beamed at me as he put me down on my feet. "Not as glad as I am. Where's Robbie?"

"He and Elena are waiting for Troy to show up for Robbie's swimming lesson, and then they're going to take him out to dinner. You'll get your big greeting from him when we get home."

I loved that Robbie and Vaughn were so close. With his children from his first marriage grown, married, and starting families of their own, Vaughn was happy to have a second chance at fatherhood.

He took my hand, and we headed for the baggage conveyer belt to pick up his luggage. As soon as he grabbed his suitcase, we hurried out of the airport terminal.

Vaughn slid behind the wheel of my car, and we headed to Sabal, twenty minutes south.

As he drove, the wind ruffled his hair—the dark, soft curls I loved to finger. He turned to me with a smile. "What's new since we last talked?"

"There's something I need to discuss with you after you're settled at home. I thought we could take a walk along the beach at The Beach House Hotel and talk there."

His eyebrows lifted. "Something serious?"

"Something unexpected, but important to me."

He narrowed his eyebrows into a V and cast a suspicious look my way. "Something about The Beach House Hotel?"

Willing myself not to blurt out anything, I simply nodded. "As I said, we'll talk where we can have some privacy away from the house."

"Hmmm, doesn't sound good to me, but I'll play along."

My nerves did a foxtrot inside me. I was eager to please him, but the hotel had been part of my life before I'd met him, and I'd missed running it. If necessary, I'd fight him for the chance to go back to it.

After playing with Robbie in the pool, Vaughn took a shower and changed into casual clothes.

"Ready to go?" he asked, approaching me in a golf shirt and shorts that nicely showed off his buff body. In his early fifties, Vaughn kept himself trim for the show. "Thought maybe we could have a drink at the hotel before coming home for dinner. What do you say?"

"Sounds good," I responded. "Robbie will be fine with Elena and Troy."

"Troy pop the question yet?" Vaughn asked.

I shook my head. "We're all going to get after him if he doesn't do it soon. Poor Elena has been waiting for weeks to officially receive the engagement ring they selected together."

Chuckling, we went out to the pool area to say goodbye to the others, and then we climbed into Vaughn's silver sports car and headed for the hotel.

As Vaughn drove through the gilded, wrought-iron gates onto the hotel property, I glanced to my right, at the little house I owned and now rented to the hotel. I loved that house. It had been such a source of pride to me to have my own place after Robert had robbed me of my home and my job. Rhonda's wish ... no, demand ... that I join her in converting her seaside estate into a small, boutique hotel had been my salvation. It had come with a ton of work, especially on my part, handling the finances and smaller details of setting up the hotel and running it.

I took a moment to study the hotel. Clad in pink stucco and with a red-tiled roof, the building extended along the shoreline like a lazy flamingo. Oversized, carved wooden doors stood guard at the top of wide, marble stairs. Potted palms sat next to the doors, balancing their height, softening their edges. Flowering hibiscus lined the front of the building, their bright blossoms a nice enhancement.

We came to a stop in the front, circular driveway and waited while a young man hurried to help me out of the car.

"It's still lovely, Ann," said Vaughn, gazing up at the building.

I remained silent. It was a beautiful place but without the polished look of welcome that Rhonda, our employees, and I had given to it.

"Welcome to The Beach House Hotel," the valet said in a bored tone of voice, holding the car door open for me.

Tears unexpectedly stung my eyes as I remembered how Rhonda and I used to run down the steps to greet our guests, our arms outstretched. I chided myself for being overly sentimental and got out of the car.

Vaughn handed over the keys and walked around the car to meet me. "Ready?

I took his arm, and we climbed the front steps together.

Pausing in the front entry, I recalled the first time I'd seen it, when Liz and I had visited Rhonda and Angela on a Thanksgiving several years ago. It had seemed so elegant, so open, so welcoming.

"Hello. Can I help you with something?"

I smiled at the young man behind the desk who obviously didn't know who I was. Tim McFarland, Bernhard Bruner, and Jean-Luc Rodin, our former Front Office Manager, General Manager, and Chef, had either been fired or quit during the past year, leaving poorly trained staff behind who were inconsistent in providing continuing, professional service.

"No, thanks. We're going to take a walk along the beach before having a cocktail."

"Enjoy," the clerk said and picked up a phone that had started to ring.

I led Vaughn out onto the pool deck, doing my best to ignore the loud rock music, the pool packed with kids, and the gossipy tones of the mothers supposedly watching their children. I loved having families at the hotel, but the clientele that now came here to take advantage of hotel package deals were people who wouldn't tolerate or appreciate anything understated.

We left the pool area and walked onto the beach.

Stepping onto the soft, warm sand, I drew deep breaths in and out, reminding myself that, to convince Vaughn of the need to take over the hotel, I had to remain calm.

Vaughn grabbed hold of my hand, and we walked up to the edge of the water. Waves caressed our toes in gentle, cool laps that kissed the shore and pulled away. We closed our eyes and breathed in unison.

This ritual of allowing ourselves a peaceful moment with the sounds and feel of nature around us had begun shortly after we met and continued to be an act of bonding. We'd even used a scenario like this as part of our wedding ceremony.

Moments later, I opened my eyes and turned to Vaughn, my heart swelling. "I love you."

He grinned. "Love you more."

It was a game we liked, and by playing it, we both won.

As we headed down the beach, I splashed in and out of the water's frothy edge. It lay on the packed sand like spun lace wrapped around seashells both broken and whole, little treasures the Gulf had offered up. Seagulls continued to cry and whirl above us, white and gray bundles of feathers dancing in the air. We'd gone about a mile when Vaughn stopped walking and turned to me. "Okay, I'm curious. What did you want to talk about, Ann?"

I faced him, my shoulders stiff with determination. "Rhonda and I want to buy back the hotel. Our contract states that we have only a couple more months when we can do that."

"But things have changed since you sold it," Vaughn said. "You both have husbands and responsibilities as mothers. And what about the freedom for you to travel with me?"

"We're distraught at seeing the hotel become ... ordinary. It's our baby, and now they're making it ugly. Besides, during the past two years, Rhonda and I have learned a lot about running a hotel on a larger scale with more staff, and I'm certain we can set things up in a way that gives us almost as much freedom as we have now."

"Aw, Ann, I know you want me to say 'go for it,' but I can't. Not yet. Give me some time to think it over. I know it's your decision, but I want things to be right between us. I want Robbie to have the mother he's had for the past two and a half years."

I stared out at the water moving back and forth rhythmically as it had always done, as if telling me that my life should continue in the same steady pattern. Ellen, Vaughn's first wife, had been a model, stay-at-home mother. But that was over twenty years ago, and times had changed, roles had changed.

"What does Will have to say about this?" Vaughn asked. "I can't imagine he'd be happy about it. He loves having Rhonda at home with the kids."

"True," I said, "but she, like me, is unwilling to let our hotel go to ruin."

"I wouldn't say it's in ruins," protested Vaughn.

My sigh held back words of frustration. "Let's go have that drink you talked about. When you look around the hotel, I think you'll have a better understanding of what Rhonda and I need to do. We've already talked to Mike Torson about it."

Vaughn's eyebrows rose in an arch. "You have?"

Unwilling to back down, I nodded. "He'll handle everything for us. It won't be easy, but I'm willing to fight for it."

His brow creased with worry, he studied me. "Let's head back and go inside. We'll talk later."

I followed Vaughn into the hotel hoping he realized how serious Rhonda and I were about getting our baby back.

About the Author

A *USA Today* Best Selling Author, Judith Keim, , is a hybrid author who both has a publisher and self-publishes, Ms. Keim writes heart-warming novels about women who face unexpected challenges, meet them with strength, and find love and happiness along the way. Her best-selling books are based, in part, on many of the places she's lived or visited and on the interesting people she's met, creating believable characters and realistic settings her many loyal readers love. Ms. Keim loves to hear from her readers and appreciates their enthusiasm for her stories.

Ms. Keim enjoyed her childhood and young-adult years in Elmira, New York, and now makes her home in Boise, Idaho, with her husband and their two domineering dachshunds, Winston and Wally, and other members of her family.

While growing up, she was drawn to the idea of writing stories from a young age. Books were always present, being read, ready to go back to the library, or about to be discovered. All in her family shared information from the books in general conversation, giving them a wealth of knowledge and vivid imaginations.

"I hope you've enjoyed this book. If you have, please help other readers discover it by leaving a review on Amazon, Bookbub, Goodreads or the site of your choice. And please check out my other books:

The Hartwell Women Series
The Beach House Hotel Series
The Fat Fridays Group
The Salty Key Inn Series
Seashell Cottage Books
The Chandler Hill Inn Series
The Desert Sage Inn Series
Soul Sisters at Cedar Mountain Lodge
The Sanderling Cove Inn Series
The Lilac Lake Inn Series

"ALL THE BOOKS ARE NOW AVAILABLE IN AUDIO on Audible, iTunes, Findaway, Kobo and Google Play! So fun to have these characters come alive!"

Ms. Keim can be reached at **www.judithkeim.com**

And to like her author page on Facebook and keep up with the news, go to: **https://bit.ly/3acs5Qc**

To receive notices about new books, follow her on Book Bub: **http://bit.ly/2pZBDXq**

And here's a link to where you can sign up for her periodic newsletter! **http://bit.ly/2OQsb7s**

She is also on Twitter @judithkeim, LinkedIn, and Goodreads. Come say hello!